A
SISTER'S
SECRET

Also by Cydney Rax

A Sister's Secret

A Sister's Survival

My Married Boyfriend

If Your Wife Only Knew

Revenge of the Mistress

My Daughter's Boyfriend

My Husband's Girlfriend

Scandalous Betrayal

My Sister's Ex

Brothers & Wives

Reckless (with Niobia Bryant and Grace Octavia)

Crush (with Michele Grant and Lutishia Lovely)

Published by Dafina Books

A SISTER'S SECRET

CYDNEY RAX

Dafina
Books

KENSINGTON PUBLISHING CORP.
www.kensingtonbooks.com

DAFINA BOOKS are published by

Kensington Publishing Corp.
119 West 40th Street
New York, NY 10018

All Kensington Titles, Imprints, and Distributed Lines are available at special quantity discounts for bulk purchases for sales promotions, premiums, fund-raising, and educational or institutional use. Special book excerpts or customized printings can also be created to fit specific needs. For details, write or phone the office of the Kensington special sales manager: Kensington Publishing Corp., 119 West 40th Street, New York, NY 10018, attn: Special Sales Department. Phone: 1-800-221-2647.

Dafina and the Dafina logo Reg. U.S. Pat. & TM Off.

ISBN-13: 978-1-4967-1542-5
ISBN-10: 1-4967-1542-X
First Kensington Trade Edition: March 2018
First Kensington Mass Market Edition: May 2019

ISBN-13: 978-1-4967-1545-6 (e-book)
ISBN-10: 1-4967-1545-4 (e-book)

10 9 8 7 6 5 4 3 2 1

Printed in the United States of America

Acknowledgments

I'm the luckiest woman in the world because I get to do this . . . again. Even though I've almost lost count on the various formats in which my novels have been published, I know it's a lot . . . I am still walking around in a daze . . . pinching my arm . . . Dreams do come true! Writing is so hard, yet so much fun. Always grateful!

FIRST AND FOREMOST: I acknowledge the Creator of heaven and earth who gave me a writing ability and an unquenchable interest in developing characters and quirky story lines.

I must also thank Leford Nugent, who emailed me out of the blue one day talking about a book with five sisters. How did he know? He was my confirmation.

Thanks to Ms. Esi Sogah, my editor, for a partnership that challenges me in ways that I never could have imagined.

EXTRA SPECIAL THANKS to: The Houston Public Library ♥♥♥♥ (esp. Darryl Kiser).

And Michelle Sloan: Thanks for setting up the social media for fans (Twitter: @CydneyRaxFans, Facebook: cydneyraxfans, Instagram: cydneyraxfans). Thanks to those that support my books: The Literary Guru, Black Page Turners, the ladies of Shawndabooklover and Friends Readers Lounge, The Tea TV Show (@jointhetea on FB—what a divine connection!! Thanks so much for the video book review), Deborah Franklin #Fempire, Kalina M. Ross Anderson, African American Literary Awards Show (thanks for the IYWOK book nomination, but if there is ever a next time, give a sista a heads-up—LOL). And Diamond's Literary World . . . much appreciated. And to each of the faithful readers across the country who contacts me and lets me know they can't wait to read the next book, etc., I am floored by your kindness. Keep spreading the words, y'all. XOXO.

MUCH APPRECIATION: The U of Houston gang— Lisa Benford ✋, Steven Burns (thanks for the animal 411), and my family members across the U.S.A. And to my author crew, the people who keep a smile on my face because you're fun, talented, supportive, and you GET IT!! Love you bunches! Marissa Monteilh, Simone Kelly (marketing genius/author/Jamaican hustler [so very happy for you]), Electa Rome Parks, Sadeqa Johnson, and Margaret Johnson-Hodge.

AND I CAN'T FORGET: Burke Wood, B Creative Digital Media, and QBR Media for producing a lovely video interview. I had sooo much fun answering those wonderful questions. Thanks for all that you do to promote AA authors.

FINALLY, let's get to reading of the first book of a new fictional series. I hope you enjoy it as much as I enjoyed writing it.

Ciao!

Cydney
booksbycyd@aol.com

CHAPTER 1

Running Her Mouth
as Usual

One Saturday morning in early September, the Reeves sisters gathered for their fifth Sister Day of the year. For the past few years, they'd congregated every two months beginning in January. Their meeting was similar to a self-instituted family holiday.

Their mother, Greta Reeves, had passed away nearly four years ago due to complications from surgery. Greta had still been in the hospital trying to recover when she unexpectedly took a turn for the worse. The doctor told the family to get to the hospital as soon as possible. And on that late December morning, all the daughters gathered around Greta's bed, standing together in a circle, clutching each other's hands, praying, crying and trying to hold it together. It hurt to realize their mother was losing her battle with leukemia right before their eyes. They knew they'd be left motherless once she took her last breath. But Greta Reeves was tired of sickness ravishing her frail body. She was ready to meet her Maker.

"Alita, Burgundy, Coco, Dru, Elyse." She struggled to talk with a voice so hoarse it sounded like a whisper.

"Yes, Mama," Burgundy replied, tears wetting her cheeks.

"I want all of you to look out for each other, ya hear?"

"We will," Dru promised and gently squeezed Greta's bony fingers.

"Stay strong, no matter how I look like now. Don't remember me like this. Remember your mom as someone that loved and feared the Lord."

"Okay, Mommy," Coco wailed, barely able to keep herself from crawling onto the bed and lying next to Greta.

"I love you, girls. Don't ever forget it." Her faint scratchy voice was barely audible. "And I want you to love each other like I love you."

Back then Elyse had just nodded. At fifteen, she was too stunned to realize what was actually happening.

Greta's final words were, "His mercy endures forever. See you girls on the other side." Then Jesus or the angels came to escort Greta, and she died in peace.

Since their mother's untimely passing, Burgundy had stepped up to the plate. She could never forget the things that her mother wanted from them as a family even after her death. Burgundy always held a deep passion for Sister Day. She put a lot into planning their special days, and her commitment and enthusiasm quickly spread to her siblings. It grew into the lifeblood and new legacy for the Reeves sisters.

Including herself there were a total of five "Reeves" sisters: Thirty-six-year-old Alita was the eldest, and Burgundy was next in line. Then came Coco, followed by Drucilla. Last of all was Elyse, the youngest at nineteen.

So it was time for the Reeves sisters to meet again. Alita complained she was low on gas, so Dru agreed to pick her up from her southwest Houston apartment, since she lived about ten minutes away from her. Then she and Alita drove on until they arrived at their favorite nail salon, which was where their meetings were typically held.

Elyse and Burgundy arrived soon thereafter. The sisters warmly greeted one another, glanced at their watches, and walked through the wide aisle of the spacious salon until they reached the pedicure stations.

"Where's Dark Skin?"

"Don't know," Burgundy told Alita, "but we are not on her time schedule, that's for sure."

Fifteen minutes later, Coco raced through the salon door.

The sisters all looked up. They were in the early stages of getting a super-deluxe pedicure.

Alita scowled at Coco, who was gasping for breath. She was breathing hard and holding her hand against her chest. Her thick hair was parted in the middle and flanked by one big Afro puff on each side of her head. She wore dark purple lipstick, and purple rouge had been dusted on her round cheeks.

"'Bout time you got here," Alita said. "Where your kids at?"

"I hired a sitter, Ms. Nosy."

Coco clumsily climbed up on her chair and quickly lowered the armrest. She pressed buttons on the remote control to start the back massager. She reclined and briefly shut her eyes. When she opened them, all the sisters were gaping at her.

"Why you late?" Alita asked.

"Don't start." Coco shot her a warning look.

"Why your forehead all sweaty and shit like you just got through fucking?"

"Maybe I did just get through—"

"Don't. No place now," Elyse murmured and covered her ears. She gave a pained expression as she trembled in her chair.

"I can't believe she spoke two sentences in a row," remarked Alita. "I need her to speak up more so we can know what's going on inside that sneaky little brain of hers."

"Leave her alone," Burgundy ordered Alita. "You know Elyse is shy. She doesn't have to be loud and ghetto like you and Coco." But Burgundy's heart felt heavy as her eyes swept over the baby of the family. Even though the girl had been living with her since their mother died, there were times when dealing with Elyse caused Burgundy's patience to wear thin. She didn't know if her sister acted withdrawn because she was trying to get attention or if she was still mourning the loss of their mother.

Elyse was average height and very thin; when she woke up for the day her breakfast usually consisted of a piece of toast and a tiny apple. She barely had an appetite for the remainder of her day, choosing to pick at her food and sneaking to throw away her dinner when she thought no one was looking.

And today, even though the temperature was high,

Elyse's tiny frame was covered by an oversize men's shirt, a pair of baggy cargo pants, and some high-top Chuck Taylors. Her uncombed hair was capped by a baseball hat worn backward.

As Burgundy returned her focus to her other sisters, she noticed that Alita was running her mouth as usual.

"Who you calling loud, B? I am not that loud, and ain't nothing wrong with being ghetto. I'm proud of where I come from. South Side, H-town, all the way. All of us was raised there. But even though you've moved far away to the suburbs, you seem to have forgotten that you started from the bottom like most of us."

"Alita, now is not the time," Burgundy replied. "I am not about to fight with you over nothing. It's going to be all love and peace today. Okay? Can we agree to disagree?"

Alita slouched in her chair and closed her eyes.

"Alita," Burgundy repeated. "I was talking to you. I said, love and peace today, all right?'"

"Alita will behave," Dru spoke up. "Now, what's the new assignment, B?"

Burgundy smiled. "First of all, how did everything go with y'all concerning the last assignment? Did you get anything out of telling each other the truth and confronting someone in a nice way? Do you feel it helped you grow as a person and especially as a sister? Did you have any struggles with this assignment?"

"Well, it wasn't a stretch for me 'cause I always tells the truth," Coco said with attitude. "That's just how I roll. It was no challenge."

"Dark Skin, you a lying ass," Alita hooted and hollered. "You only think that you always keep it real. But I know when you're lying."

The nail attendant looked at Alita then at Dru. She

quickly pretended she wasn't listening to their conversation. But Coco knew she had heard Alita's insensitive comments.

"Look, dammit," Coco complained, suddenly feeling self-conscious. "I'm sick of you calling me Dark Skin. Dru is brown skinned and so is Elyse; yet I don't hear you giving them that type of nickname."

"Uh, what?" Alita's face registered pure shock. She was so accustomed to calling Coco "Dark Skin," and seeing her respond to the nickname, that she had never thought twice about how the woman felt about it.

"Uh, nothing," Coco retorted. "I am way more than the color of my skin, and I do not appreciate you calling me that."

"But I've been calling you that since you were in elementary school."

"And now that I'm grown up, I am asking you to stop. That's not my name. My mama told me she named me Coco Chanel Reeves. And she told me that Coco means I'm passionate."

"True that," Alita said with a chuckle.

"*And* compassionate," Coco added.

"I don't know about that."

"And romantic."

Dru nodded in agreement. "Okay, now *that's* accurate."

"So anyway," Coco continued, "I want to be called by my name. You understand?"

"All right . . . Dark and Lovely," Alita said with a smirk.

"Oh, fuck it. You're lame and you're wrong."

"Funny because that's exactly how I feel about you, Coco," Alita replied. "And you just use that nickname shit as an excuse to keep us from facing the more important matters."

"What you talkin' 'bout?"

"I'm still trying to figure out the pregnancy thang."

"We on that again?"

"Yes, we are. Now. Why did you lie? We supposed to tell the truth and here you go, steadily lying."

"W-w-well," Coco sputtered. "Maybe I got good reasons for not wantin' to tell e'rything you feel you need to know."

"That could be true, Coco," Burgundy said. "But still, you should try to be truthful. Or even find a new way of telling us the truth."

"Ain't. Easy."

The room grew eerily quiet except for the sounds of bubbles splashing inside each girl's pedicure pan. Coco, the ultimate "fronter," was the one who liked to put on a façade. She wanted the sisters to think she was holding life down. Yet her life was frustrating, complex, hard, and exhausting, and she didn't want everyone commenting on it.

"What's not easy, Sis?" Burgundy replied.

Coco loudly exhaled and settled back in her chair, harboring a distant look in her eyes.

"Sometimes I wonder if it's all worth it. I already got two of Calhoun's kids. I love 'em to death. But it don't always keep him at home. So having another mouth to feed . . . I already know it won't make him act right."

"Thank you for admitting the truth." Alita sat up straighter in her chair. She loved when she was dead-on right.

"Can't really deny it," Coco shrugged.

"Take it from me," Alita replied in her piercing voice. "No-good men don't make good husbands."

"Nobody's perfect." Coco's voice was light. "Not even me. We all got issues. So I decided to accept Calhoun as he is."

Alita groaned. "Just because people have issues doesn't mean you have to settle, girl."

"Alita, why you think you know everything about my relationship?"

"Anyone with a pair of eyes and common sense can figure out you two."

"Look, you're not with us twenty-four seven!" Coco's voice trembled. "I-I know he's trying. He loves me the best he can."

Alita frowned. "Does he treat you with kindness and respect twenty-four seven?"

Coco paused. "Yes."

"See, now I know you're lying."

"All right then." Coco sighed, growing weary of the conversation. "No, he's not kind every single second."

Alita continued. "Does Calhoun get on you whenever you do something he doesn't like?"

"Yes, he puts me in check, just like I put his ass in check."

"Does he ever tell you that he'd like to seriously marry you?"

Coco said nothing as she glanced down at her feet, which were dipped in the warm, bubbling water. Coco hated being scrutinized, even if the truth was being told. She despised her sister for always getting on her about things in her life that she wanted to remain undetected.

"I could go on, Coco, and you know it," Alita continued.

"Okay! Calhoun has issues, and that's that! But

overall he's good to me. My man is young, just in case you forgot. He's got a lot more growing up to do, then he'll be all right." Calhoun was twenty-three and acted every bit of his age.

"And what shocks me is how you're fine with that," Alita remarked. "Yet you still have this obsession about weddings and honeymoons and marriage licenses? Big ole fool."

Coco snapped back, "I took this man's virginity when he was barely legal. We've been together seven years. I ain't checking for no other man. It's 'bout time I be Calhoun's wife. What's wrong with that?"

"Marriage does not work, Dark Skin. Oops, I meant to say *Coco*. Marriage can't do nothing but fail."

"Alita, *your* pathetic relationship didn't work. And you're so bitter about it that you're trying to rob me of my happiness."

"What I'm doing may feel like a robbery . . . but it's a rescue mission . . ."

"Guess what, Alita? If you are my only hope, then I'll pass on being rescued. I'd rather swallow a bottle of pills than be anything like you."

Alita's eyes grew wet with moisture, but Coco was unrepentant and downright savage. "But my beautiful sister Burgundy, she's who I really look up to. Burgundy Taylor should give all of us hope. She found a way to make a marriage do what it's supposed to do. Get over any problems and stay married . . . no matter what."

"We try. We're blessed. Thanks, Sis," Burgundy said.

"That's my whole point, Coco." Alita butted in. "Calhoun is nowhere even close to Nathaniel. Nate has a good

head on his shoulders. Calhoun doesn't use his head half
the time. And it's exactly why you shouldn't be so quick
to marry him or any other man."

"Well, whatever. This is my relationship. I want
what I want—and that's that," Coco retorted.

"You *are* a fool," Alita spat. "Word on the street is
that he doesn't even believe this unborn baby is his."

"And that's why I thought about aborting it," Coco
finally said, her voice trembling.

"What?" Burgundy and Dru yelled at the same time.

"Hell, yeah. I said I *thought* about it." Coco sighed.
"That's why I didn't want the family to know, 'cause I
had to make a decision. I tossed and turned every night
and worried myself half to death. Could I have it?
Should I abort? But naw. I ain't killing my baby. Plus, I
know it's his. Just 'cause he don't know don't mean I
don't. It *is* his."

"Are you absolutely sure?" Dru couldn't help but
ask, considering what had occurred last time.

Coco sat, her cheeks flaming hot with shame as
she mentally pondered all of her sins. She hated anything that spoke of her dreadful past; not now, when
she was ready to move forward. "Am I sure that this
new baby is Calhoun's?" Coco repeated the question to
her sister. "Yeah, Dru. I'm sure. Hell, yeah."

"Well, I'm glad it's his, and I'm happy that you're
keeping it," Dru replied. "Say what you want about the
baby daddy, but at least you two make beautiful babies."

"You got that right," Alita said.

"And that's a pretty fancy trick for a woman you think
is shaped like an elephant." Coco cheerfully winked at
Alita.

Coco's skin was as pretty as an ice cream bar. Her teeth, as white as a movie star's. Her body resembled a hippopotamus's: thighs shaped like plastic toy baseball bats that rubbed together when she walked. But her standout feature? That award would go to her enormous behind. Coco's shapely rump could capture any man's attention. No silicone. No padding. She was blessed with one hundred percent pure ass. And because of that fact, no matter what folks said, no one could label Coco ugly to her face and get away with it.

While growing up, people would say that Dru was the "look-but-don't-touch sister." And Coco was the "touch-but-don't-look sister."

Feeling satisfied that her family now knew the full state of her baby's paternity, Coco settled back to enjoy her pampering session. She hoped they'd lighten up with all their nosy questions.

"Happy. Love new baby," Elyse said in a low voice.

Coco winked at her baby sister and reached over to squeeze her hand.

"Awww, Coco loves her some Elyse," Burgundy said.

"Of course I do. I love all my sisters. Even the evil ones." Coco laughed and winked at Alita.

"Love you too." Alita rolled her eyes. "Even though you're stupid as hell."

Burgundy couldn't help but be amazed. "You are a mess. But I'm happy that we're getting some things off our chests." She sighed in contentment. "This is exactly what our mother wanted. Good job, sisters. Now, before I move on to the new assignment, does anyone have any more comments about the last one?"

Dru cleared her throat. "I have a comment."

"Go on, Pretty Girl," Alita teased.

"Oh, hush with all that. Anyway, I want to say that . . . I struggle with truth."

"You do?" Alita sounded stunned. "I thought everything that came out of your mouth was full of truth."

"I want it to be that way, but it doesn't always happen how I want. Especially when it comes to my man."

"How are things with you and Tyrique?" Burgundy said. Tyrique Evans was Dru's devoted boyfriend and they'd been dating exclusively for almost three years.

The moment that question was asked, Dru's cell phone rang. It was as if Tyrique was listening in on their conversation and wanted to make his presence known.

"I wonder if I should I take this?" Dru said.

"Go on and answer, girl. You know how your man acts when he can't get in touch with his boo," Coco laughed.

"Um. No. I won't pick up. It's Sister Day, right?" Dru laid down the phone and continued talking to Burgundy. When the phone rang incessantly, she slid her finger across the screen to power it off. She dropped the phone inside her hobo bag and zipped it shut.

"Wow. No wonder Tyrique be tripping," Coco said, looking at Dru with open envy. "He can't call just one time and give up like some men do. He'll keep trying. I *like* that."

"There's no need for him to spaz out 'cause I don't answer." Dru responded. "I don't know why he was calling, but unless it's an emergency, he should trust what he's got."

"Hmm," Coco said. "Now *that's* something I just can't completely do. I'm always scared I might get played."

"Well, an untrustworthy man can't be trusted. That's because he hasn't earned it," Dru coolly replied. "Once your man has proven himself, that he shows a lot of consistency in doing good things, he is where he says he is, then it's safe to let down your guard. You will know what you have at that point."

"Dru Boo, you should have given that speech years ago." Alita bristled. "Because I didn't know what I had till it was too damn late."

"What do you mean?" Dru asked.

Alita laughed. "Don't tell me you can't remember how Mr. Leonard Washington was acting when we first met?"

"I remember," Burgundy cut in. "You would call me and tell me that you thought you had met 'the one.'"

Alita ignored her. "Anyway, I'll never forget one day when we were together. He picked me up in his car. It was clean too. That's one compliment I'll give him. He washed that bad boy every weekend, even if it looked like it was about to rain. The inside and the outside of that car was clean."

"Okay, cool," Dru murmured. "At least there is one good memory that you have about Leonard.

"But all that good didn't last, Sis. And that's the problem. If you gonna be my knight in shining armor, at least keep on acting the way that a knight is supposed to."

Coco burst out laughing, unable to help herself.

"What, Dark Skin?"

Coco gave Alita the evil eye but continued. "That man's still got power over you, even though you hardly ever see him these days. You ain't giving up the pussy to your ex-husband like some chicks do, none of that. But

Leonard Washington is still on your brain and in your mouth."

Burgundy nodded. "I've noticed that too. It's been three years, Alita. At some point you're going to have to let go."

Alita glared at each of her sisters and cleared her throat.

"Two words," she said. "Fuck y'all."

Coco giggled. "Don't be mad. Truth hurts, Lita, right?"

Burgundy spoke up. "Life can be painful, and if any of our sisters are hurting, we should hurt too. So please let Alita continue talking, because it sounds like she wants to get something off her chest."

"She's been trying to get the same shit off her chest for years." Coco mumbled to herself and suddenly couldn't wait until this Sister Day event was over. She was wondering what Calhoun was doing, even though she knew he was at work.

Coco picked up her phone and texted Calhoun. "WYD." Then she turned her attention to Alita.

"Go on ahead, Lita, damn. You're taking all morning just to tell your little story about what happened with you and Leonard."

Alita continued in her effort to remind them about what happened. "So, as I was saying, Leonard Washington lured me in with all his fancy talk, his sweet words that I ate up like a moist piece of chocolate cake. Back then he was just starting out working in used car sales. And when he'd get off, he'd come over and spend all his free time with me. We hung out every day. He'd give me money for groceries, paid my phone bill, offered to get my hair and nails done so I could 'stay pretty,' as he liked to say. Of course, I loved that.

And I could tell things with him were getting serious. Then, *it* happened. He called me 'a trophy worth keeping.'"

Burgundy smiled. "Did he, Alita?"

"He sure did, B. A *trophy,* okay? At the time I really didn't know what a 'trophy' was, but it sounded impressive. And when he said he wanted to get married and start a family, I said yes. I went from an awkward single woman to a wife. And things were sweet at first. But I had to learn the hard way that once some men get their trophy, they admire it at first. Then when they get bored, they set the trophy somewhere high up on a shelf to collect dust. They then get busy trying to collect new trophies. Trophies with bigger boobs, a fatter ass, a better shape, you name it."

"Damn, Sis," Coco said. "That must have hurt."

"You think?" Alita replied. "At first I was in denial. I'd be at home waiting on Leonard after I slaved over a hot stove trying to cook our dinner. I'd end up putting that food in the refrigerator, uneaten. By then he did so well selling used cars that he got promoted and started working in new car sales. He'd work longer and longer hours. And sometimes I'd pop up at his job without calling. And I'd catch my husband flirting with a pretty woman that had a couple of kids with her. Or he'd be driving women around, 'test driving' is what he called it. All that wasn't necessary."

"Hmm," Coco said. "Your eyes told you what you were seeing, but you didn't want to believe it, huh?"

"I'd ask him what was up with all these women, and all I'd get was one weak excuse after another. And when I finally opened my eyes and learned who I actually married, my dumb ass thought I could change Leonard. But let me drop some truth on you. Ain't no such thing as that. I don't care if the president of the United States declares it on national television and it gets tweeted a million times, a woman *cannot* change a man. He's gonna do whatever the hell he feels he wanna do."

"If that's the case," Coco spoke up, "why doesn't Tyrique act like that? Like a bitch-ass punk?"

"Tyrique is the definition of a good man," Dru admitted. "I'll give him that. I wouldn't expect him to act like Leonard or Calhoun. No offense."

"You and I lucked out, Dru Boo." Burgundy smiled with pride. "We know what we have, and we must learn to appreciate it. The things you don't value can get taken away from you." Her smile turned into a frown.

"Like when our dear mother was here. I hate to say it, but sometimes I was impatient with her, especially when she got sick."

"I can't believe you're admitting this," Coco said.

"Well, I put on a good front for a long time, but sometimes you need to be real. That's why we do this," Burgundy said. "It helps us to face our truth." She gave a tiny smile. "And just by listening to you ladies, I'm reminded just how good I have it. Sometimes I feel guilty. Other times I don't."

"Ha?" Alita scowled. "Are you looking down on us just because of Nate? Because even though he is a good man . . . he's still a man, Burgundy."

"That's where you're wrong. He's an *exceptional* man." Burgundy calmly defended her spouse, which was what good wives did, even when they did not feel like it.

"When Nate does well," Burgundy continued, "I should back him up. When he messes up, and it's very rare that Nate slips and falls, I keep our dirty laundry in our house. I privately kiss his wounds and help him to get back up. But it hardly ever happens."

"Lucky you," Alita said sarcastically.

"You're right. It is luck," Burgundy said. "And I can't brag or feel superior, because I know my man could act like the average Joe out here. But he's not. So I count my blessings and keep it moving."

When someone has made it clear that their life is the very definition of perfection, there was nothing left for the other sisters to say. But they certainly all had a lot to think about, and for the time being they kept their secret thoughts to themselves.

CHAPTER 2

Out of Bounds

During the next few minutes, the sisters laughed heartily, recalled fond memories of their dear mother, and argued over trivial things like which sister had the biggest butt and which of them had the best boyfriends when they were younger. But as soon as their nails were done, they grew quiet and admired each other's manicures.

The ladies slid on plastic slippers and relocated to the area in which they could slide their freshly polished toenails inside the dryer. Peaceful music serenaded them. Anyone there could tell that the shop owner was serious about maintaining a feng shui atmosphere.

Once the sisters settled in, Burgundy waved her hands to get everyone's attention.

"Okay, ladies, we've stretched this out long enough. The September Sister Assignment is this: *Confront someone in a nice way and tell them whatever has been bothering you.*"

"I can confront." Alita scoffed. "But being nice?"

Dru burst out laughing. "You can be nice when you wanna be."

"Tell you what? I'ma try my best." Alita promised. "And you know who I wanna confront right now? No need to even ask."

"What, Alita? What you want now? Damn," Coco said.

"I want to know who Chance's daddy is." Chance was Coco's youngest child. At two years of age, he was a ball of energy and chatty just like his mother. He mostly looked like her. And the day after she gave birth to him, Coco told the nursing staff to put Chance Reeves on his birth certificate.

"Aw, Sis, c'mon now," Burgundy said. She knew Coco was very tight-lipped about the identity of Chance's father. "We've already been over this topic a hundred times."

"And even after all those times, we still don't know the answer. It kills me that I am his aunt and I don't know who his father is."

"And yet, you don't need to know." Coco looked riled up as she slid her feet deeper inside of her dryer. "As long as Calhoun is cool with the situation," Coco argued, "and as long as he acts like Chance's father, that's all that matters."

"Girl," Alita yelped. "Ain't no grown-ass man gonna be all right with paying for some other man's child."

"Well, apparently he is okay with it, 'cause he does pay. Damn, Alita, get off my back. I'm not playing now. You gon' make me do something to hurt you."

"What?" Alita rose to her feet and shuffled a few inches away. She positioned her long, slender legs till she towered over Coco. "What you gon' do, huh?"

"I'm sick of you. Tired of everything." Coco's beady eyes exploded into a shower of tears. She shut both eyes, blocking out Alita. She rocked back and forth in her seat and mumbled to herself.

"Alita, leave Coco alone." Burgundy immediately came to Coco's side. She grabbed Coco and pulled her face against her bosom and gently patted her back. "For the millionth time, we are sisters. We hold each other up. We don't tear each other down. We're there for each other through good times and bad. Now, I don't know what you got against Coco, but you're going to have to let it go, Alita. She doesn't deserve this type of treatment." Burgundy lowered her head until she was facing Coco's protruding stomach. She kissed Coco's belly then rubbed it. "We are family," Burgundy concluded. "And that's that."

"Just because you're family," Alita said, "doesn't mean I agree with everything that family does. That's not truthful. That's not real."

"I don't care what you say, Alita," Burgundy said in an icy tone. "In this family we *will* support each other even if we don't agree. We will learn to get along even if it kills us. You're going to have to do right by Coco whether you're feeling it or not. And remember, be nice."

Coco opened her eyes and wiped her tears. She smiled gratefully at Burgundy.

"Yes, I agree with B," Dru said. "I already asked you to ease up off Coco. She doesn't need all this stress." She asked Coco, "When's the baby due?"

"Mid-March," she replied. "March twelfth."

"So there, it's settled. She'll be a new mom in six short months from now." Dru's voice sounded incredulous. "I can't even imagine being in Coco's shoes. She needs our love and support."

Alita couldn't listen any longer. "Well, in my opinion, she should have thought about the shoes she was in before she went around fucking without making Calhoun strap up. Or she needed to stay on the pill even if it made her gain weight. Just because you can spread your legs and bring a pregnancy to term don't mean you're a fit mama." Alita strutted back to her seat and let her pedicure resume drying.

"Alita, I swear to God, you gon' make me seriously hurt you one day." Coco's angry voice nearly shook the walls. Two manicurists rushed into the room. At first they spoke in Vietnamese, then used English.

"What wrong? Why loud? You got to leave. Pay money. Then go."

"Damn, see, Alita, your loud ghetto ways are scaring everybody. They may not let us come in here anymore, and then what we going to do? Nothing and no one better not mess up Sister Day. And I mean that." Burgundy released Coco and apologized to the two employees. She promised that they'd be quieter and begged to stay a few more minutes until their nail polish was completely dried.

The two women looked skeptical and left the room but not before they fired a cautionary glance.

"Alita, see all the unnecessary hell you always raise?" Burgundy scolded. "You need to do better."

"Okay, okay. My bad," Alita whispered. She realized she was exhausted from all her yelling. Her forehead was filled with wrinkle lines. "I need a stiff drink. Need to stop worrying about family. Need to chill. Need to pray."

"You need a *man*," Burgundy answered. "And not just any man. A good man who knows how to love you just right; and one whose love can help take away all your stress."

"Ain't no man like that in the world."

"Oh, really?" Burgundy shot back. "You used to think Leonard Washington was that man."

"Yeah, I can admit he had me open back in the day. In the beginning when I was allowed to live the fairy tale. I never thought I could love any man as much as I loved him. But it all changed."

"If you had a great love once in your life," Burgundy replied, "there's a good chance you can have it again."

"True love can't strike twice," Alita protested.

"As long as you have breath in your lungs, anything is possible, Sis."

Alita cast Burgundy a doubtful glance.

"I'm talking what I know," Alita solemnly continued. "These days brothas out here rough-acting and beat-down looking. I feel like I gotta pick through the scraps after the lunch crowd has come through the Chinese buffet."

"You're wrong. There *is* a good man out here for you. In fact, I know the perfect one."

"Who is he, Burgundy?" Dru wanted to know.

"He goes to Solomon's Temple, of course."

"Church man? With me? That's like water . . . mixed with oil . . . and dynamite. Aw, hell no," Alita said.

"Sis, let me finish," Burgundy pleaded. "Stop being so negative and try to listen first."

"All right, then. Finish."

"Thank you! Okay," Burgundy continued. "All I can tell you is that this man is considerate. Thoughtful. A gentleman. And he's not the typical selfish guy who only cares about himself. He has a really down-to-earth, agreeable personality, but—he's no pushover."

"Go on."

"He has an excellent job working downtown, Alita, and he's not that needy, mama's-boy type, so there you go! That's another plus mark. Um, he's a good looking guy too, but he's no pretty boy, and we know you don't like those types."

"Nope, too cute means too arrogant. Go on."

"What else? Oh! He's into eating healthy. You won't catch him at Mickey D's or Burger King unless he's buying a salad or a wrap."

"Mmm, sounds good. I can live with that. I could stand to lose a few pounds anyway."

"Girl, now we know you lying," Coco said with a giggle. "You ain't got an ounce of fat on your bony behind."

Alita smiled and gave Coco the middle finger.

"Seriously," Burgundy continued. "This man will work with you if you really want to get back in shape. He's into fitness and sports, and I think he's a very patient man too."

Dru shook her head in disbelief. "A man with patience? Shoot, he sounds like a man that *I'd* like to meet."

"Girl, don't be greedy. You already got a good man," Alita snapped. She sat up straight in her chair, swept aside the long bangs from her naked forehead. "Um, so far he sounds all right, B. But I have two questions."

"What are they?" Burgundy said.

"If he's so damned perfect, why hasn't another woman snatched him up?"

"Hmm. I can answer that, and I don't even know him." Coco spoke with confidence. "He probably can't commit."

"You describing Calhoun," Alita said.

"Shut up, Lita!" Coco said, then continued. "Or he's a sneaky-ass, down-low man that likes to suck dick. Or he's boring as hell, a felon with a rap sheet, or he's too weak to handle a real woman," Coco said.

"You did good, Dark Skin. I like those answers," Alita said. Coco and Alita high-fived.

"Coco, nice try, but you're wrong," Burgundy replied. "To be honest, Shade told me that he fell in love with a woman that he thought was 'the one.' And he assured me that he was very good to her. But you know how there are women out here that have a good man but they take 'em for granted. Yep. Shade held on for a good minute, giving her a few chances to make the necessary changes and respond to him in the way he wanted her to. But she started smelling herself and almost dogged him out. But Shade woke up one day and like Michael Jackson, he said, 'This is it.' He cut off that woman and moved on. And, of course, now she regrets it. She sits up in church looking all depressed and suicidal." Burgundy laughed at the woman's stupidity. "But when God gives you a blessing, you better be smart enough to receive it. And, Alita, I pray to God that you will be ready. I will not have you embarrass me in front of this man, you hear?"

"I hear you," Alita said. She actually forced herself

to smile. At that moment, a sliver of hope etched itself in her heart. Maybe all men weren't the devil.

"All right. Fine," she replied. "But there's just one more thing."

"What?" Burgundy sweetly asked.

"Is he father material?"

Alita's only child, Leno, was an eleventh grader who loved sports. From the time he was in elementary school, kids from the block were always ringing their doorbell to see if Leno could go hang out. Alita would tell the little boys, "No." And she'd quickly slam the door in their faces. The boys looked like thugs, and she never wanted her child to get caught up in any bullshit.

"Doesn't Leno already have a father?" Dru asked Alita.

"Yes, silly," Alita barked. "But if you haven't noticed lately, he and I aren't together. So, if and when I do choose to date, the man will have to be good with kids. I don't want no fucking child molesters around my son. No perverted pedophiles that act nice in front of your face, but as soon as you turn your back, they try and force an innocent boy to suck his dick. Hell, no! The next man I get with has to have the fear of God *and* the fear of Alita in him before he even comes close to my baby."

"That's the problem," Coco said. "You still treat my nephew like he's a five-year-old. I'm just sure Leno is sick of you embarrassing his ass in front of his friends."

Alita's face reddened. For once she could not dispute her middle sister. She knew she'd never hesitate to say how she felt, whether it was to her son or any of his friends. She thoughtfully chewed on her bottom lip. "Well, I am his mama, so I have the right to raise him the way I see fit. You worry about your three and a half kids. How's that sound?"

Coco could only laugh. She knew it would be a cold day in hell before her sister admitted that she was wrong about anything.

The whirring noise from the dryer fan suddenly came to a stop. Coco took a deep breath and stood up. "You may tease me about my life, Lita, but it's clear that your life ain't no day at the park either. You got as many issues as me. So deal with that."

Coco grabbed her purse, told her sisters goodbye, and started to walk out of the salon so she could go check on her man.

But before she could exit, Alita ran after her.

She told her, "Hold up a sec." Then she offered her a warm hug.

Coco felt awkward as Alita tightly grabbed her around the neck and gave a squeeze.

"You my boo," Alita whispered in her ear. "I got you. I've *been* you. I just need you to stop pretending and just start . . . being."

Coco nodded. "I know. And I need you to start being . . . nicer . . . and a little less nosy."

Alita embraced Coco even more tightly. "I can try, but I can't promise you I'll be perfect." She released her sister and said in an abnormally soft tone, "Our sister assignment says we should confront someone. I'm confronting you."

"What else is new?"

"Coco Chanel Reeves?" Alita said.

"What, Lita, what?"

"Who is the father of this one that's in your stomach?"

"Calhoun! What the fuck?"

"And were you lying when you said you don't know who Chance's daddy is?"

Coco paused. Her heart was filled with pain at the memories of her deception. "Yes," she sniffed. "I lied. I know who his daddy is."

"I had a feeling you did, but it's all good. I know you got your reasons."

Coco gasped, then admitted, "I do."

"But one day, do you think you can tell us what happened? The true story, Coco?"

"Nosy-ass sister, one day you will know. But today ain't that day. Now will you leave me the hell alone, please?" And Coco shut down the conversation, told the rest of the ladies goodbye. As she walked out the door, she prayed to God that her sisters would lay off of her and let her live her life. Forget her past, allow her to have her future. And just let her breathe.

CHAPTER 3

Thotsicle

That afternoon, once the Sister Day salon appointment was complete, Dru and Alita began the drive to pick up Leno from basketball practice. They pulled up outside the facility, a moderate-size brick building connected to the high school. By the look of things, it appeared that the team was just finishing up. Numerous young men still wearing their jersey-and-shorts uniforms drifted onto the sidewalk in small groups. Alita strained her neck to see if Leno had emerged from the front entrance.

Leno was zoned to a Houston high school that had a high percentage of Hispanics and blacks. The school definitely wasn't known for its academic superiority; Alita could only pray that her child (1) got a decent enough education that would help him throughout his life; (2) left school every day without getting into trouble, or being hassled to join a gang; and (3) continue

playing ball good enough to qualify for the professional leagues.

After waiting quite a few minutes with no sign of
her son, Alita groaned and sat back in her seat. "Damn.
This happens every time. Leno's always got to be the
first one there before practice officially starts and the
last one to leave."

"Sounds like he's dedicated to his craft and is getting ready for the NBA. He could be the next Steph
Curry."

A far-off look formed in Alita's eyes. Wouldn't it be
amazing if her son made it as a superstar athlete? Even
college hoops would be nice. She could only hope that
good things would happen for Leno. Then reality settled in.

"I dunno, Sis," Alita muttered. "I just want my son
to do the best he can right here in this school and keep
his grades up. He's doing all right as a junior, but
they've only had a few tests so far. And if he keeps on
top of his studies, then he may get a full scholarship
and I won't have to come out of my pocket. Because I
already know that Leonard Washington will not chip in
two cents toward Leno's college funds."

"Wow, is he that bad? Doesn't Leonard make good
money selling cars?"

"I guess. He lies all day long trying to get people to
buy whatever car is sitting on the lot. And he's got a
PhD in lying so, yeah, I'm sure Leonard is making
bread and honey."

Dru laughed. "Alita, I think you're still upset because he convinced you to be with him. And maybe
that wasn't what you really wanted to do at the time."

"Can we change the subject?" Alita said. "I think I see my baby."

Alita watched her son take his sweet time walking out of the building. At sixteen, Leno was already six foot three and there was no telling how many more inches he'd grow. He resembled Ralph Tresvant from the group New Edition: dreamy eyes, slight mustache, and an amazing talking voice, as well as charm for days. Leno's lightweight headphones were stuck in his ears; no doubt he was listening to the latest from Drake, his favorite.

As he traipsed down the sidewalk, Leno was surrounded by six girls, three on each side of him and all of them jockeying for position. Whatever music Leno was listening to was no competition for a captive audience of beautiful, smiling, energetic young ladies. It appeared that his clique was laughing it up and having a rowdy good time. The girls were of various shapes, ages, and heights. All of their hairstyles were long enough to sit on, or they wore Ghana braids, kinky twists, or Senegalese twists. The girls sported cling-fitting shirts and short shorts that displayed their thick hips and pretty legs. One girl ran and jumped directly in Leno's path. She stopped, stuck her butt out so far he had no choice but to see it. She whooped and hollered like she was singing the lyrics to a song, then she began wiggling her butt cheeks up and down real fast. Leno stopped walking. He stared and smiled, licking his lips and nodding as he carefully observed the teasing dance that she performed especially for him. All of her braids were dyed various vibrant colors, and she resembled a dancing peacock.

When she pulled up her shirt and exposed her breasts, then hopped around like a Zulu dancer, Alita couldn't bear to watch any longer. "C'mon on, Dru. Time to run some interference."

Dru hurriedly got out of her car. Alita marched up to her son, who faced all the girls as they clustered in a semicircle.

By then the dancing girl had sense enough to lower her shirt. But Leno's eyes had turned glassy, still mesmerized by the bouncing, wild movements of her lush behind. Alita waited a few seconds, then gave Leno a forceful tap on his back.

He slowly turned around, eyes widened, then darkened.

"Um, hey, Mama. I'll be with you in a sec. I'm just finishing up."

"Finishing up what?" Alita asked. "Wasting time with these little strippers?"

A chick with purple hair and pouty purple lips rolled her eyes at Alita. Alita raised her arm up and pulled it back, ready to swing. Dru quickly stopped her. "Alita, please. Give my nephew a few more minutes. He's not doing anything wrong. Let him be a kid."

"That's the problem," Alita snapped. "I don't want *my* son out here messing around with these girls, doing shit he has no business doing, and he ends up with babies he don't need or can't afford."

Now all the girls rolled their eyes at Alita. The girl with the big booty said, "Who dis old-ass bitch? Do we know her?"

Dru gasped. She snatched her sister's arm and dragged her to her vehicle, a few yards away from Leno. She popped open the locks of her door, and they sat inside the car to wait.

"Alita, I know that's your son and you can raise him

how you see fit, but I really think you need to watch your negative words. He still has feelings."

"Mmm hmm! He has a penis too. And a big one at that."

"Really? And how would you know that?"

Alita ignored her. "My point is that these fast-ass girls can smell the money coming. *Future rich baby daddy* is what all of 'em are thinking. They're not thinking about their own careers. Leno tells me how these chicks offer to do his homework for him. Write his essays. And I think even before the school semester gets started, they've lined up to earn their spot with him. And their goal is to one day put their nasty mouths on my son's dick. Give him something he can feel."

"Oh, Alita, please. They're just kids. You're exaggerating."

"Is this exaggerating?" Alita reached inside her purse and pulled out an unopened black-and-gold condom packet.

"This," she exclaimed, "isn't mine."

Dru's eyes enlarged. "Oh, okay."

"I found it in his backpack. My little boy thinks he's a man, but fucking at sixteen is no game."

"Wow," Dru said. "I mean, he is at that age where he may want to experiment. I'm sure there are middle schoolers out here having sex. Even Coco got started early."

"And look how bad things turned out for her," Alita exclaimed.

"Just because he's talking to a few girls doesn't mean he's having sex. He practices his drills very hard every day, he obviously goes to his classes, but the boy needs a social life too."

"Are you serious, Drucilla Reeves? So a teenage sex life is now considered a damned social life?"

Dru seemed frustrated, not wanting Alita to misunderstand. "No, I'm saying Leno needs to be around girls and boys. He needs to be well-rounded."

"Look, I don't give a damn about that, Dru," Alita complained. "Fuck meeting girls on the Gram and Facebook and Snapchat, and all these other sites where these kids be lurking. I'm thinking of Leno's future. I don't want him to be like his dad and end up a lying-ass car salesman. I want Leno to make some real money, enough money to help him buy land, invest his money, and do something good with it besides buying the latest Air Jordans and a BMW or a Hummer. That is so played out, and I don't want my son to be caught up in stupid shit like some of these other boys. Leno has the chance to do big things and make enough money to get us the hell out of the neighborhood we live in. But if he gets distracted messing around with these whorish little thotsicles . . ."

"Excuse me! What did you say?"

"That's what they call them. Those hoes over there. And look at 'em. They're so young; they must learn this behavior from their mamas. I wouldn't be surprised if their mamas are a bunch of hoes too."

"Alita, are you serious?" Dru was aghast. She hated labels and seeing anyone paint a group of people with the same broad stroke of a paintbrush. "Be fair, Sis. Do you personally know any of these girls?"

"Nope!"

"Do you have a hidden cameras in their bedrooms to know what they're doing every night?"

"Don't ask stupid questions," Alita said.

"Then why would you call these girls hoes when you don't know anything about them, Alita?"

"Hello! I have two eyes. I know how girls can be sneaky and very skillful at getting a boy to do what they want. Plus, if these girls weren't hoes, their tits and asses wouldn't be hanging out, and they wouldn't be all up in Leno's face dropping it like it's hot and twerking like there's no tomorrow."

"Oh, really?" Dru sounded doubtful. "Tell me, Alita, what should the girls be doing?"

"They should be somewhere at their house helping their parents out, doing chores, or working at a part-time job trying to make their own money instead of working hard to get Leno's." She paused. "Girl, do you know that some girls tried to send Leno naked photos of themselves?"

"What? Are you serious?"

"Yes, Dru. When I get a sneaky feeling that my son is up to no good, I still look through his little cell phone because, one, he's a minor, two, I pay the bills, and three, I stay on his ass because I am concerned about him the way a good mother should be."

"As long as you respect his privacy, I don't see anything wrong with that," Dru told her.

"A minor that I gave birth to won't get privacy, Dru. I'm telling you. This is why some parents were *sooo* shocked when they found out their little teenage sons were in the garage learning how to put together home-made bombs. These innocent-faced little boys be surfing the net and reading up on domestic terrorist shit. The dumb-ass parents knew nothing and suspected nothing . . . all because they wanted to give the kid some space. Fuck space. The sure way to raise a felon is to not be involved with your kid's life and know what they are doing. Because the second you turn your back or close your eyes, that's the second they're getting into trouble."

"Okay, I stand corrected. Obviously there's more to parenting than what I thought," Dru solemnly told her. "But what about these nude photos?"

Alita took a deep breath then continued. "I was in his room picking up his laundry, 'cause God knows when he'd notice something like dirty laundry and actually pick 'em up and put 'em in the washing machine. So one night when he was taking his shower, I'm standing there in his room trying to hurry up and sort through his clothes when I hear his phone buzzing like crazy. So thinking something urgent might be going on, I pick up the phone and I see a whole bunch of texts, like five or six of 'em, with photos attached. And I couldn't help myself. I clicked on them. And yep, this chick, she couldn't have been any more than fourteen, she is butt-ass naked, vagina all out like it ain't about nothing. Dru, I actually screamed and dropped that fucking cell phone like it was on fire. I ran into the bathroom, yanked back that shower curtain, and nearly beat the shit out of him."

"Oh, Alita, I can't believe you did that. Wait, yes, I can. Anyway, what did Leno say? Who was the girl?"

"Some chick he met online. That's another thing. He has no business going online trying to meet anybody."

"Oh, my God!"

"I know."

"But, Lita, what if Leno never asked her to send the photos? She could have been the instigator. Is that his fault?"

"Hell, yeah, it's his fault. And later that night, I

went back into his phone. And Leno replied back to her, Dru. He looked and did not delete! Why not? Why is he keeping the pictures?"

"You have a good point. And I don't know why he'd leave a paper trail."

"Exactly, Dru. This shit is serious. It's scary. I don't want my son getting in no type of sex tape drama, sex photo drama, none of that. If this girl gets caught they'll see every person she sent those texts to. And these kids are sleeping with their teachers now. High school, middle school. And child predators are everywhere. Church! Boy Scouts! Chat rooms! And even the damned Waffle House! And a lot of this shit has been linked to social media and cell phones. Teachers letting kids contact them through Facebook. It's ridiculous. Anybody that shows too much interest in my son is on my watch list. So anyway, after I confronted him about the pictures, I'm fussing and cussing at Leno wondering why this chick is taking nude selfies and sending 'em to my son. Like, where are her parents? Why don't they know what she's doing? Anyway, I had to make that boy stop his long-ass shower, I thumped his ass a few times, and we sat down and I ended up having a serious talk with him. One of those talks that you never ever want to have with the child you give birth to. But that's the way of the world, and we needed to talk about how one bad decision can ruin your life. After I was done it grieved my spirit so bad that I wanted to go drink some gin and juice just to forget about all of it."

Dru was flabbergasted. "Alita, I'm so sorry you're dealing with this."

Alita paused. "You ain't the only one who's sorry. Some days it's just too much. And I-I wish I could talk to Leonard about it, but he never seems to give a fuck. That's what I get for getting caught up. Never again."

It seemed like after a very long time Leno finally made his way to Dru's car. He grabbed the door handle, hopped in the seat behind Dru, and playfully bopped her on the head.

"Hi, Auntie Dru."

"Hey, nephew. You smell like sweat. And you're messing up my vanilla air freshener."

He sniffed under his arms. "Sorry."

She laughed. "Just teasing. How was practice?"

"I did my usual. And I'm getting better."

"Great," Dru said. "I'll have to come out to one of your games once the season starts."

"That would be tight."

Alita scowled at her son. "If you don't stay focused on your studies and stay on your game, you may not even qualify to be on the main squad. They might bench you son."

"What?" Dru replied. "Are you saying what you think, or are you talking what you know?"

"Yeah, I want to know that too." Leno spoke up. "Where you hear that from, Mama, 'cause I haven't heard that rumor. You been talking to Coach?"

"Don't question me, Leno. Just be ready when I come and pick you up. You saw me waiting for you, yet you act like I'm the chauffeur or something."

"I will have a chauffeur one day," he said with a smile.

"You ain't gon' have nothing if you keep letting folks distract you. I swear to God. I won't let you make me have a nervous breakdown. Let's go, Dru."

Dru obediently started the engine.

"Mama, what you talking about, don't question you? Seems like you got an attitude with me—again."

"Let me see your phone." Alita reached in the back seat and unfolded her hand.

"Mama, not that again. Damn."

"Stop the car, Dru. Stop it now."

"Alita," Dru protested.

"Do it," Alita screamed.

The first chance Dru got, she drove until she came to an empty parking space next to a curb. They had been riding along a major street, and traffic was moving in both directions.

"You, Mr. Know It All, can get the fuck out. Since you disrespecting me as if I'm some girl off the street, you can find your own way back to the house."

"Alita?" Dru said, looking bewildered. "It is that serious?"

"Yes, it is. I won't have this little boy talking to me any kind of way. In that basketball practice, they teach these kids the rules of play. They let them know what happens when the ball goes out of bounds. Right now, Leno has crossed some lines he shouldn't be crossing, and as long as he's living under my roof, there will be consequences on and off the court."

Leno remained in his seat and defiantly stared out the window.

Alita folded her arms across her chest. "I'm going to count to ten, and by the time I'm done, your little ass better be out this car."

He gave her more stony silence.

"Did you fucking hear me, boy? Seven, eight, nine, ten. I said get out."

Looking alarmed, Leno pleaded in earnest. "Mama, please don't do this. I-I'm sorry all right? I didn't mean to disrespect you."

"That's what you said the last time you got smart with me. Now get out."

"But Mama—"

"Out, Leno. I'm not playing with you."

The boy remained glued to his seat for a couple of seconds. But then he shook his head in frustration and in a fit of boiling anger, he yanked at the door handle and got out of the car. He simply walked away, leaving the rear door wide open.

"Leno," Alita screamed. "Why'd you get out on that side of the car? Get your ass back here and close the damned door."

The sudden noise of screeching tires made her stop yelling.

Dru looked out the window. A car that had been driving in the right lane came dangerously close to taking off her door. The driver angrily blasted his horn as he sped past.

"You might as well get out and close the door, Dru."

"No!" she said. "You're the cause of all this, you get up and close my door."

"Me? Why me?"

"Because this time *you're* the one who's out of line."

Alita huffed in anger. She jumped out ran around to the rear of the car. She watched her son, curiously observed the back of him as he walked in the middle of the median that divided the street. He bounced his ball and hung his head down, looking sullen.

As she stared at Leno, a painful lump formed in Alita's throat. He'd gotten so tall lately that he towered over her by seven inches. The realization was staggering. She remembered when Leno was so pint-sized that she could easily carry him in her arms, holding

him sideways like he was a football. She changed his
diapers, taught him the alphabet, read to him as best
she could. Now he had a fresh mouth and challenged
her rules. Whatever happened to the sweet, polite
young man she'd raised?

Alita watched Leno; the sound of him bouncing his
basketball was monotonous. And it grew quieter as he
edged away from his mother. She loved him so very much
that it hurt her to have any distance from him.

Alita stepped into the street.

"I love you, son, don't you realize that?"

She screamed loud enough for him to hear but he
did not acknowledge her.

Alita returned to the car. She took her foot and slammed
the car door shut. She ran to the other side, jumped in the
front seat, and slammed her door too.

"Um, do you mind?" Dru said. "Why are you taking your anger out on my car? If this is how it's going
to be, you can drive your own car to pick up your own
kid."

"Look, Dru. I'm sorry. I'm stressed. Can't you tell
I'm stressed? Got a lot on my mind. I hate when I'm
the parent that has to handle every issue when it comes
to raising our son. Why isn't Leonard out here helping? Why doesn't he drive the boy to practices and
pick him up? Why hasn't he taught the boy how to tie
a tie? I did not sign up to be both his mama and
daddy."

"Can you stop all the yelling and calm down, please?"

"No, I can't. When you're a frustrated single mother
who hasn't been fucked good in a while, and your kid is
getting out of control, there is no calming down. I just
can't."

CHAPTER 4

Confrontation

Within twenty minutes, Dru had driven through the front entrance of the new car lot of the Nissan dealership. It was a busy Saturday afternoon with a couple dozen customers poking around the lot observing the latest model sedans and SUVs.

Dru found a vacant space, pulled in, and turned off the ignition. "Go on," she said to Alita. "It's time that you confronted someone."

"I'm not feeling this Sister Shit right now," Alita protested.

"Well, I'm not feeling how you've been acting lately. If you need to get things off your chest, do it with Leonard. You complain about him to the sisters all the time, but nothing is ever done about how you feel. Sis, I think he's the true source of all your frustration. Not Coco. Not Leno."

"Oh, Dru, c'mon, just take me home. I'm worried about Leno."

"And you ought to be. Why would you kick out your own son?"

"You are not a mother. You wouldn't understand."

"If being hateful and unmerciful to your own baby is the way mothers are supposed to act . . ." She couldn't complete her sentence. "I may never get married either. I think it's much easier to be miserable without a man without having to add a baby to the equation."

"Look, none of this is as bad as it seems. Not motherhood. Not even marriage. You just gotta make sure you're with the right person. That's all."

"Well, right person or not, I think you need to have a conversation with your ex," Dru insisted. "Go on, get out the car, take care of business. I'm going to count to ten, and by the time I'm done you better be out of here."

"Oh, Dru. Are you trying to be like me?"

"I sure as hell am not. Now go! Get out, Alita."

"I can't believe you."

"I can't believe half the things you do either, yet you still do them." Dru softened the edge in her voice. "As long as we're here, just get out and try and talk to him about what's going on. He might be able to help you."

"I doubt it."

"One, two, three, four."

"Druuuuu."

"Five, six, seven."

"You're wrong for this, Dru."

"Eight, nine, ten."

Alita defiantly remained unmoved; she stared straight ahead, looking as angry as she'd ever been.

"Ten?" Dru repeated. "You're not going to answer me?"

Alita said nothing.

"Oh, so you're deaf and dumb now?"

Alita burst out laughing.

And right then Leonard Washington spotted them and slowly walked over to Dru's car. He was wearing a headset and his mouth was steadily moving. Leonard was a tall man himself. He had rugged good looks, strong chin, piercing eyes, with broad shoulders. He resembled a younger Mathew Knowles back when he was managing the group Destiny's Child.

Leonard loved to dress to impress and give the appearance of an important businessman. He wore a decent black suit with the vest, a crisp white shirt, and a red paisley silk necktie set including matching cufflinks and a pocket square that was neatly tucked inside the front pocket. His shoes were a nice grade of black leather and perfectly polished.

As Alita gazed at her ex, she was amazed and pissed off at how good he looked. Like he was something special, and he carried himself as if he were a king.

"Um, Alita," Dru said, "I think Leonard's trying to get your attention. Don't you see him waving at you?"

"He ain't waving at me. He's swatting a mosquito or something."

"Alita, you ought to be ashamed of yourself." Dru laughed heartily at her stubborn and willful sister. "C'mon, girl. Swallow your pride, get out the car, and prove to me that you can have a grown-up conversation with the father of your child. The more we wait here doing nothing, the more the clock is steadily ticking. There's no telling where Leno is right now, and I am so mad about that I can scream. In this day and age, it's not wise to kick out a child. No matter how mad you are at him. Do it for Leno."

Dru's convincing plea made Alita feel sick and ashamed.

"All right, all right. Damn," Alita grumbled. "I will get out of your car just so I won't have to hear your mouth."

"You're getting out," Dru replied, "because you love your son."

Alita sighed, opened the car door, and slowly emerged. She nervously patted her hair and checked to see if there were any lipstick stains showing on her teeth. She wondered if she still looked as good as she had when Leonard first fell in love with her.

As soon as Leonard realized Alita was headed for him, he stopped walking and simply stood still in front of her.

She stared at him.

He stared back with no emotion on his face.

Finally he said, "May I help you, miss? Did you want to purchase a new car or a used one?"

"What the fuck?"

Alita rushed at Leonard with her hands outstretched. She came dangerously close to shoving him with all of her strength, but she stopped herself.

"Because of you," she growled, "our son has run away from home."

"Come again?"

"Leno is missing," Alita said. "I don't know where he is right now."

"Are you serious? When's the last time you saw him?"

"We drove him to practice earlier today."

"What type of practice?"

She stared at him with pure hatred. "Bas-ket-ball."

"Sorry, I didn't know."

Alita simply stared past her ex-husband, wishing he'd just disappear in thin air, never to be seen again.

"Hey, Lita," he tried to explain. "You know how it is."

She recalled how ambitious Leonard had been back in the early years of their marriage. He wanted to be the best at what he did, and that meant working hard and proving to himself and to the company that he had the skills to make them a lot of money.

"I sure do know how it is, Leonard," she scoffed. "But working fourteen hours a day is no excuse to not know what's going on in your son's life. Your only son."

He gave her a blank stare.

"Leno is your only child, right?" she asked, unable to help her curiosity.

"I know you didn't just ask me that question."

Stunned, Alita gave him the middle finger.

Leonard abruptly turned and walked away. She raced beside him, wanting to defuse the situation and stay focused on the main point. "It's nice to see you doing so well, Leonard," she said. "Your being salesman of the month or whatever award they've given you. While you're winning awards and making a ton of money, I'm doing the best I can to raise our son on my own but financially struggling like hell at the same time."

"Oh, really?" he said, sounding totally unconcerned.

"I stock products, okay? That don't pay as much as a new car salesman. I don't earn commission like some people. Plus I have two other jobs that I have to work to make ends meet."

"I don't know why. You get plenty of money from me every month."

"Ha! That chickenfeed ain't enough for a growing teenage boy."

Leonard stopped walking. "Like hell it isn't. I do my part, and the money you get should be more than enough to take care of him."

"Well, I'm telling you, Dumbass, it's not. That chump change barely covers expenses. He eats like a horse and an elephant. A pregnant elephant. As an athlete, Leno has a very healthy appetite. I can't just give him a hot dog and call it a day. He eats four of them suckers at a time. With all the works. And he demands I make chili for him, not the stuff that comes out the can."

"Maybe he should help out and get himself a part-time job."

"Hello? He has no time for no damned job. He has to practice, all the fucking time. And speaking of practice, Leno's big feet won't stay the same size for longer than a month. They know us by name at Skechers and Finish Line and New Balance."

Leonard grinned. "You say his feet are big, huh?"

Alita wanted to punch him. "On top of that," she continued, "I have to scrape up the funds to send him to summer basketball camps and athletic clinics. Been doing that since he was in seventh grade. And he's been begging me to let him take a driver education course; that costs at least five hundred dollars."

Tears filled Alita's eyes, but she dared them to slide down her cheeks. She toughened up. "So you see that doing your part is more than just paying the State of Texas. It's driving him around. It's keeping up with his schools. Making him do his chores. Taking his ass to the barbershop. Ha! You should see the new haircut Leno has these days. He wants to be all fancy and shit and stand out, so he has this Mohawk thing going on.

The bottom part of his head is dyed brown like his natural color. And the crown is like a fiery blond color. It stands up several inches high. He calls it his signature hairstyle. Ha! Our son looks like that fucking Dennis Rodman, only he's a hundred percent more handsome. I hope he won't end up being as controversial as Rodman but it would be nice if he makes a grip of cash—" Alita shut her mouth. She wanted Leonard to know their son was good, but she wasn't ready for him to know how great he was at playing ball.

"Okay, Lita. It sounds like you have a lot on your plate. Well, I'm doing what I can do. But if you work hard like I work, I don't believe that you have time to do anything else for Leno. So tell me something. What's really going on? What are you actually spending time doing besides spending all the child support money?"

"You cheap-ass bastard," she said. "I know you're good at what you do. Selling people a bullshit dream just like you did me years ago. So I know you making plenty of commission on these car sales. Thanks to President Obama, the interest rates are very low. So yeah . . . lots of people are being approved to buy all kinds of cars these days."

"So?"

"So you can afford to give more money to your son."

"Don't you mean give more money to his mother?" Leonard rolled his eyes and stormed away from Alita. She ran and caught up with him again.

"The older he gets, the more things cost. He'll be a senior very soon. And he needs money for graduation photos, a class ring, the prom, the class trip, and when he goes to college, that's even more money."

Leonard stopped. "You said he plays basketball, right?"

She wanted to say "yes, idiot" but she said, "Have you been listening to anything I've told you?" She sighed. "Leno plays ball. And he's pretty good at it too."

"If he's as good as you say he is, then he'll qualify for full scholarships."

"Is that what you're hoping for? Because if you believe that a full scholarship will replace your daddy duties, you are dead wrong, asshole."

"The name is Mr. Washington."

"You may have Denzel's last name," she argued, "but you definitely don't have his class."

"That wasn't necessary, Lita."

"What's necessary is you stepping up and knowing you should be helping out more with our son. And yes, you should be contributing to his college fund and not automatically think he'll get a full scholarship."

"Well, if my son is busy, then guess what? I am too. I'm doing everything that it is humanly possible to do based on the schedule I have."

Alita looked at Leonard like he was crazy. "You're doing the best you can? Like, even though you work long hours you can't call Leno once in a while? And you don't work every Sunday, so surely you can squeeze in some time for him."

"Look, I know what I'm saying makes no sense to you, but you're on the outside looking in. I have so little personal time that I usually sleep in on Sundays. I do stuff around the house, taking care of my car, doing laundry. I have to live my life too."

Alita bit her bottom lip. Everyone was busy. But some people had excuses while others got things done.

"Lita, don't worry about Leno. He'll be all right.

And if you're as dedicated a mother as you say that you are, then you two should wind up just fine."

"I'm glad you're so confident," she said sarcastically. "But we could do even better with your help. This isn't just about me. It's about your own flesh and blood."

"If things go good for him, then you probably won't need my help. Just keep doing what you're doing. He'll get that scholarship, sweetheart. And I'm sure when he does, it may be one of the answers to your many desperate prayers, Alita."

She wanted to punch him, throw him to the ground, kick him in his nuts, and then kick him in the face with some spike heels. But she remembered their recent Sister Day assignment: *Confront someone in a nice way and tell them what's been bothering you.*

Alita knew that so many issues bothered her, she didn't know where to begin. But she knew she had to start somewhere.

Be nice be nice be nice.

She softened her voice and tried to smile. "Look, Leonard, I know you take your job very seriously. You're good at what you do, and I know that and I am impressed."

"Thank you."

"I see you're very busy, and I honestly did not come by here to argue or fight or start any trouble."

"Then why are you still here? And why are you still harassing me? I'm at my place of employment. If you could hold down a decent job, you might really understand me."

Alita slugged him before she realized it. Her closed fist bopped him on top of his head. Leonard felt as if he'd been hit by a boulder. His face contorted with

anger. And Alita instantly had scary flashbacks of
Leonard yelling at her. Shoving her against a wall . . .
his fist crashing through the living room wall and
tearing a small hole into it.

"Oh, shit, my bad. I'm so sorry." She immediately
felt regretful. Two men dressed in security officer uniforms quickly approached her.

"Mr. Washington," one of them said, "is everything
all right?"

"We're good," he told them. "I got this. We'll be done
in a minute. Thanks, guys." After they left, Leonard
asked Alita to come walk with him. They headed toward
the very end of car lot. Leonard found a private space
in between two Nissan Armadas. The vehicles' height
was so high, it felt like Alita was surrounded by sky-
scrapers.

She eyed Leonard suspiciously. Maybe she was
about to get her ass whipped right there on a parking
lot. "Why'd you bring me over here?" she asked.

"Stop thinking the worst," he replied.

"Can't help but think that when you've been known
to raise your fist at me."

"As I recall, Alita, you've assaulted me way more
times than I've hit you. I still have a scar on my knee
from that one time when you went batshit crazy. All
because I got home five minutes and thirteen seconds
late."

She glared at him.

"And you're very lucky that I never pressed charges,"
he concluded. "So if I were you I'd just chill."

"All right, okay."

"Let's get back to business," Leonard said. "You
came out here to see me, and I know it's pretty serious,
because the last time we talked you screamed into the

phone 'I never want to see your black ass again.' Do you remember that, Alita?"

"What if I do?"

"I'm just saying that I know you, woman. I know how hell-bent and crazy you get when you're passionate about things. You tend to stress out over stuff that can be solved if you just give it a chance."

She nodded. "Go ahead."

"And I know that it's only because you think Leno has run away that I will give you a pass for acting like an ass back there."

"Oh, wow, thanks."

"And be forewarned, the next time you won't get a pass. You need to get over whatever you're angry about, because it takes two to make a marriage work, and we know you were not the perfect wife."

"Why are we talking about me?" Alita said.

"You're right. This isn't about you. The main thing you should be concerned about right now is our son, where he is right now, and you should definitely forget that idea about giving you more money. Maybe you can get a better paying job."

Tears threatened to fill Alita's eyes, but she wouldn't allow it. "It's not just the money, Leonard. You're not around when I see my son run fast toward a basket . . ." She could barely speak. "I suffer through the worry and the fear . . . all by myself, Leonard. Can't you understand that?"

Leonard shifted his eyes and refused to look at her.

"Money helps, but your presence is better. Maybe you can help him out with his homework, for example. Leno tries to do his best to pass his classes, and so far he's done all right. His school ain't about shit, but that's because we're zoned to it, and that can't be helped unless we move. And I do work, by the way, and you know it. I have to. If I depended on the little bit of money you give me, both Leno and I would be out on the street pushing around a shopping cart and looking for someplace to sleep under a tall bridge and competing with the pigeons for food."

He sneered. "You really know how to turn on the dramatics, don't you?"

Alita almost wanted to laugh. "I'm keeping it real, Leonard."

"You're trying to manipulate me, Alita, and it won't work. Not anymore."

She felt like slapping him one last time. "Leonard, you were an ass back then, and you're still one. I'm glad we're not together anymore."

"You're not the only one. I'm glad about a lot of things too." He stopped talking and realized he was sweating so hard that he needed to remove his suit jacket. He took it off and neatly folded it over his arm.

"Look, what's done is done. Our only concern right now is our son," he said. Leonard glanced at his watch. "Tell you what. I can take a short break and try to figure out where he is. I'm sure whatever is bothering him is only temporary."

"How can you be so sure of that?"

"Because he has my genes. He is resilient. He is a smart boy and is not inclined to do too many stupid things. At least he doesn't get that from my side of the family."

"If you trying to throw shade at my family, don't! They love Leno and care about him and everything he does."

"Good for them."

As if right on cue, suddenly Dru's cute face came into view as she slowly walked past the two Armadas.

Leonard saw her and whistled. "Hey, over here."

Dru smiled and walked over to Leonard. She extended her hand. "Well, hello there, brother-in-law."

"Don't call him that," Alita scoffed.

Leonard smiled at Dru, reached over, and gave her a pleasant hug.

"You're still looking just as beautiful as I remember you, Dru."

"Why, thank you."

"Oh, girl, if you fall for that lie, you're really stupid. Only stupid bitches fall for stupid lies."

"Um, excuse me," Dru said. "Don't forget I'm your ride. You can't be talking crap about the limo driver. She will drive off and leave you. Then who's going to look stupid?"

"And if you do leave me, with all these new cars around here, honey, I'll be just fine," Alita said.

They all started laughing and broke up the tension that threatened to make Alita explode with rage. She calmed down and turned. "Leonard, I don't want to fuss and argue. I've called Leno ten times on his cell. He didn't pick up. I know he's mad at me, and it kills me when he ignores me. It hurts so badly."

Feeling drained from all the drama, Alita found herself collapsing in Leonard's arms. He nodded his head, patted her back. His display of sympathy actually made her feel even more emotional, but she didn't want to break down in tears.

He let her lean on him for a minute then gently pushed her away.

"I'll help you, Alita. Give me a minute," he said and began to move from in between the SUVs.

He quickly departed, leaving Alita and Dru to themselves.

"Hey, everything all right?" Dru asked.

"I honestly don't know," Alita said. "Welcome to my life. Shit always bound to happen, and this is just the newest thing to deal with."

Dru placed her arm around her sister's shoulder. They walked toward the dealership showroom to catch up with Leonard. Ex-husband or not, Alita was forced to team up with him and figure out what could be done to save her son's life.

CHAPTER 5

The Lord's Day

Burgundy Reeves Taylor, the modern-day superwoman, was on a constant mission: From the time she was seven years old, she strove to be the best at everything she did. Burgundy made all A's from elementary school through twelfth grade. She quickly enrolled in college and graduated early thanks to the blessing of a full scholarship. Burgundy always wanted to be her own boss; she earned an undergraduate degree in business administration and minored in marketing. Although she did pledge Delta Sigma Theta when she was a sophomore, Burgundy refused to seriously date while she was in college. She hung out with her sorors, but she was mostly single-minded, and her studies always came first in her life.

But she crossed paths with Nathaniel Taylor when she was twenty-one years old, shortly after she finished college. Burgundy knew from their first date that there was no other man for her. Nate was a perfect gentleman, he seemed to have a good head on his shoulders, and he didn't nag her for sex like most young guys did. He had just opened his brunch business and seemed to be on the path to success. The qualities he possessed made him stand out. Burgundy became serious about Nate rather quickly, acting fast before any other woman could grab on to him. They became engaged within that first year, and she married him nine months later. Burgundy's wedding was attended by two hundred people and included her sorority sisters and his frat brothers. The wedding was paid for by Nate's family. They were featured in the *Houston Chronicle* and became the talk of the town. Nate and his parents split the costs for their Hawaiian honeymoon. As lovely as that trip was, after they returned to Houston and settled in, Burgundy decided that would be the last time she'd let someone else pay for anything major on her behalf. Burgundy had a brilliant mind and could easily brainstorm when it came to business and marketing ideas. She and her husband made an enviable team. They excelled at whatever venture they started. She was determined to be the best wife she could be and grew more determined after she gave birth to his two daughters: Natalia, who was six, and Sidnee, who was four years old. And now she was embarking on the normal quest that had become her life.

It was Sunday, one day after the Sister Day meeting. Burgundy woke up early, around five-thirty. Burgundy lay next to Nate, who was sound asleep. It felt so good whenever she could reach over and caress her husband. Knowing that he was inches away from made her feel calm and peaceful. She drew her strength from realizing she had a good man.

Burgundy started talking to him even though she figured he couldn't hear her.

"Hey, baby. God is good. He woke me up this morning and blessed me to see another day." She smiled and pressed her lips against his warm cheek. Nate mumbled and shifted to spread out on his side.

She softly laughed then continued. "I want you to know that I love you very much, baby. I thank the Lord for you, for my kids, our life."

She sighed in contentment and refused to wipe the huge smile from her face.

Right then she heard her cell phone vibrating. She rolled her eyes but reached over to grab it off the table.

"Hello, Lita," she answered. "Is everything all right?"

"Sorry to bother you."

"You're not bothering me."

"Girl, stop! I know you're up already. You probably about to run on that treadmill or suck Nate's dick so he can wake up and fuck, fuck, fuck you real quick since he's always working and you always doing something."

Burgundy grimaced. "Watch all that foul language, please. It's the Lord's Day."

"What's that supposed to mean? Y'all don't fuck on Sundays?"

"Lita, *please*. Hold on a sec."

Burgundy was ready to groan. Although she had not been thinking about nibbling on her husband's penis, she figured that Alita was right. If Burgundy was going to sex him up, it probably would have to be done on Sunday morning while he was asleep, because God knows when she'd have time to do it otherwise.

But right then hopping on the treadmill instead of on Nate seemed more probable.

Burgundy got up and pressed the phone to her ear.

"I was just getting up. I need to do a thirty-minute cardio walk and lift that set of barbells that Nate bought me for my birthday."

"That's what he bought you?"

"He sure did," Burgundy said as she began to make her way to their home gym. It was located on the second story of their spacious stucco home. The house had two staircases, one in the front as soon as you walked in the door and the other in the kitchen, which provided a shortcut if you didn't want to walk all the way to their huge foyer.

Burgundy and Nate's bedroom was located closer to the back staircase. She made her way up the stairs trying to listen to Alita's chattering.

"Anyway, girl," Alita continued, "I had to fill you in on what happened yesterday. Remember? I called to tell you about the drama I went through about Leno and his daddy and those fast-ass little girls and how he called himself running away?"

"Yeah." Burgundy yawned. "What happened?"

"So at first his daddy couldn't get the boy on his phone either. But after about thirty minutes, Leno called him back. I was glad he did that. Sometimes he gets in these moods where he is mad at his daddy for long stretches and he'll ignore him."

"I wonder where he gets that from."

"Funny. Anyway, Leno talked to his daddy and they actually had a decent conversation. It gave me hope, you know? I just want them to have a strong relationship."

"I don't know what to say."

"Yeah, tell me about it. I was shocked too," Alita continued. "So father and son talked, and Leonard was able to get away from his job to go and pick up my baby. And I wanted to go too, I really did. I begged Dru to drive me over to where Leno was, but she flat out said no. Can you believe that shit? That little heifer gets this unhelpful attitude sometimes, and I can't stand that. If you nice, stay nice. Because her acting like a dick when she's really a pussy just confuses me. Hello? B? Are you listening to me, or am I talking to myself as usual?"

Burgundy laughed. "Girl, stop. I'm listening. I have you on speakerphone while I'm doing my walk. But since no one can ever predict what will come out of your mouth, I may have to take you off speaker. There are some people that just can't be on speakerphone."

"Oh, fuck you, B."

"See what I mean? What if Sid and Natalia wander in here?"

"They're used to me. They know how their auntie Alita rolls."

"And that is exactly why you can never babysit my girls."

"Oh, you're so wrong for that." Alita laughed. "I'm just so glad that my nieces are still very young." She paused. "I'm telling you, B. Enjoy them while you can. Let them be little girls. Don't try to force them to grow up too fast. None of that letting them wear lipstick when they're four and six years old. I can't stand that ghetto-ass shit."

"But I thought you loved ghetto life?"

"I do, but there is a such as thing as being *too* ghetto. You know what I mean, B?"

Burgundy knew exactly what Alita meant, but she had no time to go into it. She was running on a tight, systematic schedule. Everything had to be just so in Burgundy Reeves Taylor's life. She knew that after she did her walk and lifted the weights, it would be time to run the bubble bath. She'd takes a few sips of her favorite hazelnut coffee and study a couple of scriptures as she soaked in the tub.

Every minute of her day was always accounted for. She believed this is what her husband loved about her. She wasn't one to lie around waiting on her man to pay constant attention to her. Burgundy was always on the move, being a good mom, wife, and businesswoman, plus helping most of her siblings sort out their love lives and family drama.

"Anyway, I hope you're listening to me, B, but even if you're not, it's all right, because saying things out loud helps me to process stuff. So Dru acted like an ass and refused to take me to where Leno was."

"Why can't you drive your own car?"

"That piece of shit car is real half-assed. It's on its last legs," Alita complained. "I really want to get a new car, but I can't afford even a mountain bike right now. Shit. I need a man."

"You need a man?" Burgundy asked.

"Well, I will as soon as I'm off of my man break."

"I think you've lost your mind, Alita. I really do. Coco says you're love challenged."

"She might be right, because I'm on strike right now. Everybody who knows me knows that. If I want to be miserable, I'll do it by my damned self."

"But why do you have to be miserable just because you're in a relationship, Alita? You can be happy and attached and fulfilled . . . You do realize that, right?"

"Ha! All I know is screaming, fighting, fucking, cussing, bullshit, and aggravation."

"I give up. How soon they forget." Burgundy smiled to herself. She wanted to rub it in and remind Alita how often she used to call her during the earlier times of Leonard and her relationship. Back then Alita seemed happier than she'd ever been in her life, constantly gushing about this perfect man that she had. But Burgundy wasn't in the mood to get cursed out so she kept the "happy Alita Washington" memories to herself.

"Um, I have fifteen minutes to go to burn some calories, so hurry up and finish your little story, Alita."

"All right. Let's see. Where was I? Oh, so Leonard tells me that Leno was actually over at one of those girls' house. The one I was telling you about? The one with the big booty who was practically gyrating against my son in public? That little pedophile about to get arrested, she keep messing with my son."

"Oh, my goodness. How old is she?"

"See, B, these days the girls lie and say they're fifteen or sixteen, but they're really like nineteen or twenty. How many times have I told my son, do not believe it when a girl tells him their age. They need to pull out a driver license or some type of government ID before I believe their lying asses. Oh, girl, you don't know how stressed out I am about finding a condom. I don't need him to be fucking little girls left and right. I'm only thirty-six, too young to be a grandmother. Sperm don't care how old you are; if the dick works he can get a girl pregnant. And because of his little hormones I stay worried every single day until he's back in my sight safe and sound."

"You can't live life that way, Alita. You can't monitor Leno twenty-four hours a day."

"Do you monitor Nate?"

"Um, no. We don't roll like that. We trust each other. We give each other personal space."

"I don't believe that, because last time I checked,

you two have a joint Facebook and Instagram accounts. Are you serious?"

"Nothing wrong with joint social media! I have nothing to hide, and neither does he."

"So you mean to tell me you actually share passwords and can read each other's messages?"

"Yes!"

"Sick."

"Not sick! Smart," Burgundy insisted. "We share passwords for all of our email accounts too. Don't forget we have a lot of business ventures. And if anything ever happens to either of us, it won't do any good to be locked out of emails when we need to tend to business. It's just something we do."

"Don't tell me. Nate came up with that brilliant idea, or did you come up with it?"

"We both did."

"Hold on a sec," Alita ordered. Soon Burgundy heard her sister making vomiting noises. She laughed at her sister's proclivity for extreme reactions.

"You're a hot mess," she told Alita. "I heard you making those disgusting sounds."

"That's 'cause you disgust me."

"You're just jealous, Lita. I get it. You are a hater. Haters gon' hate."

"What I hate," Alita replied, "is that you are so blinded by love that you feel the need to know his password to his email. Tell me something. Do you know everything about your husband? Do y'all keep any secrets from each other?"

"We talk," Burgundy explained. "That's what we do. We get our feelings out. I'm not hiding anything from him, and I hope he's not hiding anything from me. But if he is, it just means that I need to be more understanding so that he feels comfortable enough to come talk to me. About anything. At any time."

"Girl, bye. I feel my dinner rising up in my throat, and I need to find a toilet and let it out so I won't mess up my good carpet."

"Before I let you go vomit, I wanted to hear the rest of your story about Leno."

"All you need to know is that he is now home where he belongs. And I'm not letting that boy out of my sight till he turns twenty-six."

"You, Alita, are one crazy mama."

"I sure am. I have to be." Alita sighed with relief. "Leonard Washington actually came through for me this time, but I'm sure I won't be able to depend on him every time."

"That's why I want you hook you up with that friend; I told you about him. We work together every Sunday at the church bookstore."

"That's nice."

"We've worked side by side for years, and I've gotten to know him pretty well."

"So what?"

"Alita, you're single. He's single and looking."

"I ain't looking, though."

"And his name is Shade Wilkins."

"Are you serious? His name is Shade? That sounds messed up. Nope. Mm mmm. Not interested."

"At least give the guy a chance and meet with him before you turn him down."

"I'm not giving no man a chance to hurt me." Alita spoke with defiance and finality. Love could feel so very good when everything fit well together, but when love wasn't right it could hurt like hell: a devastating pain that Alita did not enjoy.

"Just one date!" Burgundy pleaded.

"Thanks for the offer, Sis, but right now my heart is on lock, and I'm the only one that holds the key."

"Really?" Burgundy said, sounding doubtful.

"You damn fucking straight."

"Oh, God. I told you no profanity. It's the Lord's Day. Respect my wishes."

"Respect mine and stop trying to hook me up with your church friends. I don't care how angelic they sound. I don't care if they have wings and harps. I don't care if they've been baptized three times. I don't give a fuck!"

Burgundy gave up. "All right! You win. Talk later. Smooches, Ms. Potty Mouth."

"Okay, then before you hang up, let me ask you one more thing."

"Yes, Alita?"

"Is bitch-ass a bad word?"

"*What?*"

"How about asswipe?"

Click.

Burgundy hung up on Alita; she was ready to get on with her tightly scheduled day.

When she returned to their bedroom, Nate was still spread out underneath the covers on their king-size bed. She went into the bathroom and proceeded to fill the tub with water. She took a seat and reviewed her next week's calendar while she waited.

Soon she heard Nate yawning. From where she was standing, she saw him open his eyes. Burgundy sprang to her feet.

"Hi, babe," she said to him as she approached the side of their bed. "Did I wake you? I know you like to sleep in on Sundays."

"It's fine." He sat up in bed and stared at his wife. Burgundy was completely nude and was trying to cram her long hair inside of a large bath towel.

"Need any help, baby?" he asked.

"No. I got it." She blushed. But she struggled to wrap her hair so that it was completely covered. In seconds Nate fled to her side.

"Here, let me get that." He stood behind Burgundy and managed to neatly stuff her long strands of hair into the towel so that none of it was showing. When he was done, he stared hungrily at her ass. He reached over and caressed her soft bottom. He instantly felt himself getting aroused. He stroked his penis.

"Babe?" he said in that husky voice of his.

Burgundy yelped and scooted away. "No. No. Not right now. Gotta take my bath and get the girls up, and you know what a hassle that is. We're trying to make it to Sunday school on time this week."

They attended Solomon's Temple, a megachurch located a good forty minutes from their house.

When Burgundy excused herself, she dashed to the bathroom, opened a cabinet door, and retrieved her favorite brand of bubble bath. She screwed off the cap and squeezed the liquid into her iron claw-foot tub. This was the place she went when she needed to relax. Once the water filled up high enough to suit her tastes, Burgundy lifted up one leg and lowered herself into the tub.

She listened for any sounds coming from her bedroom. She knew it had been a couple of months since she'd let her husband touch her.

Nate came and stood in the doorway.

"Burgundy, we need to talk."

"Can it wait?" She was seated in the tub and situated in front of her bathtub caddy. It was sturdy enough to hold books and her coffee mug. Burgundy picked up a file folder that she'd laid on the caddy. She opened the folder and waved sheets of paper.

"I'm multitasking. Going over this week's schedule. Baller Cutz is running out of razors, clippers, and neck strips. I'll pop in at the Warehouse Salon first thing tomorrow. Then I'll need to pick up the new menus from the print shop around ten." She inserted the papers back into the folder and waited.

Nate sat in a chair next to her. She hid her body underneath a mountain of white bubbles.

"I thought we weren't supposed to think about or even talk about business on Sundays," he told her.

"Well, you *don't* have to talk about it . . . but I just like to stay on top of things."

"I need you to stay on top of me, Burg."

"What else is new? All men ever think about is sex."

"That's not all we think about. Plus, I'm not men. And according to that Bible you love to read, you owe me some booty. You're not supposed to deny me."

"What? Where is that scripture?"

Nate got his cell phone and clicked on a Bible app. "First Corinthians chapter five, verse—"

"Oh, whatever, Nate. I'm fairly positive that a man came up with that rule. Am I right?"

"Thank God that he did."

"I don't care what that verse says." She picked up a sponge and starting cleaning her arms. "Right now I'm getting ready—"

"Getting ready to go to church," he said. "Wouldn't it be something if Pastor Solomon preaches about *sex* today?"

"If Pastor Sol did that, it would be a miracle. And

you'd better not call him and put any ideas in his head either."

Nate stood up and forced a laugh. What did Burgundy expect him to do? Masturbate until his penis fell off from exhaustion?

"Hey," he finally muttered. "I tried. What can I say?"

Nate left the room, got back in bed, and slid underneath the covers. He conjured up an image of a naked body in his mind. He vigorously rubbed his penis and hoped it would just stop hurting.

Burgundy finished her bath and got dressed. When it was precisely seven, she gently kissed Natalia and Sid out of their sleep. She oversaw them taking off their pajamas, then she coaxed them into their own bathtub and thoroughly bathed them. They dried off and put on underwear and sat at their vanity mirror. Burgundy patiently combed the girls' hair until they resembled adorable child models. She went to their closet and selected two matching red dresses and raspberry ballerina flats. She helped the girls get ready while engaging them in delightful conversation.

"How are my perfect little angels?" she asked. Burgundy wanted her daughters to have the best self-esteem ever, and she always endeavored to speak positivity and treat them like royalty.

"I love you girls so much. You are my life. Both you and your daddy, of course."

"Mommy, I love that new baby doll you got for me." Sid was the clingiest child. "She talks and she cries and when I give her the pacifier, her mouth moves around like she's a real baby. I feel sad when she's sad."

"That's nice to hear," Burgundy said. "But this doll is not real. Those aren't real tears. It's all just pretend."

"Sid is such a baby," Natalia said. She was daddy's little girl and always wanted to prove how grown up she was. "I don't play with dolls anymore," Natalia said.

"Don't be like that, Nat," Burgundy gently told her. "It's okay for you to play with a doll."

"I don't like dolls." Natalia's voice had a snobbish tone. "My daddy's going to buy me some better toys than that. Sid can have all my old toys."

Burgundy dismissed her daughter's haughty statement. She finished combing Sid's and Natalia's hair and then went downstairs and prepared a light breakfast for her family to eat. She completed all these tasks before seven-thirty. It was customary for her to attend to the girls while Nate slept in. He always preferred to show up at the church in time for the eleven o'clock service.

Once she was satisfied that the girls had eaten and were quietly playing in the upstairs playroom, Burgundy bounded up the spiral staircase. She timidly knocked on Elyse's bedroom door. When she didn't hear a response, she attempted to turn the knob but, as usual, the door was securely locked.

"Elyse, baby, you going to church with me or are you riding with Nate?"

She didn't hear a single sound and impatiently noted the time. It was getting late. Burgundy was ready to drive her daughters to children's church and needed a few extra minutes to check them in before she could join the eight-thirty a.m. service.

She figured that Nate was still in their bedroom. Knowing him, by now he'd officially gotten up for the day and was probably using their landline to make one phone call after another. Nate was always checking up with Jordan Andrews, Morning Glory's manager, to make sure that the restaurant had opened precisely at six a.m. and that the cooks had arrived for pre-preparations of their breakfast specials.

"Honey," Burgundy yelled. "I'm about to go, all right?" Her voice traveled down the hallway as she busily scuttled the girls downstairs. "I'll see you at church in a couple hours. Bye!"

She didn't hear Nate's reply, but was too preoccupied to follow up. She and the girls settled in her vehicle and within minutes were headed in the direction of Solomon's Temple.

Elyse was hidden away in her bedroom closet. All the lights were lights off, and it was eerily dark inside the small rectangular space. Although it was quite warm inside of the house, the girl wore three long-sleeved shirts, two pair of sweat pants, and two pair of underwear. Her clothes clung to her skin and felt slick with perspiration. A big baseball cap covered her hair. She reached up and patted her forehead, which was dotted with sweat. She sniffed herself and smelled the dirtiness on her skin. She purposely had not taken a bath the night before. She badly wanted to clean herself in a scorching shower. But she couldn't. She sat in the dark on the floor of the closet listening for sounds. Earlier, she clearly had heard her sister Burgundy call for her; she had wanted to answer her, but didn't. She wasn't in the mood for her sister's cheerful ways.

Besides, Elyse had been too busy praying. Crying.

Shaking uncontrollably. Burgundy may have loved Sundays, but Elyse hated them. She hated the routine. She hated everything about the Lord's Day.

She heard knocking at her door. She fumbled around in the dark until she found her pillow. She pressed it against her chest and squeezed her eyes shut.

"Elyse? Elyse?"

It was Nate. She didn't reply. Her hands covered both her ears. She quietly hummed and drowned out the sound of her name, dismissing everything except the sound of her own voice. After she stopped humming, she was glad Nate wasn't calling her anymore. She just wanted everybody to leave her alone. Forget about her and allow her to exist in peace. She wanted to stay undisturbed until she blissfully fell asleep.

CHAPTER 6

Wifey

Coco spent the week focused on Calhoun, frequently reminding him of his responsibilities to her and their kids.

Even though they lived together, his driver's license listed his mother's address. Her name was Henrietta Humphries, and she was always in her son's business. Henrietta would ask him if he was spending the night at "home." And he'd tell his mother "yes," but seventy-five percent of the time, at Coco's insistence, he would sleep over at the big house.

Later that week on Wednesday, Coco reached Calhoun by cell phone. "You coming straight home right after work?" she asked.

She knew he was in his company truck delivering cases of soda to various stores around the Houston area. Calhoun assured Coco that he'd come directly home and help her with the kids, no problem. Satisfied with his answer, Coco ended the call and began to do one of the things she loved the most: season and fry some chicken, whip up a bowl of mashed potatoes, and cook her family a pot of mustard and turnip greens. She cooked her butt off, and when she was done, she sat down and waited on Calhoun. Forty minutes after he completed his shift, Calhoun breezed through the doorway.

"'Bout time you got home."

"Don't give me that attitude, Coco, you know how it is out here."

"No, I don't. Especially when I can't get you on the phone so I can ask you what's happening."

Calhoun gave her a disapproving look. "Work. Damn. Do I need to explain to you everything I'm doing all day long, from the time I punch in till the time I punch out?"

"Yeah, you do. I'm your real boss," she said, partially teasing him.

Coco gave him a huge, silly grin that made him crack a smile. Then she dutifully honored him with a passionate kiss and made him go sit down at their wobbly dinner table.

She watched him devour his food; she could barely eat anything herself while she stared at him.

"Did I do okay? You like it?" she asked.

He nodded, his mouth full. "I always do," he tried to tell her.

"Good," she responded with a smile. "That's all I need to know."

They ate their meal and afterward retreated to the living room to watch a *Fresh Prince of Bel-Air* marathon.

Calhoun sat with his long legs spread out and resting on top of the coffee table. Coco went and got Cadee and Chloe and made them sit up under their daddy.

They all snuggled together while Coco positioned Chance right next to her, the girls on the other side.

She brimmed with happiness, there with her ever-growing family.

"How was work, baby?" she asked as her eyes focused on the television show.

"A'ight."

"You meet any new people while you were delivering?"

"Coco, c'mon, we having a good time chilling. Why you gotta bring up who I meet at the job? What difference that make?"

Her smile faded slightly. "I just wanna know how your day went."

"No, you don't. You wanna know more than that. I know how your mind thinks."

She was amused. "You think you know, but you don't."

"Women like you . . . hell, I can see right through all this shit you doing. Cooking for me. Serving my plate. Making me sit here with the kids and watch wack-ass Will Smith. I feel like I'm in prison."

She stopped smiling. "Calhoun, how can you say that shit in front of your kids? You're supposed to wanna be with us, kicking it with us. It's your damn kids."

"Except that one." He pointed at Chance.

"Hush your mouth with that." Coco was so mad she wanted to slug Calhoun. "You raising him like he yours. And that's what counts."

"True."

"Then there shouldn't be anything you wanna do more than be with your family."

Calhoun knew he ought to shut his mouth, but his feelings were boiling over. They always did whenever Coco pressured him.

"There you go again, Ma, telling me exactly what I should be doing to be happy. How you know what makes me happy?"

She shrugged.

"You ever ask?" Before she could reply he blurted, "You need to stop focusing on me so much."

"Why?" she challenged him. "What makes you say that, Calhoun?"

"Huh?" he asked.

"You trying to tell me something?" she demanded. "As hard as I work to make us a family? As many hours as it takes to keep the house clean, keep the kids in line, wash your uniforms, and take care of our business? If I didn't focus on you, on us, who the fuck else would? Huh?"

"Stop raising your voice."

"You better hope I don't raise my fist."

By then two-year-old Chance had crawled on her lap. He wanted his mom to hold him, ease his fears. Their frequent loud yelling and aggressive talk made him antsy. But in anger, Coco pushed Chance off of her like he was a frisky puppy.

"Stay off my stomach," she told him. "That hurts your mama."

Coco then struggled to stand up. Chance started screaming, angry that he wasn't where he wanted to be.

"Pick me up," he hollered.

"Shut your mouth," she screamed back.

Cadee and Chloe clung even tighter to their father. Things grew so chaotic by then that even Calhoun begin to feel pissed off.

Coco came and stood in front of him, hands on her hips.

"See what you've done?" she said. "If I didn't have

to deal with so much stress about you and what you doing when you not here, and how you supposed to be helping me out more, none of this would be happening."

"Oh, really?"

"Yes! I get tired of doing everything I can for you, just for you to treat me like shit." She stared right at him and blocked his view of the television.

"Get out the way," he said. "I can't see the show through your big ass."

"I thought you didn't like Will Smith?"

"I don't like you raising your voice at me and acting like you want to throw down."

She angrily stared at him. Some days she loved him with more passion than she ever thought she could feel. Other days she wondered if what Alita had been telling her was true . . . Calhoun Humphries wasn't the best man out there . . . that she was settling for scraps when she could have better . . . that he wasn't a decent boyfriend, no matter how you sliced it.

Dru had told her one time that when it came to Calhoun, she acted too controlling. She informed Coco that men can't be controlled. The more you try to lock them down, the more they want to escape. But she couldn't imagine Calhoun not being in her life.

Coco felt her heart giving in, and she swallowed her pride. "Baby, look. I-I'm sorry. I know you work hard at what you do. You don't have time to be hollering at every woman that passes by you at these damned grocery stores. Plus, why would you wanna holler at them when you have me to come home to?" She gave him a hopeful grin.

He ignored her. She yelled at Chloe and Cadee. "Get up. Move out the way."

They leapt to their feet in an instant and stampeded out of the way.

Coco waited for Calhoun to shift to the side a few inches so she could sit next to him. He stared right through her as if she were invisible.

"Dude, you bugging." She lifted his long leg, moved it out the way, and sat next to him. She scrutinized his handsome face, his thick, smooth lips; rugged, brittle skin. She raised her hand up to gingerly caress the cheek area right by his beard. It felt warm yet hard.

"I love you, Calhoun. That's why I do what I do. I just want . . . us."

He finally gave in.

"I know that," he said stubbornly.

"But do you like that?"

"Yeah, damn, Coco. Now go on and go somewhere so I can look at TV."

She smiled at her man, her heart filling with love for him. "Good. That's all I want to know."

That weekend, Calhoun had the day off from work. Coco needed her man's help. She was on public assistance. And her Texas EBT card balance was down to twenty dollars; in order to feed the kids, she needed about two hundred fifty dollars' worth of food.

"It's 'bout time you took on more responsibilities," she said as she fussed at him. "I'm tired of footing a lot of the bills. Thank you for the little bit you do, but you gotta do more."

"Okay, all right," he complained. "I'll do anything to shut your nagging-ass mouth."

Calhoun agreed to take her shopping without complaint. The grocery store was especially busy on this Saturday afternoon. Coco filled her basket with fresh fruits and vegetables, plenty of chicken, fish, and red meat, cereal, butter cookies, hot dogs, and potato chips. She also made sure to get the foods that Chance would want to eat.

Once she filled her basket, Coco stood in line with her hands perched on the grocery cart; she mentally calculated the total.

"Hey, hold on a sec. I need a six-pack," Calhoun said. He promised that he'd be right back. Chance was sitting in the baby seat of her cart. The other two little ones, Cadee and Chloe, were standing right in front of the basket.

"Y'all stay outta people's way," Coco yelled at her kids.

As Coco stood there, all she could hear was people standing around her conversing in Spanish. Folks waited in front of her, and a long line of folks was behind her. Lots of noise and crowds irritated Coco. She began placing her food items on the conveyer belt. Soon she was in a grim mood, since the salesclerk had rung up her food but Calhoun had yet to arrive.

"Damn it," she cursed. "I'm out of here. I get sick of waiting for his ass." Coco was ready to abandon her groceries.

But then she saw Calhoun running toward her. He grinned as he squeezed past the other women and stepped up to the register.

"Sorry, baby," he said.

"What took you so long? You had these chicks looking at me like I was crazy."

"I bought a couple of scratch-offs." He triumphantly held two validated tickets in his hand. "Today's my lucky day. I won five hundred."

"Stop playing. Really?"

"Yeah, Ma. My hand been itching for a minute. Finally paid off."

"Oh," she said, stunned.

"And I got us some more shit," he explained. Calhoun retrieved his credit card from his wallet. Then he handed the cashier a big box of shrimp, two cases of beer, and a slab of ribs.

"Add this. And this. And this." He gave a woeful smile like he was really didn't intend to hold up the line.

"So if you won," Coco said, "where's the money? Why you using your credit card?"

He looked both ways then opened his wallet. He showed her that his winning tickets were validated for the entire five hundred dollars.

"I gotta go to this claim center off the North Loop to pick up the cash. I'm calling in sick tomorrow and going to get our money."

Coco's eyes enlarged. "For real? You won?"

"Would I lie to you?"

When Coco realized that he hadn't tried to hide his new windfall from her, she began to giggle. Then she gave him a high-five. She wrapped her arms around Calhoun's neck for a hug, then she backed up off of him when she heard the women behind her sighing real loud.

"Calhoun, you took so long I didn't know what had happened," she explained. "Man, I could kill you sometimes," she said. "I swear to God."

"Hey, you swear you want me as your man. This is what you gon' get when you with Calhoun Humphries."

"I guess it is."

"Stick with me, I'm gon' take us places."

At hearing Calhoun's proclamation, Coco felt in a daze. She wanted to call Alita and mock her for every time she had called her man a loser.

Because right then, it felt as though Coco's dream of him being her husband was a reality. She kissed him on his lips and sucked his tongue right in front of everybody.

Calhoun broke off from her kiss.

"So, Ma, I'll prove it to you that, when the time is right, I'll make things legal for us."

She nodded and proceeded to finish the transaction so they could go and celebrate his winnings.

Coco felt no matter what he did, if she really loved Calhoun, she'd forgive him as many times as needed. Because of his personality, she knew that number would be astronomical.

CHAPTER 7

Men Are Men

"Are you completely positive you want to do this?" Burgundy asked. Alita was sitting in Burgundy's sedan. She securely fastened her seat belt and gave herself a moment to think. It was Friday at the top of the lunch hour. And not too long ago Alita had clocked out from her stock clerk job. She worked in the health and beauty department of a major grocery chain and she'd been on the job exactly six months. Today, Alita decided to take care of some business and now she was taking the rest of the afternoon off.

Alita examined her hair in the car's vanity mirror.

"Did you hear me ask you a question, or am I just talking to myself?" Burgundy asked.

"Yeah, girl, I heard you. I want to do this. I took time off from my job just to take care of this. So thanks for coming to get me, B. I was not in the mood for catching no damned Metro bus. Ain't nobody got time for that."

Burgundy laughed. "No problem, Sis." Alita slammed the car door shut, and they were on their way.

"Lita, are you hungry? You want me to stop by Wendy's?"

"No, I'm not thinking about no hamburgers."

"And you're one hundred percent sure you—"

"Hello? How many times I got to tell you, B?" She reached inside of her purse. "You see these papers here that I've got to fill out and get them notarized?" She read the name of the document out loud: "'Original Petition for Change of Name of an Adult.' That's one form that's ready to go. And there's this other one that the judge will sign. So yes, I want to go get my name changed back to Reeves. I'm not feeling Alita Washington anymore."

Burgundy knew not to try to persuade her sister to take time to think. She paused. "Lita, I know you been thinking about this for a minute. So please tell me everything that happened that makes you want to do this."

"I'll tell you, but first let me munch on this piece of fruit I brought with me. You know it's gonna be a long-ass wait at the county clerk's office."

"I thought you weren't hungry."

"I said I have something important to do. And I can eat some fruit on the way there."

Alita reached inside her tote bag. The contents included her divorce decree, birth certificate, Social Security card, a copy of the *Waiting to Exhale* sound track, and an apple.

"Hey, can you pop this CD in for me, B?" She handed Burgundy the jewel case. It had tons of scratches on it.

"You still listen to CDs?"

Alita glared at her. "Can you pop in my CD and play track seven please, ma'am?"

Burgundy did as she was told. Soon Mary J. Blige was wailing the song "Not Gon Cry."

"So anyway," Alita continued as she took a huge chunk out of her apple, "Mister Leonard Washington is straight out tripping. Like, I remember when we were about to get divorced, I could have changed my name back then. But I decided not to do this. I would keep my married name. Figured it was no big deal. My son is a Washington, and I wanted me and him to share last names. But now I know it's time. Y'all were right. I need to let this man go."

"Are you serious? This is what you really want to do?"

"I do. Because you gotta be careful what you wish for."

"What are you talking about now, Alita?"

"I'm getting to it. Now, as you know, Leonard helped me out in that last situation with Leno, right. And so he actually started taking time to be with his kid a little more. It's only been a few weeks since they've been hanging out. He's picked our son up from our apartment and taken him to the barbershop, taken him to the gym, or the mall. And I was shocked but happy—at first. Him spending time with Leno gave me a much-needed break. But I think in that short a time, he put a whole lot of negative shit in Leno's head. And my ex began to ask Leno questions."

"Questions like what?"

"Like how would he feel about staying with his daddy? How does he like being raised by a woman? Doesn't he want to know what it's like to be a man? And didn't he want to be told 'man stuff' by a man in-

stead of his mama? Leno came back and told me everything they talked about."

"Everything? Really, Alita?"

Alita ignored her. "And from what Leno told me, I
do think he's feeling everything his daddy has put in
his head. Said he's going through some things, and he
wants his daddy's opinion on things I can't talk to him
about. I don't know where he gets that from. I can talk
to that boy about anything under the sun." Alita's voice
sounded hurt, slightly betrayed. "And it's like the things
I've taught him, built up in him, might be all taken away
because the boy has stars in his eyes."

"What do you mean? Because of the basketball?"

"No, because he finally has the one thing I hadn't
been able to give him: a relationship with his daddy."
She rolled her eyes. "Leonard Washington will get all
the praise, even though for a minute he was nowhere to
be found. And my son thinks he's the greatest thing
since Blu-ray."

Burgundy's heart went out to her sister. She knew
how fiercely protective Alita was. But she also knew
how she viewed life through a narrow window. "Alita,"
she replied carefully, "I've seen you raise Leno. He's a
good kid. And if it weren't for you, he would not be the
ball player that he is. And sweetie, he's almost a man.
And I know you do the best you can. But a young man
needs his father's influence. And it's never too late to
get that."

Alita wanted to cut off her sister's head with hateful
words. But even she knew that Burgundy was partially
correct. She knew that Leno enjoyed being around his
dad.

"I hear what you trying to say, B. But when you

think about it, Leonard's timing is very suspect. Here, take a look at this."

Alita pulled out her cell phone. She went on the internet and pulled up articles that she'd saved as favorites: Yahoo Sports, Sports Illustrated, CBS Sports, SB Nation.com, and NCAA.com. Each of them had posted news story after news story about the best NBA prospects in U.S. high schools. They posted rankings and all the top basketball recruits. And in every single article Leonard Washington, Jr., got grouped in the top three. They mentioned his position, height, weight, age, city, high school, his stats, and of course, there was that professional headshot that displayed Leno's fabulous smile and his signature haircut.

"I think Leno made the mistake of letting his daddy know how hot he's getting and the name he's been making for himself as a basketball player. And those scouts have been hounding my baby. I don't know how they got his number, but we been getting calls from Villanova, Syracuse, Duke, Michigan State, and North Carolina. It's only gon' get worse if he keeps his game up the way he has. See, here are articles on Leno Washington, the future of high school basketball. They say he is the best guard in the state."

"Ahh, so now his dad is suddenly taking a stronger interest in him."

"Yes, he is. But I think it's his way of locking down a relationship with Leno, just in case the boy really does blow up and gets rich and famous. If it ain't the little skeezers at school, it's his own daddy trying to make a buck off of him."

"But I thought that his daddy's schedule was too jam-packed for him to spend any real significant time with him."

"That's the thing. You see, in his own way, Leonard is a superstar himself. He does very well at that car dealership. So when he asks for a little bit of time off, they don't complain. And I could shoot myself in my own head because I'm the one who has asked Leonard for a couple of favors lately. Like I needed him to pick up Leno from school and take him to his doctor's appointments and dentist. Things like that."

"Excuse me, Alita, but that isn't called doing you a favor. That's part of his fatherly responsibility. He shouldn't get a clap on the back for that, or even child support for doing it."

"That's what I'm talking about. Not when the child lives with me one hundred percent of the time."

"Okay, so this is why you suddenly want to change your name back to Reeves?"

"Yes," Alita said stubbornly. "I hate his ass, and I don't want his name attached to my name."

"But, sweetie, you should really think this out carefully before making such a life changing decision." Burgundy understood how Alita felt, but she was leery about her habit of making emotional decisions that weren't thoroughly considered. A lot of people cut off their nose to spite their face and cause more harm than good.

"I've thought about it. I want out."

A little while later they arrived downtown. Burgundy pulled up in front of the county clerk's building. But she took one look at Alita and decided to circle the block.

"Alita, I'm sorry, but by the look on your face, you don't seem like you're in any position to go up there and demand a name change. I think you should give it some time. There is no need to rush through this, baby. You are angry, and your pride is hurt."

"Why is he doing this?" Alita asked with sincerity. "Oh, what the hell. Why am I asking you about why men do fucked-up shit? Look at who you're married to. Y'all's relationship is so perfect I want to go jump out of a window."

Burgundy smiled and secretly felt so very relieved that she did not live Alita's life. She felt sorry for her sister in ways she could never imagine.

"Hey, Nate is a good man, but we do have our little issues from time to time."

"Oh, don't tell me," Alita said sarcastically. "You argue about which way the toilet paper should be placed in the bathroom. Or you argue about what color to paint the kitchen. Stupid shit like that, right?"

Burgundy squirmed in her seat as she thought about how off base Alita was. "You're partially right. Most of our disagreements are minor, but sometimes we get into it. Mostly about financial stuff."

"Nate is cheap as hell, isn't he?"

"Nate is conservative," she answered carefully. "My husband mostly insists on socking away a lot of money in savings and investments. And I have no problem with that. It's smart to save some of what you earn. But we work hard for our money, and I enjoy splurging and treating myself now and then. And I love spoiling the girls, but he's not really down for that. He hates to overdo things when it comes to the Natalia and Sid. If it were up to him he'd give them two birthday presents and that's that. But I like to buy them like six or seven presents. Make their birthdays really memorable and special."

"Wow, how can a daddy that makes as much as he makes scrimp out on his own daughters?"

"Don't get me wrong. Once in a while he will spend," Burgundy explained. "But he hates to buy things like the toy replica Mercedes-Benz cars that you see all the time on Instagram. Nate doesn't play that at all. He will plug away tons of money, though, for the girls' college funds or for us to take a nice family vacation or two every summer and winter."

"Hmm. Well, I may need him to give me a loan or something, because this name change shit's going cost me two hundred dollars. Maybe he can help me pay that fee."

"You can forget about Nate helping you out on that. You know how he feels about mixing money and family." Burgundy laughed when she imagined her sister going to Nate for a handout. "Knowing him, my frugal husband would make you sign a promissory note to make sure you pay him back. With interest. And if you didn't pay up, he'd take you to small claims court and not think twice about it."

"Okay then," Alita scoffed, "if he's that petty and cheap, he's way more of a bastard than I thought. Just like a man!"

They fell into silence. The county clerk only processed name changes between one-thirty and two-twenty in the afternoon. Alita knew the line would be long; everything that had anything to do with the government always took forever. The clock was ticking; Alita had a decision to make.

She spoke up. "I've made up my mind. Alita Washington has too damned many syllables. I'm going back to Reeves. I get sick of calling some company, and when I try to tell them my name they cut me off before I can finish. Plus, this'll piss Leonard off if I do this."

"You're so silly," Burgundy muttered. "I know I am a Reeves even though I'm married. You really shouldn't make this decision simply because you hate Leonard. Think about how it's going to impact everything. Bank accounts, personal checks, changing your driver license, car insurance, your tax returns. Alita, I think you should give it more time, all right, sweetie?"

"See, this is the shit I try to warn stupid-ass Coco about. Marriage is way more than sharing a last name. She's such a fool to want to marry that guy. He isn't ready. She's not either."

"Alita, whether we like it or not, Coco is grown." Burgundy chose her words carefully as she slowly drove away from the county building and hoped her sister didn't notice. "Just like you have the right to make your own decision about going back to your maiden name, Coco has the right to decide if she wants to stay single or be married."

"But it's a mistake," Alita insisted.

"And even if my middle sister makes a mistake and falls flat on her face, let her do it. As long as she doesn't kill herself in the process, let her grow up in her own way."

Alita simmered in her seat, not acknowledging the fact that Burgundy seemed to be making her decisions for her. What did it matter to Burgundy if Alita wanted to change her last name and go through the hassles of doing something she felt she needed to do for her life?

She moodily stared out of the window as they drove farther away from the county clerk's office.

Burgundy cleared her throat. "I will take you back

home, Big Sis, unless there is someplace else you want
to go."

"There is," Alita replied. She sat up in her seat. "I'm
starving. That little piece of fruit just didn't do the job. I
want something to fill up my stomach."

"No problem. We'll go to Morning Glory and check
in on things."

Moments later the ladies were walking through the
restaurant that Burgundy and Nate owned. It was a one-
story facility that seated seventy-five; located in a busy
part of town, it catered to the middle class and the
working class. The lighting was bright yet soothing,
furnishings modern, and atmosphere comfortable.

All the staff greeted Burgundy as she blew through
the front area, past the wide display table that showed off
samples plates of various menu items. They headed
straight into the kitchen.

"Hello, Mrs. Taylor," said Darius, the breakfast chef.
He was a nice looking man, with a bald head, goatee
mustache, and in his late-forties. As she and Burgundy
walked by Darius, he stopped and openly gaped at
Alita.

"Excuse me," she barked. "May I help you with
something?"

He grinned at her and continued staring until Alita
dashed out of his sight. They ended up in the business
office. It was an oversize space with an executive desk,
three comfortable guest chairs, a credenza, standard
bookcase, and no windows. Several security cameras
monitored the cash registers, kitchen, hallways outside
the restrooms, plus the front entrance and the parking
lot.

"Ohhh," said Burgundy as she took a seat in her

swivel chair. "It looks like someone here was checking you out, Sis." She kicked off her pumps and stared at Alita for a moment or two.

"Are you serious? Girl, please. I'm not thinking about that man."

"Good," Burgundy replied and took a seat at her desk. "Because Darius is as married as I am."

Alita stopped in her tracks. "See, that's the shit I'm talking about." She twirled around and stormed back toward the kitchen.

"Hey, Lita, please don't."

But it was too late.

By the time Burgundy reached her, Alita's long skinny finger wagged in front of Darius's reddened face.

"Don't you dare try to holler at me with your cheating, married ass."

"What did you say?" he replied.

"You heard me. Let me see your hand."

Darius refused to comply. Alita snatched his left hand and stared. There was no ring.

"Um, ain't you married?"

"What I am is nothing you should be concerned about." Darius seemed furious, but one look at Burgundy's face and he thought twice about telling her off.

"Well, I heard you were married," Alita hastily explained. "And I don't fuck around with married men. If they cheating, they lying, and if they lying, I don't want their monkey asses. They immoral and they dicks probably don't even work half the time. That's why the wives ain't putting out and y'all gotta go around searching for side pussy."

"Whoa whoa whoa. Side pussy? That's what you think?"

"That's what I know."

Darius threw up a hand. "Okay, Sister, sheesh. I get it. You hate men and you aren't ashamed of it. Now, can you let me get back to doing my job?"

"That's what your ass should have been doing in the first place. Minding your business, cooking pancakes, and keeping the hell away from me."

A few of the other kitchen workers tried hard to not burst out laughing at Darius. He was the type who, while he was cooking, liked to look out inside the eating area to see what pretty ladies had entered the restaurant.

Burgundy yanked her sister's arm. "C'mon, Alita. Everyone, please get back to work." When Alita turned her back, Burgundy whispered, "Sorry" to Darius. But in her mind she was thinking he got exactly what he deserved.

The two women returned to the business office, and Burgundy closed the door solidly behind her. "Alita, I swear to God, you will never get a man acting the way you do. I really wanted to introduce you to my good friend Shade Wilkins. But now I'm having second thoughts."

"Good. Don't even waste your time. Told you I wasn't interested anyway."

Burgundy crossed her arms over her chest. "You are going to need an attitude readjustment, like real quick. I know you despise Leonard, but you can't allow so many negative feelings rile you up. Why can't you take a compliment?"

"B, you told me that man is married."

"He may not have been wearing his ring, but yes, he is *married*, not blind. Men are men. And the ones that have a wife at home may still look at a woman whom they find attractive. They're just admiring her beauty. It doesn't mean they're outright dogs. You could have simply ignored the guy."

"Does Nate take long looks at women? Flirt with 'em? Undress 'em with his eyes?"

"Not in front of me," Burgundy assured her. "He is way too respectful to let me catch him doing anything like that. But, hey, it doesn't mean that he's not above admiring a nice looking woman from time to time. Houston has a million pretty women, and a lot of them like to eat here."

"Does your husband walk around Morning Glory checking out pretty women?"

"What type of wife would I be if I had to keep my man on a tight leash?" Burgundy sounded defensive. "I'm so busy doing what I have to do, working and taking care of the things concerning Natalia and Sid, and the barbershop and the restaurant; shoot, I really don't have time to keep an eye on Nate. He's grown and he will do what he wants to do. But I'll bet anything that ninety-nine percent of the time, my husband chooses to do right by me."

Alita's voice was icy. "A lot of men would give anything to be married to a naïve, trusting bitch like you."

"Now wait just one minute," Burgundy protested. "I have never ever cursed you, Lita. And not because you haven't deserved it."

"I know, B . . . sorry. I didn't mean it."

"No, you always say exactly what you mean, and that's your problem. You need to think before you speak. You're the type to bite the hand that feeds you. I don't have to take time out of my busy day to drive you around taking care of your personal business. Nor am I obligated to do half the stuff I do for you. Family or no family."

Burgundy's angry outburst at her sister was rare. Alita knew that if nothing else Burgundy was always down for her sisters. Her biting words stung Alita beyond belief.

"Oh, I don't know about all that," Alita said, feeling embarrassed and indignant at the same time.

"Well, it's time that you learned. You can't treat people any type of way and expect them to want to be bothered. This includes strangers *and* family."

Alita wanted to clap back at Burgundy, but for a rare moment wisdom kicked in. Burgundy was kind and generous in many ways, but Alita knew even she had her limits.

"Ooh, those paintings nice, B. I like 'em a lot. You so cultured. How much they set you back?"

Burgundy ignored Alita and focused on reviewing data on her computer.

After ten minutes of staring at paintings, Alita nearly screamed. "I can't stand keeping quiet and feeling ignored. I'm bored to death."

"No problem. I thought you were hungry anyway. In fact I hear your stomach growling and sounding like wailing cats. Go to the kitchen and tell them I said to make you a special. Tell Jordan Andrews. He'll hook you up."

"You sure?"

"Yes, I'm sure, silly rabbit."

"Thanks, Sis." Alita happily bounced to her feet. It sure felt good to have a relative who was in charge of her own restaurant, and a good one at that, for Morning Glory was known throughout the city for its mouth-watering food.

Alita forced herself to smile with confidence as she entered the kitchen. She looked around warily, hoping no one remembered the scene she had made in there fifteen minutes earlier. She even waved at Darius when she ran into him, but he simply rolled his eyes and made sure to scoot out of her way when she walked by.

Alita located Jordan Andrews, whom she'd met on a previous occasion. She greeted him pleasantly and sweet-talked him into asking another cook to prepare her a French toast special.

"Make sure anybody except that Darius guy cooks my food."

Once Jordan solicited help from another worker, Alita happily wandered into the dining area and found an empty seat. The place was nearly packed, as usual.

As she waited for her order, Alita kept herself pre-occupied by examining the menu that she was already familiar with. She beamed with pride at the impressive food offerings and at the tiny color photo of Nate and Burgundy located on the back.

As happy as she was for Burgundy, why was she the sister with enough talent to create something so good that people were willing to pay for it? When Alita surmised that she didn't have anything that people would buy, she laughed to herself.

"I only got one thing that people would pay to get, but hey, that ain't for sale."

When she felt the presence of someone quietly standing next to her, Alita became startled and hoped to hell it wasn't Darius.

It was Elyse. The girl had a sullen look on her face and seemed to be submerged in thought. Seeing her there was shocking. It was very rare for Elyse to be found anywhere outside of Burgundy's house.

The girl wore a long-sleeved gray shirt that had the name of the restaurant embroidered in pink on the left pocket. She also sported dark gray slacks and black loafers. She even wore a name tag.

"You work here now or something?" Alita asked.

Elyse shook her head.

"Is that a yes or a no? Damn, girl, I wish you'd open up your mouth and talk." Alita wasn't in the mood for Elyse's weird behavior. "Why is all that sweat on your forehead? You look like you burning up."

Elyse avoided eye contact with Alita.

"Well, you look like you just robbed a bank and scared the police about to come pick your ass up." Alita cackled. She swiped a few napkins from the dispenser, stood up, and dabbed the sweat from the girl's head.

"No," Elyse told her, trying to dodge Alita. "Don't."

Elyse rolled up a shirtsleeve. She scratched her arm repeatedly. She looked like she was suffering from a bad case of eczema.

Right then Nate started to walk past them.

"Hey, brother-in-law," Alita yelled. He waved and came over.

"Hi, Alita. Hi, Elyse."

Nate placed his hand on Elyse's shoulder. She stared into space, scratched her other arm, and ignored him.

"How's my favorite sister-in-law?" he said, looking at Alita. "And what brings you here?"

"Your sweet little wife brought me here to get something to eat. You know how us poor folk love getting a handout here and there."

She stretched out her hand.

He laughed, then closed her hand and balled it into a fist.

"Isn't this more like your style, Alita?"

Alita cackled with him then sat down. "I was just playing anyway."

"Sure you were."

"Nate, can you tell me why is my baby sister is here in a work uniform?"

"That's the thing. Elyse isn't a baby anymore. She's a grownup that needs to do something with her time. That's why she's now on the payroll." He gave Elyse a friendly hug as her eyes fell to the floor. Beads of sweat returned to her forehead.

"Okay, she's a new employee, but I swear she don't look like she wants to work here, Nate." Alita was troubled by Elyse's despondent mood. And being around people that rarely talked much made Alita nervous. She never knew what was going through her sister's mind. Was she depressed? Was she going insane? Was she plotting to shoot up the place?

"Elyse, baby, talk to me," Alita said, feeling nervous and despondent. "You all right with this? Is working here what you want to do?"

Elyse rubbed the floor with the bottom of her shoe.

"See what I mean?" Alita said, exasperated. "How in the hell is she going to be working here when she can't even form a basic sentence?"

"Don't worry. She won't be a server and work with the public," Nate replied. "We'll keep her in the back, out of sight, where she can wash dishes. Or she can set condiments on the table when we run out. We'll keep her busy doing things that won't require much interaction."

"I don't know about that. After Mama died, it was nice of you to take Elyse in. But when she got older, I thought y'all just wanted her to help out with Natalia and Sid and be there when they get home from school?"

"She can do both. It's not good for her to just lie around the house playing video games all day."

"Yeah, you're right. Hell, if Leno takes a break from his homework and plants his feet in front of that damned TV too long, I make up any type of chore to keep him busy. Or I ask him 'how's that homework coming along?' Kids! Anyway, I won't hold you up from your work, brother-in-law. See you later. Elyse, smile or something. Hell, stop looking like you about to go to a funeral."

Elyse, unable to tolerate Alita's negative barrage, abruptly stormed away.

"I guess I'm pissing off people left and right," Alita said to herself. "Maybe I should do like Burgundy said and think first before I speak."

She thought about it. "Hell, no! That ain't happening."

Soon her food was brought to her, and she devoured the breakfast and seriously considered the state of her life. Her ex-husband, her lack of a love life, her son, and her future. By the time she was done thinking, Burgundy came and took a seat right across from her.

"Well, Sis. What have you decided about going back to Reeves?"

"I'm not going back," Alita said. "I need to move forward."

"What?"

"I need to face the fact that I made the decision to become Mrs. Washington. I need to put on my big girl drawers and just deal with shit. Grow up. And prove that I am a woman that's strong enough to accept the hand I've been dealt."

Burgundy looked taken aback. "And what brought on this sudden turnaround? You've only been here maybe thirty minutes."

"See, it's like this. I sat alone at this table. And at first I didn't know what to do with myself. I wanted to try and play it off and act like I was waiting on someone to join me for lunch, right? I don't want to look like the loser woman who is single and has no date, no man in her life that loves her. And I felt like everybody in this restaurant was staring. Feeling sorry for me. Hell, I think one of your servers came to my table at least five times asking me if I was okay. He was trying to make conversation with me, and I know exactly why." Alita rolled her eyes. "But no one has to feel sorry for me. I'm okay being divorced, without a man in my life. I don't have to prove anything to anybody, including changing my name back to Reeves."

Burgundy smiled in admiration. "There must be something in the French toast today because this is the most grown-up thing I've heard you say in a long time, Lita."

"I know. And hopefully it won't be the last one. Somehow, some way, I'm getting my shit together. Starting today." Alita lifted her glass of freshly squeezed orange juice, took a tiny sip, then stood up.

"You ready to go yet, B? 'Cause I am. I got things to do. I want to get home and try and crank up my car, kick it, lay hands on it with some anointing oil or whatever I need to do so I can go pick up Leno from school."

"Wait. Can't he walk home or catch the bus?"

"No. My son is a target. He's black, he's a future superstar athlete. I don't feel right unless I know for sure where he is."

Burgundy got up so they could get ready to leave the restaurant. She hurried into the kitchen.

"C'mon on, Elyse," she yelled. "I might as well take her home with me. You do wanna go home with me now, right?"

"Home. Right now."

"Humph, I see that she can talk when she wants to," Alita said. Burgundy agreed to let Elyse punch out and get off the clock. They all left Morning Glory and drove away.

While in the car, Burgundy activated the telephone in her car. She got Shade on the phone but begged Alita to keep quiet.

"Hey there, friend," she said when Shade answered.

"What's up, Burgundy?"

"Nothing much. I'm in my car. I have my little sister here with me, and we're on our way home right now. How has your week been so far, Shade?"

"I'm living the life."

Alita's eyes grew real big.

Burgundy easily laughed. "I'm sure you mean something very nice and positive when you say that, right? You haven't been on any hot dates or anything like that?"

"Nah," Shade uttered in his very pleasant deep voice. "I had a hot date with the gym. That means I got to hit the gym four times," he said with a laugh. "I'm trying to get in shape so I can eat all the good food I want during the upcoming holidays."

"Sounds good. I'll try and bake an extra pie or two for you, my friend," Burgundy said.

"You do that. Hey, I don't mean to rush you off the phone, but I'm on my way to a meeting. We'll talk later this week? Or I'll just see you at the bookstore?"

"Sure, that'll work. Bye, Shade."

She hung up.

"What ya think, Alita?"

"Girl, please. You can't tell nothing 'bout no man just by listening to his voice on the speakerphone."

"Then that means you're going to have to meet him in person. I'll think of something for the two of you."

"You need to quit," Alita complained. "Just stop it."

Burgundy laughed. "Never that." Soon she dropped Alita in front of her apartment.

"Thank you, B, for everything." Alita waved good-bye and watched her sister drive away. She hoped that she could start up her own car and try and change the oil herself before she left to get Leno. His school let out at three, and she wanted to come home and relax a few minutes before handling her car maintenance issues.

Alita inserted her key in the door and closed it behind her. The chilled apartment felt like a walk-in freezer; its quiet as still as a country road in the wee hours of the morning.

She kicked off her shoes and decided to get dressed in something more comfortable. Alita walked down the hall toward her bedroom. She stopped at the door and was about to enter it when she heard a snicker.

Then a moan.

Did I leave the TV on?

The moan grew louder. Alita ran across the hallway and found a baseball bat that she kept in between the washer and dryer. She crept down the hall, braced herself, and opened her door.

All she could see was the silhouette of a female sitting on top of a body that was stretched out on her bed. The woman arched her back then wailed.

An acidic aroma hit Alita's nostrils as soon as she entered her bedroom. The odors of semen, vaginal secretion, sweat, baby oil, and honey clogged the air. She drew her hand over her mouth. Tiny pieces of French toast rose up her throat. She swallowed her lunch back down, then yelled, "What the fuck is going on?"

The female jumped out of the bed. Then, not knowing what else to do, she yelped and got back in bed. She slid underneath the covers and pulled the blanket over her body.

Alita flipped on the light switch and yanked a string. The ceiling fan made whirring sounds. Alita went and opened a window.

"Damn, it stinks in here. Leno?" she screamed.

But she didn't hear Leno speak a word. Alita snatched the covers off the bed. The girl was crouched in a ball; her hands covered her face. But the boy lying beside the chick wasn't Alita's son.

"What the hell is this?" Alita demanded.

The guy was speechless. He looked to be around seventeen. The chick was very skinny, and Alita couldn't tell how old she was. Upon a closer inspection, Alita recognized the young man. He was Phil Proctor, one of Leno's teammates. Phil's nickname was "P Square." And Alita knew his mother, Kennisha, because she had a reputation for being a shit starter up at the high school when she got reprimanded for trying to date one of the married assistant coaches.

"Phil, if you don't get your nasty ass out of my bed! Where's Leno? And what is this little whore doing here with you?"

The girl screamed and finally hopped out of the bed. She placed the cover on her like it was a cape. She wildly searched for her clothes, picking up a shirt and tossing it back on the floor.

"Nasty-ass whore, get the hell out of my house and never come back. You don't belong here!" The girl was crying. She dropped the comforter from her shoulders and tried to simultaneously pull on a shirt plus a pair of shorts.

"Phil," Alita screamed. "I asked you where's my son?"

Phil gave her a blank look.

Furious, Alita stormed out. She was headed for Leno's bedroom, which was on the other side of their split apartment. Before she reached his door, she passed the bathroom that was primarily used by Leno. The sound of the shower stopped her.

"They better not be taking a shower."

Alita turned the knob, but the door wouldn't open.

"Leno, get your narrow ass out of that bathroom right now. I come home trying to get ready to go and pick you up, and you're already here? Why the hell you taking a shower at this time of day? Who you got in there with you? Why aren't y'all in school? Are you trying to ruin your life, son? Is that what you're doing?"

It took several minutes for Leno to open the door. His big brown eyes grew even bigger as he walked out of the bathroom dressed in a bath towel.

Alita ran in the room. The shower curtain was drawn. She yelled, "Come the fuck out, you little whore." She yanked the shower curtain to the side. No one was there.

"Mom, what you doing?"

She said nothing. Leno walked through the apartment, and Alita followed him.

"Mom, where are my friends?"

"Your friends are the last thing you should be worried about. I want to know what Phil was doing in *my* bed with that little girl. And you in here showering? What were y'all about to do? Have a threesome?"

Alita clapped her hands over her mouth over that quick slip of the tongue. She wished she would have thought carefully about what she wanted to say before it she said it. Leno was smart enough to know what a threesome was, but she prayed her son had never had one.

"Boy, I swear to God if you weren't already naked I'd whip your ass with an extension cord. That's what my mama used to do to us before it became illegal to discipline your kids the right way. By putting the fear of God in them."

The plans she had for Leno seemed to be falling apart. That could not be happening.

"Leno, you're going to have to do better, son. You don't understand it now, but I'm trying to save your life. And you're bent on trying to destroy it. You and Phil ought to know better. And before you even ask, yes, I am going to tell his mama about this."

"Mom, please leave Miss Kennisha out of this. She don't need to be all up in our business."

"Leno, you don't have any business, okay? Only business you have is to take your ass to school, go to practice, and come straight home. You already know the rules, but since you enjoying breaking rules, you are now on a punishment." Alita found herself laughing. The whole thing seemed ludicrous. Could she put a boy his size on punishment? A boy who was an internet sensation?

"I wish I could whip your ass with a lead pipe, but

grounding you is the best I can do right now." She stopped pacing and flung herself around to face her son.

"Phil," she yelled, "get in here." Alita knew that the naked girl had left by then, but the young man still hung around. Within seconds Phil came and stood next to Leno.

"Wait here," Alita demanded. She hurried to the kitchen and came back with a butcher knife.

She waved it around. "You know what I feel like doing right now? Huh? Since you two wanna be so damned grown and go around fucking little girls. Do you even realize what you're doing?"

"Ms. Washing—" said Phil.

"Shut up," she screamed and continued to jab the air with the knife. "You need your little penises sliced off. Mm hmm. Because that little itty-bitty thing is what gets a lot of men in trouble. Especially guys like you. Young men that have talent but who have no common sense. Young men with parents who are constantly pushing them to succeed and working hard to make something good out of their lives." Alita thought about men who were in the public eye: athletes, politicians, actors, and so on. Men who were filled with incredible talent and an amazing ability to touch the world with their God-given gifts. Yet they ruined everything because they were weak when it came to sex and gold diggers, chicks who were skilled at having their way with men. Physically unattractive men who were uniquely gifted, but if they did not have money and fame, these women would never even look their way. These chicks were professional men fuckers, and the cost to be with them added up to millions. The men fell for their lies time and again, thinking the woman was down for him. But the lying chick knew that she had her eyes on his bank account all along.

"Your little penises can get you in big trouble, you hear me? And you're too young to be caught up in the bullshit. Excuse my French, but I always keep it real with Leno. I have to. Sugarcoating shit and trying to call it sugar won't work around here."

Leno looked like he was so angry at his mother that he could knock her upside her head. But he stood and listened.

"Leno, did you have sex with that girl? Did you?"

"No, Mama. No. I was taking a shower."

"Why take a shower in the middle of the afternoon? Do you think I'm stupid or something?" She thumped Leno hard upside his head. "You're a man, and you'll get horny. But have you ever heard of masturbating? It's a lot less drama involved. Because when you mess around with chicks like the one you brought in my bed, *my* bed, you little prick, you can end up with diseases that you can never get rid of. You can get a girl pregnant, and you may not even stand her ass after you find out she's having a baby. You think you're in love, but you're much too young to know what love is."

"Ha," Leno said. "If you really knew what love was, you wouldn't have run my daddy away."

Alita pushed Leno against the wall. "You don't know what you're taking about. I did not run him away; he ran me off with his behavior. He was acting like you, except he was married with a child and had zero dick control."

Leno burst out laughing.

"Ain't nothing funny, Leno. I'm trying to tell you what your daddy hasn't."

"You don't know what he's told me."

"You're right. I don't know. But regardless, you two boys will not mess up your lives."

"You're not my mother," argued Phil.

"As long as you in my house fucking in my bed, Phil, you best believe I will tell your little stupid ass what to do. And Leno, until you work, pay all the bills, and make the decisions for my house, you are not a man. Having a dick does not make you a man. Being responsible does. I get so sick of stupid know-nothing kids trying to tell grown-ups what to do."

Alita felt so angry that she began to perspire. Her skin actually heated up. She wiped her forehead and was blind with rage.

"Who was that little girl? Is that your woman, Phil?"

"Hell, nah. Just some girl."

"Does the girl have a name?"

"Uh, I dunno."

"By not telling me her name, I hope that means you're trying to protect her. Because if you really don't know her name but you're trying to have sex with her, then that's a damned shame."

Phil looked as if the girl's name just didn't matter to him.

"Oh, Phil," she said. "This is bad. And it hurts me, and I'm not even her."

How could young men start the disrespect of women as early as sixteen years of age? The notion of it all frightened Alita. She never wanted to think that the son she gave birth to did not know how to honor females.

"You're too young for this player shit, Phil."

"Mama, can I get dressed, please?" Leno asked. "This sounds like an A and B conversation. I didn't do anything anyway."

Alita desperately wanted to believe that her son, her

baby boy, had not had sex with the young lady. But she had no proof. She wanted to take Leno at his word. But she despised being made to look like a fool.

"Come with me, you two." As much as she did not feel like doing it, Alita returned to the scene of the sex crime. The overhead light was still on. She walked over to the trashcan next to her bed. She emptied its contents. There was a black-and-gold condom packet right there for all to see. She picked it up. "At least you had the good sense to strap it up. Now whose was this?"

The two boys pointed at each other.

"Somebody's lying," Alita remarked. "And I'd love to call Kennisha and ask her if you're a pathological liar."

"Leno's lying," said Phil. "He is as guilty as I am. It was his idea to smash that girl. He thought you'd be at work—"

"Wow, you've become the little snitch, haven't you?" replied Alita. Leno looked as if he was about to burst out of his skin. "Wait. This is all wrong. You two are friends. I don't want you to snitch on each other, so spare me the details, Phil."

"He's lying on me, Mama. It wasn't my idea. It was his idea since his mama is at home. He asked if there was anybody here, and I told him no. So he got me to come over here and invited that girl too. We haven't even been here long."

"Long enough to almost get your nut, huh, Phil?" Alita massaged her temples. "I can't believe we're having this conversation. I don't know everything that happened here. But I know one thing. You, Leno, and I will have a conference with your daddy real soon."

"If I go live with him, I wouldn't be going through all of this."

"Well, hopefully he could talk some sense into you."

"But didn't you tell me one time that I am starting to act just like my dad?"

"Yeah," Phil blurted. "My mother tells me boys will be boys every time I do something she don't like. And she'll just give me a pass."

"If Phil's mom is nice enough to understand what we go through, then why can't you be like her, Mama?"

"She's not nice, she's stupid."

Phil raised his eyebrows.

"What I meant to say is I'm not her, I'm me."

"I thought so," Leno replied. "That's why every day I'm around you, you just make me want to go live with my dad even more."

"Hush you mouth, boy." Leno's words hurt Alita to her core. She had always been afraid that this might happen, that her son would turn on her once he got older and perhaps began to miss his father.

Phil told Leno he'd hit him up later. Leno said, "No, don't leave. Wait for me."

"Leno, if you walk out that door, you better not ever come back."

Leno scowled at Alita. He ran behind Phil and swiftly left the apartment.

CHAPTER 8

Three-Way

On the same day that Alita dealt with her drama, Calhoun got out of bed earlier than normal. He ate breakfast with Coco and the kids. Then, before he left for the day, Calhoun broke her off with an extra six hundred dollars.

"Here," he said. "Go buy the kids some clothes and shoes. And get something for the new baby too."

"Where'd you get this money from?" she demanded. "You won the lottery again?"

"Don't worry about that. Just have fun spending it, Ma."

Coco jumped up and down in exhilaration, her breasts flopping like tennis balls.

"Woo hoo! No more PayLess and Wal-Mart. I'm about to hit up Macy's, Dillard's, and Kohl's."

"You do that."

A few hours after Calhoun left for work, Coco gathered up the children and drove away from home with a contented smile. Finally, her man was halfway acting how she wanted him to. But after she shopped for hours and had a satisfying lunch, returning to an empty house left her feeling worn out and discontent.

The time for Calhoun to come home came and went. Coco stared at the clock on the wall. She wondered how long it would be before Calhoun would insert his key in the front door.

Feeling restless, Coco sat on the couch.

"Cadee, come in here and turn on the TV and find me something good to watch."

Six-year-old Cadee instantly obeyed.

"You like this, Mama? How about this show? Let's watch this."

"Okay, Cadee. Great job."

But then Chloe ran into the room and snatched the remote from Cadee. Even though she was only three, Chloe knew how to change the station to a Disney channel. Cadee shoved her sister, and little Chloe fought back.

Then they magically all sat together, their eyes glued to the colorful characters on the screen.

Coco couldn't believe how quickly her kids could disobey her orders. "I told you to find something that I'd want to watch. I don't wanna look at no damn Disney movie."

"Mama, please let us watch, please," Chloe cried.

Coco slapped the remote out of Chloe's hand and watched it fly across the room. At once all the kids began to cry and kick their feet angrily in the air.

"Forget this," Coco said to herself. "I'm about to tell your daddy how bad you been acting."

She grabbed her cell phone and voice-dialed Calhoun. She felt excited at the thought of even hearing his voice. His line rang six times then stopped.

"Where the fuck are you?" she yelled into his voice mail then hung up.

Leaving her man seven messages in three hours with no return call made Coco feel irrelevant, and that was the last thing she ever wanted to feel.

It was now almost midnight. The kids had long ago fallen asleep. The girls slumbered in one twin bed, and Chance snoozed in the other. Although the house had three bedrooms, Coco wanted the kids to share one room, figuring it would be easier to keep track of them. The third bedroom had been converted to a nursery.

Coco checked each child and made sure they were securely tucked in. She shut the door securely behind her and returned to the living room. The only sounds she heard were a drippy kitchen faucet and the ticking of a battery-operated wall clock.

She went to her bedroom, and she pulled out a messy black wig and slapped it on her head. She grabbed her denim shoulder bag, cell phone, and scooped up her keys.

Coco quickly exited the house, making sure to not slam the front door. The dim streetlights cast a menacing shadow on her noisy street. She lived on a main boulevard that was filled with traffic. Music from passing cars banged so loud that she felt the concrete vibrate underneath her shoes.

Once Coco got in her car and began to drive, her mind raced. Where was he? Who was he laid up with this time?

Coco promised herself to do a quick drive-by and come right back home.

"I swear to God if things keep going this way, I may seriously think about dumping his ass. Sick of this shit," she said, talking to herself. She dabbed her wet eyes with her thick fingers.

Coco slowed her car to ten miles an hour as she approached Henrietta Humphries's house, a mere ten blocks from hers.

She craned her neck and checked out every car parked out front.

Behind her, a person driving a pickup truck laid on its horn real loud.

Startled, Coco jumped in her seat and peered in her rear-view. She saw the outline of what looked like a man wearing a hat. When the horn loudly sounded again, she rolled down her window.

"Fuck you, you asshole. Go around me." Coco stuck a finger out the window and flipped him the bird.

The pickup advanced forward, moving close enough to tap the back of car. She lurched forward, then stopped and grabbed her door handle. Before she knew it the vehicle backed up, sped past her, its tires screeching. She heard the whooshing sound of a stray bullet, but it was a bad shot and completely missed her.

"I hope you get in a wreck and die," she screamed again before calming down and rolling up her window. She continued spying on Calhoun's mother's house, noting every vehicle in the driveway, across the street, and parked down the block. She didn't see her man's Dodge. A lot of times, even though she and Calhoun lived together, when they got into a quarrel, he ended up crashing on Henrietta's couch. But that didn't seem to be the case tonight.

As she felt sick with dread, the hole in Coco's stomach enlarged and began to fill with a familiar aching pain that made her want to bend forward and puke.

"Why can't he act right?" She drove away, slowly inching down the street, any street, in search of her man.

Not caring about the lateness of the hour, Coco dialed Dru's cell phone.

"Hey, Dru, what you doing?"

"I was asleep!" Dru rolled over and quietly got out of bed. Tyrique was instantly alert and sat up.

"What's wrong?" he asked.

"It's Coco," she told him. "Go back to sleep. This shouldn't take long."

"That's what you said the last time Coco called at this ungodly hour."

"Well, I have to take the call. She's family."

Tyrique nodded. He knew. "Do what you have to do. I'll try and go back to sleep."

Dru told him, "Good idea." She got up and slid her feet into some house slippers and went downstairs to the first floor of their townhouse.

"Hello?" Coco could be heard saying. "You still there?"

Dru sighed and went to open the refrigerator. She grabbed a bottle of Coke and took a generous swallow. It was a drink she despised, but she figured she'd need the caffeine. She flipped on the light switch and stood still for a moment.

"Dru, you hang up?"

"I'm here, Coco. Trying to stay awake. What's up?"

"I'm calling about . . . him."

Dru knew the topic without her sister even speaking the man's name.

"What about him? Is he all right?"

"I don't know. The Negro not even home yet."

"That's a shame," Dru said with a loud yawn. She started to ask Coco if she'd tried calling Calhoun, but right away knew that was a pointless question.

"What have I ever done to him?" Coco lamented. "Does Tyrique ever stay out late?"

Dru laughed out loud.

"Am I not sexy enough for my man? Why can't Calhoun act like he got some sense and stop worrying me half to death?"

Coco hated herself for bringing her messy business to her sister, but she knew Dru would listen to her.

"I don't know why he does what he does," Dru mumbled, sounding drowsy. "Some men are . . . are strange."

"Some of 'em? Shit, all of 'em fucked up in the head."

"Yeah, yeah. Maybe. Maybe not." Dru took a seat at the breakfast bar and tried to get comfortable. "Are you in your car, Coco? Sounds like you're driving."

"I'm almost home," she lied.

"Oh, okay. Where are you?"

"Hell if I know."

"Huh? Girl, you're scaring me." Dru sat up straighter on the barstool. "Why don't you know where you are?"

"I meant to say, I'm in Houston; I'm just not familiar with this street."

"Please don't tell me you're doing *that* again." Dru's heart ached for her sister. This is why she herself was so pragmatic about her own relationship. What she and Tyrique shared was infinitely less histrionic than Coco and Calhoun's relationship. Nevertheless Dru had decided a long time ago if she had to endure tons of drama just to have a man, she'd rather be by herself. Everyone wasn't destined to meet the love of their life, even if that's what they wanted more than anything.

Dru pleaded with Coco. "Sis, leave that man alone. You cannot control an adult."

"He's a big kid."

"Stop acting like his mother, because folks will do exactly what they want to do."

"Not on my watch, he won't. He acts like he don't know I'm having his baby."

Dru wanted to be supportive, but sometimes love meant being firm.

"Coco, what exactly do you want from Calhoun?"

"Love."

"Be more specific."

"I just want him to think about his family. Put us first all the time instead of some of the time."

"Um, can you be even more detailed? Give an example."

"Okay," Coco said stubbornly. "I prove my love to my man by being there whenever he needs me. I take care of our children. I try my best to keep the house clean and give him home-cooked meals. I am with him when he's sick and will go to the pharmacy and pick up whatever medicine he needs, no matter what time of the day or night."

"That's nice," Dru agreed. "You are showing him support and love when you do all these things . . . but, and I want you to be honest, does he reciprocate?"

"Huh?"

"Coco, how does Calhoun act in return? Like, how does he make you feel most of the time?"

This was the part that hurt Coco to her core. She could tell Dru the truth, but she knew it would sound too damning. So she let her know the partial story.

"Well, he went to a Louisiana casino last week, and I think he won some money. I couldn't go because I had morning sickness. Anyway, so like, this morning he gave me a lot of cash to buy the kids some clothes. But you would think that he'd want to know what his money bought. And we buy a lot of nice stuff and I go straight home after we went shopping. And I wait on him . . . for hours . . . so excited to lay the clothes out on the couch. Cadee and Chloe wanted to model for their daddy." She laughed wistfully. "But the longer I waited, the madder I got. And I called him, but instead of him calling me right back, he ignores me. Not once, not twice." She swallowed deeply, and her tonsils throbbed with pain. "He acts like I'm in this relationship by myself. Like I gotta beg him to do shit that should happen naturally if a man really loves a woman." Her voice fell to a haunting whisper. The echo of her words made her feel conflicted. She wanted to tell Dru about the times when she'd tell Calhoun she loved him. And there'd be that unbearably awkward silence between them. Like Calhoun was thinking of other things.

"So tell me," Dru said. "Why chase someone who seems to be running away, and who isn't giving you everything you need?"

"Because sometimes he does." Coco defended Calhoun even though there were moments she wanted to crack his head with a sledgehammer. She reminded Dru that he helped pays her doctor bills, bought her gasoline, washed and detailed her car, and gave her money to buy things for their new baby.

"If he was really worthless," Coco said, "he wouldn't even do what he does."

"But is the little bit that he does worth all this heartache?"

Coco couldn't answer. Her brain felt as if it was being twisted over and over like a long, wet, filthy rag. She couldn't see clearly due to the tears that spilled from her eyelids. When you're lost in love, how else are you supposed to behave? Right then she felt torn between two highly volatile emotions: love and hate. At times they almost felt identical.

"I just want him to act more right. Hell, even fifty percent of the time would be cool." She didn't care that Dru heard her blubbering and sniffling. "When he loves me the way I need to be loved, we're cool. We're on top of the world, on top of the mountain. I just want us to stay on top."

Dru thought Coco sounded like a hopeless nut. "Oh, my God. This is crazy. I'm concerned about you, Coco. I hate hearing you sound like this. Pull yourself together."

Coco rummaged through her purse, and whisked out some facial tissue. She blew her nose and wiped it dry.

"Dru Boo," she sniffed. "I know you think my man ain't worth all this. But hell. Nobody's perfect, not even your precious Tyrique. That's just life. It can't always go the way we want."

"What does Tyrique have to do with this?"

"Nothing." Coco snapped. She was beyond irritated that no man could be compared to her treacherous Calhoun Humphries.

"Your man ain't nothing like mine," Coco said sarcastically. "Yet he ain't no saint. There has to be something wrong with him, just like any other man."

"Wow," Dru muttered. Why did she have to try to throw Tyrique under a bus? "Seriously, Sis. Perfect. Non-perfect. Angel. Demon. It really doesn't matter. Because you being out here in these Houston streets all over a man is dangerous—and extreme."

"So you're telling me you've never done this before over Tyrique?"

Dru had to laugh, but it was a tickled kind of laughter. "Sweetheart, it's been a long time since I've allowed myself to feel that type of emotion over any guy, let alone my boyfriend." She carefully considered her words. "If someone makes me feel crazy in the head, I take as a sign that they aren't meant to be with me. Love shouldn't make you do crazy things . . . think insane thoughts . . . lose your common sense. Oh, I am aware that's how it all starts out, you think he's the one because of the crazy emotions you have, but emotions can be deceiving, Sis." She said what she felt, but she didn't want her sister to think that she was calling her crazy . . . even though Coco was loco.

"I know because your heart is so very involved, you can get caught up. We do that at times," she allowed herself to say. "And I-I know a little bit of drama can happen at times. As long as I'm with Tyrique, I prefer to avoid the drama."

Coco remained silent. Her throat felt dry, and her head pounded harder with her relentless migraine.

"Coco, are you still there?" Coco did not reply, but the hairs on Dru's neck rose. She felt an eerie presence behind her. She jerked her head. It was Tyrique, staring at her. She placed the call on mute.

"What's up?" she asked him.

"I heard my name . . . twice."

"Seriously? You're listening in on my conversation with Coco?"

"Sound travels, Dru."

Tyrique offered her a hug from behind. His squeeze felt nice and comforting. She felt a little guilty that she'd shut him out and escaped downstairs for some privacy. Why did love mean having to give up parts of herself that she wanted to keep?

"I'm good, Tyrique. We're not finished talking yet, but we should be done soon."

"Just checking. As long as you're okay."

"I'm fine, really. Go back to bed. I'll be there in no time." He gave Dru a droopy smile, kissed her on the mouth, then disappeared up the stairs. When she heard the sound of their bedroom door close, she took the call off mute.

"Hello? Coco?" Dru said. The call was still connected, but her sister failed to answer.

Dru felt guilty and hoped she hadn't made things worse. She knew Coco acted hard, but the girl could still be supersensitive. Maybe she felt like Dru treated her like she was bothering her.

"Sis, you're scaring me again; please answer and let me know you're still on the phone."

"I'm here," she finally heard Coco say.

Dru glanced at her watch. It was really getting late, and she needed to go to sleep so she could wake up for work in a few hours.

"Coco, where are you now? Please tell me you're almost home."

"No, I'm not."

"Fine. How long will it take for you to get home? I really hate to picture you dragging my nieces and nephew around this late."

"Mmm, yeah. I know."

"Coco?"

"What?" she snapped.

"W-what are you doing? Where are you again?" Dru demanded.

"Huh?"

"Stop acting like you don't know what street you're on. You aren't that stupid. Now tell me!"

Coco paid no attention to her sister's jabbering. Her eyes were now free of tears. Her mind was fuzzy, but she needed to get focused. She continued driving until she arrived at a familiar spot. That's when she finally saw Calhoun's Dodge.

Coco slowly pulled up behind her man's car. Her mind began to race.

Why didn't he come home? Is he all right? Is he up to no good?

Calhoun was over at Q's, one of his partners. His given name was Quantavius Mitchell. Q hardly ever got any sleep because he preferred to be up all night and mostly slept during the day.

Coco turned off the ignition and waited. Her heart pounded so wildly she could hear it. She felt relieved that she found her man, but was pissed off to see that he'd rather hang out at Q's instead of being with her and the kids.

Coco unlocked the door and stood next to her car. She heard the loud yelps of several neighborhood dogs. Part of her felt ridiculous and low-life, but when it came to her man, she was way past acting dignified and sensible.

After a long period of silence, Dru finally asked, "What are you doing? Are you still there?"

"Yeah, I'm here. I need a big favor, though."

"What?" Dru said, sounding annoyed.

"I need you to do a three-way. Call Calhoun for me."

"No way."

"Please, Dru, this is urgent."

"Girl, do you know what time it is? I'm not calling that man at one-thirty in the morning."

"Come on, Dru. Damn, just do it. It ain't no big deal. I just need to holler at him for a sec. He won't answer if he sees that it's me calling. I don't know why he does me so dirty. I'm getting sick of his shit, but I need to talk to him."

Coco wondered if he was making love to another woman. Maybe that's why he wouldn't pick up. Or maybe he hadn't forgiven her for having sex with another man and he wanted to pay her back by stepping out on her. As she imagined Calhoun's tongue licking another woman, a manic pitch dominated Coco's voice. "Go on and call him real quick. I'd do it for you."

Feeling sympathetic yet livid at the same time, Dru hesitated. "Okay, Sis, hold on," she said.

Coco closed her eyes and snapped them open the second she heard Calhoun answer his phone.

"Hi, Calhoun," Dru said. "I'm sorry to bother you but—"

"Yo, wassup, Mommy?"

"Um, uh." Dru didn't know what else to say.

"Where you been, you slimy motherfucka?" Coco yelled out, feeling irritated. As she pressed her phone closer to her ear, she could hear the thunderous sound of music playing in the background, as if her man was having a good old time partying without her.

"Coco?" Calhoun asked. "What the fuck?"

"Don't 'what-the-fuck' me! Why didn't you answer when I called your bum ass a hundred times, but when my sister called you picked up? What type of shit is that?"

"Look, woman, calm down. I ain't doing nothing. I got off work and headed straight over to Q's, since you want to know my every move."

"Oh, really?" Coco felt herself calming down. She felt good that he told the truth. Yet Calhoun had one of those convincing voices that she did not want to completely trust. "Hmm. That's where you been posted up all this time?"

"Yeah, fool. I already told you. What the fuck?"

"Okay, then. I hear you." She paused. "Is it just y'all two or does Q have company up in there?" Coco squinted in the darkness. She could clearly see Q's apartment window from where she was standing. The lights were on. But that in itself did not mean much.

"Why the hell you asking me if anybody else up here?

"'Cause I wanna know, that's why. Who else is there? Just Q?"

"Hold on. This ain't yo fucking house. So whoever else is up here, even if was King Kong, it ain't your damn business."

"It damn well is my business. We are in a relationship, Calhoun. I won't have you disrespecting me, and I know you. I know how you do."

"You bugging, Coco. Not disrespecting you, man."

"I know one thing. You better not have no bum bitches up there with you in Q's spot."

"Hey, Q," Calhoun yelled over the loud music. "Any bum bitches up in here?" Coco listened while Calhoun and Q laughed hysterically.

Their degrading reaction made Coco's cheeks burn

with anger. She felt silly checking her man, but she was used to acting like a female James Bond when it came to Calhoun. He could be conniving and blow her off, and she hated when he did that. Her love wasn't a game, and her heart wasn't to be toyed with.

Right then, Coco began yawning; her eyes felt so heavy she could barely keep them open.

She wanted to go get some rest. And from all outward appearances it seemed like Calhoun was telling the truth for a rare change.

"Well, baby," she said, trying to sound sweet and repentant, "I'm really sorry for blowing up your phone like I did. But you saw I called you, but you didn't holler back. So I was worried. And I just wanted to check on you."

"We know all about that checking on me shit. What else is new?"

She thought she heard the sound of a female's voice.

"When you gon' be home, baby?" Coco wanted to know. "My kitty cat is purring and it's ready to be licked."

At hearing her seductive words, Calhoun moaned appreciatively.

"I'll be home soon, baby girl. And I'ma take care of you real good. Get that kitty cat good and wet for me, and I'll lick it all night long for you."

Coco grinned widely as if Calhoun was standing right in front of her and could see her pleased expression. Her heart gradually softened, and Calhoun's raspy voice easily tore down all the hostility and coldness she'd been harboring for him. Every day she questioned why she was with him, and each time the answer was the same. She loved her man to death. Rough neck and all, Coco wanted to be the only woman in Calhoun Humphries's life.

"Okay, then. I'll head home and get ready for you. Bye, Calhoun." She paused, still feeling stupid as hell. "I-I only do these things 'cause I love your ass."

"I know, Ma. Stop stressing so much. You need to start trusting me."

Coco promised him she'd try to trust him more.

"I love you, Calhoun," she said again.

She heard him cough, a laugh, and then the sound of music blaring even louder.

"Aw shit," Coco remarked. "My man is too lit to hang up."

Coco felt alarmed when she saw "CONFERENCE CALL" still displayed on her phone. "Dru, you can end the call now."

Dru happily disconnected Calhoun.

"Damn, that was extremely difficult to listen to," Dru responded in a daze. Her eyes were very droopy; it felt like she was in a dream state. She drank some more Coke and forced herself to stay alert.

"I'm sorry!" Coco said. "I didn't mean for you to hear all that."

"Of course you didn't." Her sister sure had it bad. The dysfunctionality that Dru witnessed in other people's relationships made her question if being in "love" was even worth the trouble.

"Glad it's all over," Dru continued. "You finally got to talk to your man, and you know exactly where he is at this very second. Feel better now, Sis?"

"Much better." Coco sighed then giggled. She slapped her cheeks several times and was ready to end the night.

"Excellent!" Dru stood, about to hang up.

"I guess I need to drive my drowsy ass on to the house." Coco began shuffling toward her car. Then she abruptly decided to lay her hand on top of the Dodge's hood. She lightly touched the hood, which felt cold to the touch.

"Good," she said and smiled. "That means he's been posted up here a good minute. Maybe he's telling the truth for a change."

"What did you say?" Dru asked.

"Nothing. Don't even worry about it." Feeling lighthearted and joyful, Coco had just started walking toward her own vehicle. Then a sudden movement caught her eye. Coco went and stood close to the driver's-side window of Calhoun's Dodge. She retrieved her key ring and flicked on the mini flashlight. She shined the light on his front seat. She squinted some more and detected a long-haired, light-skinned female crouched down in the seat.

"What the fuck?" Coco was fully awake now. She banged her fist against the window. "Who the fuck is you?"

The woman cowered further in the seat and covered her face with her hands.

"Ain't that a bitch?" Coco said. She let go of her purse and it hit the concrete. She grabbed the door handle. It was locked. Coco violently yanked on it; her fingers burned with pain.

"Open up this door, bitch. What you doing in my man's car?"

The woman squeezed her eyes shut even tighter, resisting the urge to acknowledge Coco.

Coco fished around in her purse for her phone. She dialed Calhoun's number, but the call went straight to voice mail.

Screaming, Coco raised her foot and kicked Calhoun's car several times. A small dent was left in the
side door.

"See, this what I'm talkin' 'bout," she wailed.

"What in the world is going on?" Dru asked. She
went and opened a new bottle of Coke and took a few
sips. "Why are you crying again?"

"This dude ain't right. But he gon' get right, you
best believe that," Coco declared. "Bye." She abruptly
hung up from Dru and tried to think. She debated
standing outside till the sun came up. Then she would
be able to see clearly who the woman was. But Coco's
mind forced her to envision her kids. It had been almost two hours since she'd left them. As much as she
didn't want to leave, she knew she had to go check on
her babies.

Coco wept all the way home. When she arrived at
her house and emerged from the car, her neighbor, Sil-
via, was standing outside her front door.

Coco hesitated and then said, "Hey, Silvie."

Silvie glared at her. Coco tried to ignore the woman
and went to insert her key into the door.

"Um, Coco. Next time you wanna desert your babies, you better think twice about it."

"What? What are you talking about?"

"You know good and well what I'm talking about.
About an hour ago I came outside to walk my dog. We
start going down the block. I get a few houses down
and see something white running toward me. Something so small it looks like a little ghost. And guess
who I run into at twelve-thirty in the morning? A little
boy with no shoes on. No clothes. Just a big white dirty
diaper . . . His eyes were big and scary looking. He'd
been crying. He—"

Coco held her breath. It felt like oxygen was leaving her body. She bolted her big self toward the door and managed to turn the key.

"Chance?" she screamed as she pushed open her front door. "Where you at, baby?"

Silvie followed Coco inside.

"Coco—"

Coco's big feet pounded across the floor; she made a left and galloped to the kids' bedroom. He wasn't in his bed.

"Your baby is at my place. I fed him, he fell asleep, and he's safe. Good thing my dog kept barking like he had to go use it or else . . ."

Coco nodded. What if Chance had gotten hit by a car? What if someone snatched him up and she never saw her baby again? The entire night weighed on her. She covered her face with her hands and burst into tears.

"I didn't mean to do it, I swear to God. I love my baby. I love my son." Coco Reeves, big belly and all, clumsily fell into Silvie's arms. Silvie could barely breathe as she tried to comfort the anguished woman.

Silvie angrily hugged her. "You ought to know better than that. You better have had a good excuse for leaving your kid like that. A damned good excuse."

Coco had no good excuse to offer. She opened her purse and tried to give Silvie a ten-dollar bill. Silvie refused.

Coco thanked her, pulled herself together, and went and got her son.

CHAPTER 9

You Must Think I'm Psycho

A few days later, Alita called Coco on the phone. She waited until she knew Calhoun would be at work.

"Hey, Sis," she said. "You got a minute?"

"Whassup, Alita?"

"Dru told me how you got her caught up in the middle of your shit the other night."

"Wasn't no shit."

"Excuse me, Dark Skin? You out past midnight driving through the streets of Houston looking for this fool like you the police working the graveyard shift? Sounds exactly like a whole bunch of shit if you ask me."

"And that's the problem. 'Cause nobody asked you. I can't stand Dru with her big-ass mouth."

"She doesn't have a big mouth. But she did tell me how you cursed out some chick that you found in Calhoun's car. What was up with that?"

"Oh, girl. That was so crazy. His mama happened to be peeking through the window the night I drove past her house. I guess she put two and two together."

"And she gave her son the heads-up? That Henrietta Humphries is a hot mess . . . just like her son."

"My future mother-in-law."

"You need to stop saying that. Based on everything Dru told me about what happened, you two clowns won't be getting married anytime soon. That's for sure."

"Dru don't know what the hell she talkin' about. She needs to stay in her lane."

"Are you seriously getting an attitude, Coco?" Alita wanted to reach through the phone line and choke her sister. "And stop blaming Dru for your nonsense. You drug her into that mess and got the nerve to get mad because she wanted to talk to me about it."

"Ugh." Coco felt impatient and annoyed. She'd just gotten Cadee off to school, and she wanted the other two kids to lie down for a nap so she could get some rest. When you were a mother with young kids and had a man that acted like a kid, life tended to be overwhelming.

"What you calling my phone for, Alita?"

"Why you chasing a man? Don't *chase*. Replace."

"Oh, girl, please. Until you replace the one you had with a better one, you ain't in the position to lecture me. So save it."

"I don't even have to have a good man to know what's going with you. I'm just saying, as usual, you making yourself look like a fool."

"Okay, it's official. I'm a fool. I do what fools do, remember?"

"Dark Skin, I'm not trying to crack on you, but—"

"The name is Coco!"

"All right . . . Coco. As I was saying, I don't want to crack on you, but—"

"But what?"

"Okay." Alita paused. "I'm going to try real hard to be nice as I can as I say this."

"What, Lita, what?"

"You better stop leaving your kids alone in the house while you running them fucking streets with your retarded ass."

"Why you talking to me like that?" Coco was screeching by now. "Don't you dare talk to me crazy, Alita."

"Trust me, I could have talked to you a lot worse. And how I talk to you ain't the main issue. Like I said, stop leaving your kids alone or something bad will happen. Don't tempt the Lord with your bullshit. Just like he blessed you to have those kids, that same Lord can take your blessings away." Alita slammed down the phone before Coco could hang up on her first.

It was a Saturday afternoon in mid-October, a couple of weeks after Leno had been caught in his little sex scandal. Alita managed to convince her son to be more responsible with his life, and he promised to do better as long as she lightened up with the threats of punishment.

Once things calmed down with that situation, Alita let Burgundy in on what had happened with Leno. Burgundy decided her sister needed a nice little diversion from her parenting issues. Quite frankly, she knew Alita needed a man. And she nagged her sister until she gave in and agreed to meet the man she'd heard so much about.

The sisters were in the car and on their way to see if they could bring some positivity, and some good companionship, into Alita's life. During the drive, Alita barked questions at Burgundy, who was driving frantically during mid-afternoon traffic.

"B, are you sure he's not going to be a waste of my fucking time?"

"Alita, dang, girl, you won't know till you try."

"That's what I don't want. I can't afford to take another risk. I'm getting too damned old for this shit."

"You're not old. Some women get remarried at fifty, sixty, and even seventy years old."

"They're fools. Shit, Oprah has been with Stedman forever. You don't see her chasing him down trying to sing, 'Put a ring on it.'"

Burgundy couldn't help but laugh. "You, girl, are going to have to calm down and take things a step at a time." She paused. "If you end up finding love again, Sis, it'll be worth it. There's nothing like being in love and having someone who is your rock, your lover, and the father of your kids."

"What?" Alita said. "Who said anything about having more kids?"

"Calm down . . . I was just—"

"You're just doing way too much trying to run your big sister's life. You better hope I don't regret meeting this man."

"You," Burgundy replied in all seriousness, "had better hope I don't regret you meeting him either."

Within minutes they arrived at their destination, Morning Glory.

"Shade Wilkins, meet my oldest sister, Alita Washington." Burgundy beamed at her sister with immense pride. Alita was wearing a slim fitting sleeveless black dress and wore a knitted shawl that Burgundy had carefully arranged over her shoulders.

"Hello, Ms. Washington."

Alita slid the shawl off and extended her hand. "I hate this damn thing, it's so pointless. Anyway, hi, Shade. Good to meet you. But I go by Alita. Not Washington. Just Alita."

"Kind of like Ciara?" Shade asked. He curved his top lip into an amazing, beautiful smile that made Alita feel warm all over.

"What about her?" Alita asked.

Shade continued. "Ciara likes to go by one name, but now that she's married, maybe all of that has changed."

"Hmm," Alita replied. "I wish I was as great as that woman. She really lucked out after going through hell with all of her exes, especially that awful baby daddy of hers. Thank God he's in Ciara's past, which is where all badass men should stay . . . forever."

"Shhh," Burgundy pleaded. "Let's not start all that wasting energy on people we don't even know and probably will never meet face to face. We're here to celebrate my sister, Alita. She's turning thirty-seven tomorrow."

"Yeah, ain't that special?" Alita said.

"Happy pre-birthday to you Ms. Alita." Shade's lip curved into that beautiful grin once more. He grabbed her hand and pumped it several times.

"Mmm hmm," she remarked. "Happy damned birthday."

Shade was cordial and skillfully ignored her comment. "Say, ladies. Why don't we go sit down at the booth over that way?" he suggested, then invited them to walk ahead of him. They formed a single file as they strolled through the restaurant. When they had nearly reached their destination, Shade hurried past them. He waited next to the booth and gestured at Alita to be seated.

Alita stared. "Are you serious?"

"I'm very serious."

"A man with class. All righty then." She sat down and watched him welcome Burgundy into their booth as well.

They took a seat in a corner of the restaurant where the atmosphere was more intimate, light slightly dimmer, ambience very relaxing.

"Shade, dear, I've been wanting to get you two together for the longest, and I've already told you a couple of things about my sister, but I felt it was important for you to meet her and form your own opinion."

"May I ask something?" Alita blurted to her date.

"Feel free to ask whatever you want," he replied.

"Is Shade your *real* name or is that some type of fake-ass name 'cause you got something to hide? You a felon?"

Burgundy burst out laughing. "Whoa. She's started already. I think that's my cue to leave."

"Noooo, B," Alita begged. "Stay with us. Please."

"Of course I will," Burgundy promised.

"I mean," Alita explained to Shade, "I never heard of anybody with that name before."

"I've never heard of the name Alita before . . . until I met you."

"Look. I get it all right? We both have unusual names. But I didn't know if your mama named you that, or if that's your street moniker or what."

"None of the above," he laughed good-naturedly. "Not at all. And yes, Shade Wilkins is my government name courtesy of my maternal grandmother; it was her father's name, Ms. Washington."

"Ugh," she complained. "If we're going to be around each other, and I'll let you know once this date is over, you need to call me Alita. I thought I already told you that."

"You're right, I forgot." He laughed. "Alita."

Shade was acting with such decency toward her that she began to feel won over. Not knowing what else to do, Alita took a sip of the ice water that had been placed on their table. She allowed herself a moment to look deeply into his eyes. The eyes spoke volumes. Alita noticed that his twinkled when he smiled. They appeared kind, open, and welcoming.

"I must admit, the last time I had a blind date . . ." he continued. "I swore I'd never go on one again."

"Oh, really?" Burgundy said, intrigued. "Was it that bad? What happened?"

"Her name was Jennifer. We met for dinner and a movie. I quickly determined that she and I had nothing in common. The conversation felt cold . . . like a struggle. Usually I can bond with just about anybody, but that woman, woo, she was steadily looking at the exit door . . . staring at her phone, not really giving me eye contact. Very disconnected."

"Whoa," Burgundy said. "Makes you wonder why she'd even agree to go out with you if her body language suggested she wasn't interested. Just say you aren't feeling the man and move keep it moving."

"Right," Shade agreed with a sigh. "That's why today, I was hesitant—"

"You don't have to hesitant with me," Alita snapped, unknowingly mispronouncing the word. "We could cut out right now, and I'll call it a day."

"Alita, would you stop embarrassing the hell out of me?" Burgundy had just about had it. "You will sit here and be as sweet and friendly as I know you can be. Now. Chill out and stop stressing so much like you're a teenager. You deserve to relax and be in the company of a good man," she insisted.

Alita knew she needed to be more adult about this with her almost thirty-seven-year-old self. "Oh, Jesus. I'm sorry, Shade. I'm flipping out."

"No problem, I understand," Shade assured her and acted like what she'd previously said did not bother him.

"I wasn't directing anything at you, Alita," he explained. "I was just saying that this is about my third time going on a blind date and . . . well, I guess I shouldn't be going into the past just yet. Let's focus on right now."

"Thanks for saying that, Shade," Burgundy said. "Brand-new day for both of you."

Alita wished she could relax and just be able to chitchat and not feel so uptight as if she were at an important job interview. But in spite of his encouragement, it felt like a ton of weights were in her stomach. Since Alita's divorce several years ago, she had not been on one authentic date. Falling in love felt scary. And she'd rather get attacked by a Rottweiler than face rejection or be hurt again.

Shade handed Alita the menu. "Take a look at what you might want to order." Then he apologized. "Oops," he laughed. "I guess I'm as nervous as you, since I'm sure you've probably memorized it."

"I know about it but trust me, I sure haven't eaten all of it."

They both laughed easily and placed their orders for a breakfast special.

Shade seemed very down-to-earth and he made her feel so good that she wanted to give him a chance. His admiring glances eased her anxiety.

Alita's hair was swept up (something Burgundy had insisted on) and she wore an Afrocentric scarf around her head that bore a dozen striking colors. Outwardly she looked elegant, but on the inside she felt ratchet and as wild as a rattlesnake.

"Well," Shade said to her, "I must say you're looking mighty fine this afternoon. You're not wearing any makeup, are you?"

"Nope. No foundation."

"A natural beauty."

"My sister is a beauty, isn't she?" Burgundy remarked. "I always told Alita she could have been a model. She definitely has the height." Alita had long, slender legs, but her wide, sensual hips kept her from being considered model thin. Her hairless arms were smooth and pretty. And she was blessed to never have to wear tons of eye shadow, blush, or things like fake eyelashes. Her natural lashes were so lengthy there was no need to buy any.

"I guess being a model wasn't in my future."

"Well, hopefully, if I'm a lucky guy, I will be that future."

Alita froze. "Look, wait a second, man. Why would you say that when I only met you five minutes ago? See, that's why I didn't even want to go on this funky date. I hate when some men tell women the shit they think we wanna hear. Just bullshit promises that lead to nothing."

"Alita, would you please show some respect?" Burgundy said in disbelief. "This man goes to my church."

"Oh, and now I'm supposed to change the way I am to please this man that goes to church? Hell, the church-going bastards be some of the worst devils out here. So noooo." She pronounced the word as if she was saying "Noah."

"I won't act any different with him than anybody else. I guess since he reads the Bible his ass don't stank and he's perfect like you pretend to be? I don't think so."

"Alita, please—" Burgundy prayed that the humiliation would soon end. "I'm sorry, Shade. I warned you she's a little outspoken."

"Burgundy, look. What she's saying doesn't bother me at all. I love it when a woman speaks her mind. It's important to know where I stand." Shade turned to Alita. "You don't have to act fake around me. If you like to cuss, cuss on. I wasn't born baptized. And it's not like I've never used profanity when the right occasion came up. If you read the New Testament, even Peter cussed, and Jesus was cool with him."

"All righty then," Alita replied. "Call me the female Peter, 'cause I like to cuss."

"Yes ma'am," he replied. "We now have that understanding. You are a cussing saint, and there's a lot of 'em out here these days."

Alita calmed down and actually felt embarrassed. She knew she was no saint. She fiddled with her hands and couldn't even look Shade in the face. She wasn't sure if he was just messing with her or if he was serious. But his eyes twinkled as he grinned at Alita. His eyes felt safe, even though she may have not deserved it.

Shade lifted her chin and forced eye contact. "Alita, I didn't mean to offend you. I'm not trying to run game. I honestly want to take time and get to know you better. The real you. That's my thing. I love people."

"It's true, Lita," Burgundy replied.

"Oh, okay," Alita said, her voice trembling. "I'm sorry for going off. I could use a stiff drink right now."

"Girl, you know Morning Glory doesn't serve anything stronger than ginger ale and root beer."

"Well, y'all need to change the menu." Alita was partially joking. She inhaled. Exhaled. As she sat there she realized that Shade Wilkins had an intoxicating masculine scent, fresh and clean. As the minutes passed, they locked eyes a couple of times. He intensely watched her as she unabashedly eyed him. A tiny butterfly flapped its delicate wings in her belly.

By then their plates had arrived: scrambled eggs, fried wings, a large golden brown waffle, and various beverages.

"I, um, I guess I'll have to stick with drinking this lemon water. It's better for my skin anyway," Alita muttered.

"And you do have some lovely flawless skin," Shade told her. "You don't look your age at all. Black ain't cracking on you whatsoever. And no, I'm not running game because you already know you're a good looking woman."

She let his sweet words sink in, let the sweetness of his compliments ease her troubled soul.

As Shade began to devour his meal, he discreetly watched Alita with compassion. He appreciated what he saw: an attractive and desirable woman who, in her past, had been inappropriately handled, perhaps rough enough to get bruised, but who still held tenderness inside her broken heart. He plainly saw the beauty underneath the tough façade.

"Alita," he continued, "I am not trying to rush you and or put pressure on you. But I am the type who knows what I want from jump and I'm not afraid to admit it. If I have a hunch I'm feeling you and I turn out to be right, cool. If I'm wrong, I can deal with that too."

"Nothing wrong with that . . . I can give it a fair chance," Alita said. Her voice was a humble whisper.

"Excellent. Let's get to know each other. I'll start first. I'm from Louisiana."

"Which part?" Alita asked.

"New Orleans."

"Why don't you have a Cajun accent?"

"I was born there, but we came to Houston when I was three."

"And he's now thirty-three. He's been here a few decades. So officially that means Shade's a Texan, and he's not a saint," Burgundy said teasingly.

"Yes. I claim Texas. I haven't liked the Saints since Reggie Bush defected. So I've lived here, and worked for Shell Oil Company ever since I graduated with a BBA . . . from Rice University."

"Rice?" Alita remarked. She'd never known anyone to graduate from Rice, and she knew it was one of the best colleges in the nation. Why would a man like Shade be interested in her? They seemed complete opposites.

Educated. Refined. Sophisticated. Professional job.

Her confidence threatening to crumble, something compelled Alita to stay and listen.

"Now that you've learned a little bit about me," he said, "what about you?"

Alita gave Burgundy an incredulous look as if to say, "Why'd you bring me here to meet him?"

"Ah, ah, ah," Shade scolded her when he saw Alita give Burgundy "the look."

"What I've shared with you are my credentials on *paper*. But if you want to know about the real me," he explained, "I've gotten a few speeding tickets, I've been arrested for walking in civil rights protests, and um, I cheat at Monopoly."

Alita frowned. "That's it? That's your faults? Hell, the shit that I've done and been through is like Armageddon compared to your little confessions."

"We still have time to get to know the dirtier sides of my life." Shade turned serious. "Alita, sweetheart. Everybody has issues. Your family, your co-workers, your neighbors. White folks, black folks, Asians. All of us have good and bad . . ."

"But there is way more goodness inside of you than bad, right, Shade Wilkins?" Burgundy shamelessly asked. She hoped she hadn't pumped this man up just to find out he'd been hiding an evil side. "You don't sleep with little boys or anything like that, do you?"

"No," he laughed. "Nothing like that. But I just want Alita . . . excuse me, I want *you* to know, sweet lady, that it's okay to be who you are regardless of who or what I am. I'm not here to judge you. And guess what? I don't need you to judge me either."

"That's fair," Alita replied, for she had nothing else to say. She concentrated on eating her meal.

"Again," Shade continued. "What's your background? What do you like? What do you hate? If you could write your own ticket to the type of life you'd want, what would it be?"

Now this was something no one had ever asked Alita before.

"Okay," Alita said and laid down her fork. "I have had one failed marriage, and I'm sure you know all the dirt about that. I have a kid, a very handsome, talented teenage boy that we call Leno. I love him to death. He's my heart and soul, and I'm doing my best to raise him right. Um, I, shit, what else can I tell you about me? I love family . . . yeah, that's it. Family keeps me sane when I want to go crazy. And about that ticket that I could write? I'd want what any other woman would want . . . a damned good relationship with the right man without the drama, the bullshit, the lies, the excuses, and the man's fascination for hooking up with the next chick even when he's still with you. Oh, yeah, another thing, in addition to being a mother, I hold down three part-time jobs. My main job is to stock the shelves at a grocery store. And my other gigs don't have regular hours, but I get to work when I can. One job has to do with harassing people to pay their bills. Yeah, me, Alita Washington, the one who struggles to pay her bills, is a bill collector. That means straight commission, and if I don't convince folk to pay up, it's like I've worked for nothing. But my third gig is more normal. Another telephone job, but this time I take catalog orders from people that want to buy clothes and stuff but they can't stand the internet. So in other words, I get paid to run my mouth. Between taking care of Leno and going to these funky-ass jobs, a sister stays tired. And one of my dreams is to come into lots of money so I never have to work a day in my life. I'd want to be in great health; I never want to have health issues like my sister Coco. And I hate looking at the news, because it's always something crazy going down like terrorists losing they damn minds, or the police losing they damn minds, so yeah, my dream is just to be safe from the evils of the world, and just to not be bothered with the bullshit that I see out here. That's about it. Those are my dreams. Now tell me something, Shade. Are you going to give them to me?"

"Welp," Burgundy said, round-eyed at her sister's big revelations. "I think she's covered just about everything, don't you think, because she sure talked without taking one breath."

"I enjoyed listening to every word," Shade admitted aloud. "She's something else, and I like her already. Crazy-ass woman."

Burgundy gasped. All Alita could do was genuinely laugh out loud. She reached over and touched Shade's hand. He quickly grabbed her hand back and squeezed it.

Alita wondered if she talked too much, and it felt like she'd just delivered her first speech in public, and she hoped that she aced it.

After Burgundy calmed down from the shock of Shade using profanity, she watched both of them resume their conversation; she began to feel a warm fuzziness take over. She felt more assured, less tense.

"Excuse me, you two," Burgundy said and stood up. "Please continue to eat and enjoy your meal. I need to use the ladies' room. Then I gotta go to the business office and make a few phone calls and check on some other matters. Be right back." She discreetly left the table.

Shade leaned back in his seat and calmly continued.

"You know, Alita, life can drop-kick any one of us in the knees and make us fall down. So please don't feel bad about whatever you've been through with your ex. That's your truth, you know what I mean? And each of us is the product of our past experiences, good or bad. So far, I do like you, and I barely know you. Now I must disagree with you in that you said think I'm a typical man that tells a woman what they want to hear. But I try to say what's in my heart. You can't knock a brother for that, can you?"

Alita believed that Shade talked a lot; she wasn't sure if she should trust every word he told her, but she sat on the edge of her seat eagerly listening.

"No, Shade," she mumbled. "I won't knock you for being you. And I-I'm sorry for prejudging. This dating stuff . . . I'm out of practice, ya know? All I really want to do is have a good time and escape from my worries." She looked apologetic. "I feel so nervous right now. It took me hours to get ready for this date."

"Hey, don't apologize." He held up his hands. "No pressure. No expectations. I may never see you again after we leave here, but not because I don't want to. I'm a strong advocate of fate."

Alita stared at him wide-eyed, not being certain of the definition of "advocate" but hoping it was something good.

"If it's meant for me and you to know each other, we will," he assured her. "We can hang out. I'm not about to run away from a pretty woman. But I definitely won't tolerate one that doesn't treat me right either."

Alita respected what he was saying, but at the same time listening to his direct way of talking made her feel slightly intimidated.

She paused. "You seem like a cool guy. And I can't promise you that I will treat you like the king that you probably are every single day of the week."

He laughed. "That's honest."

"I'm not finished."

"Sorry."

Alita nervously toyed with her hands. "I-I've never been on a college campus except to take my son to one so he can see what they're like. I only earned a high school diploma. College just wasn't my thing."

He hunched his shoulders as if that didn't matter.

"I've been working since I was seventeen," she continued. "Got married when I was twenty. Had the baby when I was twenty-one, and even though my ex—Leonard is his name—even though he had a good job when we first got married, I wanted to help out. I like to stay busy. And back then, I worked at Mickey D's, child care centers, receptionist jobs, whatever I could do to pay a few bills. I felt we were a team."

"I admire that."

"I ain't finished."

"Sorry. Go ahead."

"At first things were good," she continued. "I loved being married. Loved being loved. I felt safe. Safer than I'd felt in a long time." Her eyes gleamed at the fond memories. "But after he got the job at the dealership and started bringing home a lot of money, life changed. Leonard is competitive. So he put in the hours, tried to be the best. And that caused some problems in our relationship. He'd say he was so tired from working fifteen hours a day that he had no time for romance. I got lonely. Then I got angry. And he got into flirting around with his female customers." She stopped momentarily, carefully choosing what she wanted to reveal. "And so it went from playful flirting to one out-right affair that he had with this single woman. He got her pregnant. She miscarried, but I didn't care. I was through after that. We were married twelve years. Then boom, it was over. It was a nasty divorce too. Some of my sisters tell me all the time, they say, 'Lita, you walk around like you got a big-ass chip on your shoulder.' I get mad at 'em and I tell 'em if they had survived what I have survived, they'd have big chips too. But my sisters and I, make that a few of them, are very different. Burgundy, humph, she's probably more your type than me. But she's very married."

"Are you done?" Shade asked, looking serious.

"Maybe."

"Let's pretend like you're done for now, Alita. First of all, I am not here to compare you to other women, not to your sisters, not anyone. I'm simply here in this fine restaurant, eating this good food, just so I can take a moment to get to know you . . . for you. And never apologize for what you've survived."

"I don't!"

He laughed. "What I'm trying to say is you don't have to write yourself off based on a few superficial things like education and or lack of money. Some edu-cated rich folks are complete and utter fools."

"You right about that," she blurted, even though she did not personally know anyone like that.

Shade continued. "I like and appreciate real. Your path was your path. All you can do is be upfront about your life. Only an idiot would blame you for where life has taken you. And, Alita, I'm no idiot."

This time it was Alita's turn to grow quiet. She did not know what to say, she could only look at him. Shade's eyes twinkled, and he gave her the warmest smile she'd experienced from a man in quite some time. Was he talking just to be saying something, or was this his true personality? Alita curiously stared at her date; she felt a strong urge to jump up and run. Many guys started off great, appearing like someone that possessed everything a woman could desire—till they quickly showed their true colors.

"Why ain't you married?" she blurted out to him.

He thought carefully. "Why marry if I'm not ready? Why rush to be with someone just to make her happy? Just to make my relatives happy who, by the way, ask me every other week, who am I dating? Just the sound of that: being tied down . . ." He had to laugh out loud. "That in itself doesn't even sound like anything a rational person would want to do. So, to answer your question, young lady, before I make a major mistake, I'd rather take my time, be single, enjoy the life I have right now, than rush into a mistake. Then I'd be an ex-husband, the very type of man you'd be complaining about."

She nodded.

"Although I came very close to getting married one time, Alita, ultimately the situation didn't work out. I hate to call it dodging a bullet. And sometimes I still think about what would've happened if we had stuck it out."

"You still see her?" she asked, waiting to hear how he'd answer.

"Yes," he exclaimed, "but only because she still attends the church. But hey, it's a big church, thousands of people are there every week. So once in a while we run into each other. It's always pleasant." He made a face, "She gives me that look like she wishes we could reconcile, but nah, that ain't happening. Once I'm done, I'm done. You had your chance, you blew it. Now I have a chance to be somebody else's blessing. I don't have time to be messing around with a woman that doesn't know what she wants; one day she wants me the next day she doesn't."

Alita eyed Shade carefully and concluded he didn't fit the description of a BS artist. She spoke in a humble tone. "I feel you on that one. I'm not down for the okie-doke either. And since my divorce I'm trying hard to learn who I am." At that point her own thoughts about herself frightened her. "You know, sometimes I think this person I've become, it ain't completely the true me. I feel like the real Alita is hiding somewhere deep in here." She rested her hands over her heart. "As old as I am, she's someone I'm still getting to know."

"Well, I believe the real woman, the better woman, the seasoned woman, is in there somewhere, young lady. That's the one I'm hoping to know too. How 'bout we get to know her together?"

Shade's voice sounded welcoming. And his words touched her heart so deeply that she hardly could believe what he just told her.

"I want to know your story," Shade continued. "Your truth. It's not where you've been but where you're going."

His words proved to be a doorway through which Alita Washington could safely enter. And for the next ten minutes she found herself gradually opening up to Shade. She tried her best to just tell him about her life and leave bitterness out of her voice, but at the same time, she had to expose her life.

"Love played a cruel trick on me."

"Why do you say that?"

"Because," she said, "I believed it. My ex, Leonard,

was probably the third serious boyfriend I had. The third man I ever slept with. Third time's a charm, my ass."

Shade chuckled at her way with words. "Who doesn't want to give love a try?"

"Only a fool, Shade. Only us fools." Her heart felt lighter, and she to admit, it did feel good to have a man to talk to. She'd learned it was much easy to get a man to tell you the truth when he wasn't trying to sleep with you.

"Seriously, though, Shade. When you fall in love with the person that you think is the one, it feels so damn good that you're scared . . . scared it's not totally real. And when things fall apart, that's when you wonder if you imagined the whole thing. That shit seemed like a counterfeit dollar bill, and you were a fool for thinking it was the real deal."

Alita told him how, after their divorce, it seemed as if their arguments escalated. Things got nasty. Hurt tried to increase the hurt. And when Leonard came around less, and even more so as time progressed, to her wounded ego it felt like her ex-husband had disowned his namesake.

"If you absent, if you gone, it's like you're saying to the kid 'fuck you,' like I hate ya mama and I hate you too. Because I think some people, and yes, even men do it too, they don't want to see the kid anymore. They want to pretend like the kid doesn't exist, and like they can be happy without that little boy . . . little girl. They act like you made that baby all by yourself. And I wonder how they would feel if their daddy or mama did them that way." Even though she knew that Leonard was now making up for lost time, it seemed so unfair. He already missed so much. And she questioned his motives for wanting to develop a close relationship with Leno all of a sudden.

"Sometimes the ones that abandon people are repeating what happened to them," Shade told her.

"Bullshit. Leonard Washington grew up with a mama, a daddy, and one sister. He has no excuse."

Shade could only look baffled. "I can't make excuses for a man I don't know."

"Right, you don't know him. I know what he used to be, and what he has ended up being. I know he can be better." Her voice was a faint whisper. "I always hoped it could be better for Leno."

"What do you want him to do?"

She laughed. "Be active. Be there when it counts. Come to the games, his practices. Let people know that you're proud of your son. Let your son see how excited it makes him when you show up to the game. Love is a two-way street." She wanted to cry when she thought of all the times that he had looked up in the stands searching for his father's friendly face. Her heart hurt for any young boy whose daddy was missing in his life. "Boys need their fathers. Is that asking too much?"

"No."

"Thank you," she told him. "You're a great listener." She smiled and was happy to have Shade to talk to.

"I try."

But the more she thought about Leonard, the sooner her smile vanished. It was tortuous, like she was trapped in an eternal well from which she could not escape. She wanted to think about the good, but the bad continued to haunt the woman.

"I don't see how any father can deny his flesh and blood. I don't care for my sake, but for my son's sake? I would kill for Leno."

"I believe that."

Shade didn't mean for his words to sound humorous, yet Alita burst out laughing. She laughed for a few minutes, nearly gasping for breath. When she was able to calm down, she said, "This has to be the most horrible first date ever. You must think I'm damned psycho."

"I don't," he insisted.

"You sure?"

"I am."

"You're not saying that just to make me feel better?"

"I swear to God, and if I had my Bible with me, I'd swear on that too."

She giggled some more. Relaxed.

By the time Burgundy returned, Alita was enjoying listening to Shade tell her about his life, and she didn't even get pissed when he eventually took her hand in his and held it with the most gentle touch she'd ever felt. It wasn't sexual. It felt human. Like he cared, even though he had no good reason to.

Their date ended with a promise to hook up again. As much as she enjoyed spending time with Shade, Alita had her doubts. She remembered the things she had told him about herself and felt afraid. She hated the despair that had taken over when her had marriage ended, even though she was the one who divorced Leonard. It had happened years ago, and she continued to nurse the pain and remember the great sense of loss. She only wanted to be married one time to one man. But she was a divorced, single mom. And she desperately wanted to move past it.

Burgundy and Alita waved goodbye to Shade and watched him leave the restaurant.

"How'd I do?" Alita asked.

"Let's not even go there."

"Was it that bad?" Alita wanted to know.

"Sis, I'm surprised he didn't walk away while he had the chance."

"Oooh, I didn't mean to—"

"Alita, it's time for you to be real," Burgundy told her in a no-nonsense tone. "Yes, you did mean it. You said what you meant, and you acted the way you wanted to act."

"But I did not mean—"

"Let me share some advice coming from a woman that's been married a long time," Burgundy said in a gentle voice. "Watch your words, Sis. And guard your thoughts, because a lot of times they are outright negative. And I wanted to warn you that whatever you *think* about a situation is exactly what you're going to have. Because your thoughts and your words will set out to create your reality. Words have power."

Alita looked visibly uncomfortable. Suddenly it felt like Burgundy was acting like her all-knowing mother instead of her inexperienced younger sister.

"I also wanted to say," Burgundy continued, "please don't judge Shade based on whoever else you've dated. Because if you're going to do that, what's the point of agreeing to go out with a new man?"

Alita could only hunch her shoulders.

"Lita, give Shade Wilkins the benefit of the doubt until he proves that he's not the type of man you want. Everybody deserves a chance. Even you."

Alita was silenced into humility. Again, she felt like she had messed up big time. Would there ever be a moment in her life when she'd get it right?

"Thanks for the advice, B. I won't judge him. But are you trying to judge me?"

"Oh, Sis, don't be mad. I'm trying to help you."

"I don't need your help, Queen B," she snapped.

"Apparently you do. When's the last time you were able to get a date on your own?"

"I know I can get a date on my own." Alita stood up. "I don't need any favors or lectures from you, baby sister."

"See, that's what I'm talking about," Burgundy rushed to say. "You are way too sensitive, got your feelings all on your sleeve. All I've ever done is try to help you get your life together."

"Oh, now the truth comes out. You pretend like I got it going on, and you try hard to convince your little church boy associate that I'm a good risk, but you honestly don't think I'm good enough for him. Or else you wouldn't be trying to change me on the slick." Alita snatched up the shawl that Burgundy had bought for her. It was very pretty and sophisticated, unlike any article of clothing Alita had ever owned. But she took it and dropped it on top of Burgundy's head.

"I hate this corny looking shit. I'm no Princess Kate."

Burgundy discreetly removed the scarf, folded it up neatly, and placed it on the table. "You don't have to be an actual princess to want nice things. This cost me a lot of money, Lita."

"So what? No one asked you to be my wardrobe assistant or my stupid-ass makeup artist either. I can see who I want to see and be the way I want to be and dress how I want to dress. That's what grown-ups do."

"Fine, Lita. All right! I'm just saying that if you continue with your attitude, you'll end up a bitter, lonely woman. I want the best for you. And if you want to be with Shade, you'll have to step up your game."

"You don't really know what he's like behind closed doors, right?" Alita hated a know-it-all who didn't really know much at all.

"I won't even dignify your dumb question with a response." Burgundy glared at her sister, despising her negative ways that constantly made her life unbearable.

"My question isn't dumb. It's the truth. You can assume you know a person, B, and you can believe with everything inside you that you really know Shade Wilkins. But unless you've fucked that man and seriously hung out with him, and I'm not talking about at the church bookstore, then you don't know him."

"Sweetie, there is no way on this planet that I'd hook you up with a man that I know isn't going to be good for you. You'll have to trust me and you'll have to trust him. And we'll see where this goes."

Furious, Alita wanted to take both her hands and aim for her sister's neck . . . the neck with the diamond jewelry around it . . . the neck that held up the head of a beautiful, successful, professional black woman who seemed to hold it all together . . . with her perfect life as if she was part of an updated *Cosby Show* family.

In that moment, as she compared her life to her sister's, Alita resented Burgundy. She felt envious of her decent life and her decent husband, the two adorable kids who had two solid parents raising them; the well-to-do family who owned a house that was practically an estate with its four acres, four-car garage, two staircases, and sixteen televisions. She hated how Burgundy Reeves had enough money rolling in that her kids would never know the pang of hunger causing a growl to rumble inside their little bellies. The kids wouldn't know how it felt to use the same raggedy tooth-brush for a couple of years. They would never wear the same clothes over and over again, clothes that had been machine washed so often that the bright colors began to fade. Alita knew it was unfair, but she resented her nieces, who couldn't help that they had been born to responsible, hardworking parents. But in that moment of hate, Alita mostly hated herself.

Could she really blame all of her problems on her ex-husband? On the fact that she did not pursue a col-lege degree and thereby limited the amount of money she could make? Or that she was in the habit of making bad decisions, and the result of her judgment was what had really caused her life to plunge into the depths of despair.

I can't blame the white man, the government, stupid-ass men, or anybody except myself for the choices I've made, everything I've done.

It hurt to admit that perhaps Burgundy was right. Once her divorce was final, Alita knew she had scared away men who never even got a chance to ask her for a date. If she were honest with herself, she knew she was fortunate that Shade Wilkins even allowed her a couple of hours of his time.

"Well, if I'm a fuck-up, I better make the most of it. I guess he'll never call my negative ass again. See if I care."

Alita turned around and walked away; she hoped that Burgundy felt regretful for speaking to her like she was nothing. Even if it was the truth, no one on earth wanted to be treated like they were nobody.

CHAPTER 10

New Lovers

It was a Sunday in October. And the day before, Leonard Washington had called Alita to see if it was all right for Leno to spend the night. Even though Alita had full custody, she would have thought that Leonard would have been eager to get their child every two weeks, per the custody agreement. But most times he didn't, or couldn't. Alita was baffled.

"All these years, and now you want him to sleep over?" she said to her ex. "Isn't he kind of old for that type of thing?"

"He's never too old to hang out with his dad. I happen to have some tickets to the Texans game. And if he sleeps over, we'll get up early in the morning and go tailgate. It'll be fun."

"Hmm," she said, sounding suspicious. But isn't Leno bonding with his dad, the thing she'd been wanting? Trying to be nice, she told him, "How thoughtful of you. I guess it'll be okay. Have fun."

Leonard had picked up his son from Alita's the night before without incident. And now it was Sunday evening. Time was steadily passing. Alita thought her son would've returned home by now. But she hadn't heard from him or his dad.

After trying to get in touch with Leonard four times with no response, Alita was itching to do something. She cranked up her car and went to over to the big house to see Coco.

"Please go with me over to Leonard's," she begged. "I don't feel right going over there by myself."

"Girl, don't drag me into your mess. I got my own messes to deal with," Coco protested.

They were both standing in Coco's doorway. Alita could hear all three of her kids screaming their heads off like they were out of control.

"See what I'm talking about, Lita?" Coco said as she glanced into the house at Cadee, Chloe, and Chance. They were all running around barefoot.

"I made a chocolate cake for Calhoun's mama, but they talked me into giving them a big slice, and now they're losing their minds."

Alita shook her head. "You'll learn one of these days. Don't let them badass kids control you, Sis. But forget about them for now. I need to borrow you for about an hour. Is your baby daddy at home right now?"

"Yeah, my *husband* is home. What about him?"

"Ask him if he can watch the kids. They are always up under you, and he needs to do his part when it comes to letting you out the house."

"I can't argue with that. Wait a second. Be right back."

Within minutes Coco was bursting through the front

door. "If we gonna do this, let's roll like right now. Calhoun is on the toilet, and he wasn't too happy to know I was leaving without giving him a heads-up. But he'll be all right."

Alita noticed, though, that little Chance was attached to Coco's hip.

"Why is he going with us?"

"I just want him with us, that's all. Let's go. Hurry."

They hurried outside and got into Alita's dented-up Impala. The scratches and dents were due to years of neglect. But it got Alita from point A to B.

"Ohh, I will be so glad when you get you a man. I can't believe that you let Leonard take the newer, nicer car when y'all got divorced."

"Who you telling?" Alita replied. "I ended up taking that cash payout instead of keeping the nicer. And I should have took both. I definitely got the short end of the stick in my divorce settlement. I think I was being too nice."

"You? Too nice?"

"Yes! Me! It happens."

Coco laughed.

"Plus, my attorney wasn't the best. And had the nerve to charge me all that money just so I still ended up being screwed."

"You're just an inexperienced whore, that's all." Coco laughed.

"I guess I am."

With Coco living in Third Ward and Leonard staying on the Southwest Side of Houston, it took the ladies thirty minutes to reach his house. He lived in a small gated community that consisted of fifteen houses spread out on two residential blocks. Fortunately for

Alita, another vehicle happened to be entering the complex, which allowed Alita to speed up before the gate could close.

"Girl," Coco said. "You know you supposed to punch in the code, or call first."

"I know. I don't care. He never answered my calls, so that's why I gotta do it this way."

"This definitely ain't the nice Alita."

"Shut up, Coco."

Within minutes Alita located the house, a lovely tan two-story stucco. As they came to a stop and parked, Coco gasped. "I've never been here before, but damn, he look like he's rolling in the dough." Leonard's house looked stunning from the curb.

"Ain't that a bitch?" Alita said as they got out of her car. "Look at how well he keeps up his property. The bushes are all neatly trimmed. They just flowers, yet he won't give me extra money to buy Leno decent clothes. I want to shop at Macy's but the money I get keeps me at Target."

"Well, that's who you picked, Lita. You wanted to marry him." Coco enjoyed echoing the advice that her sister often gave to her. "What did you see in him anyway?"

Alita rolled her eyes. "None of it matters anymore. C'mon. The sooner I get my kid, the better. I can't stand being forced to see how good my ex is living when he knows we're struggling."

As they walked up short the pathway leading to the front door, Alita noticed a late-model Mercedes in the driveway. She thought it couldn't be Leonard's car, since he was loyal to Nissan and had been driving his Maxima for years.

Alita rang the doorbell and heard its shrill sound from outside. At first she maintained her patience. But after five long minutes of standing around, she had to open her mouth.

"What's taking him so long?" she asked. "Now I'm getting nervous, and it's not good when I feel nervous."

Alita hesitated, then banged her fist against the door. Seconds later, the door squeaked open. A woman answered. Petite, short hair, well dressed, quite attractive. Her makeup was impeccable; her large doe-like eyes lit up when she smiled.

Upon seeing the woman, Alita involuntarily opened and closed her fists. She felt Coco's hand attempt to soothingly rub her back.

"Hi," the woman said. "May I help you?"

Feeling facetious, Alita asked. "I know I have the right house, but I sure didn't expect a strange woman to answer. Who are you?"

The woman looked at her questioningly. "I'm Desiree."

"Desiree what?" Alita demanded.

"Who wants to know?" The woman gazed Alita up and down, and the friendly smile disappeared from her face.

"I'm Alita *Washington*. I've here to pick up my son, Leno. Is he here?"

"Oh, the baby moms. I've heard a lot about you." She snickered but quickly stopped.

Alita raised an eyebrow. "Hold on. Did you laugh?"

"No!"

"Yeah, you did. What's so funny?"

Desiree said, "Nothing." She twirled around and abandoned Alita and Coco; the glass storm door was closed, but the interior door was still ajar. They had a clear look inside the house, and Desiree was nowhere in sight.

"Can you believe that? What's up with her?" Alita opened the storm door and motioned at Coco to follow her.

Alita eye's widened as she stepped foot inside Leonard's new house. The few times that he did hang out with his son, he'd been the one to come to her apartment to pick up Leno.

As she ventured farther down the vast hallway, it was immediately obvious that Leonard had moved up in the world. The home that she had shared with him was a typical house: one story, three large bedrooms, living and dining areas, a den. Nice but nothing extravagant. But his new dwelling had impressive craftsmanship.

Alita took in everything, and she nearly gasped at the upscale, carefully arranged contemporary art. Artwork lined the walls of the foyer, living room, dining area, and even the kitchen. Alita felt herself growing smaller and smaller as she walked from room to room. The house felt like a museum with its exhibition lighting, beige walls, and pristine high white ceilings. The more she saw, the more she felt like she never knew the father of her child.

"Hmmm," Coco said. She also perceived that this setup was drastically different than when Alita had been married.

"This is just unbelievable, sickening in a way," Coco mumbled to herself as she eyeballed the paintings. "No wonder he can't afford to buy my nephew new clothes. He has to put all his money into useless expensive shit that's supposed to impress people, but all it's doing is collecting a whole lot of dust."

Alita came to a stop at the corner of the living room. She finally found something that she could tolerate seeing: black-and-white photos in picture frames. A few were of Leno when he was ten years old. and some were from when he was an infant and a toddler. A couple photos were of Leonard and Leno during an elementary school field trip when they traveled by bus to San Antonio.

There were no photographs that featured Alita. It felt as if she had never existed.

Her throat swelled up. "Hell, I guess he created Leno all by himself." She picked up one photo and set it facedown.

"Girl," Coco said. "I know you ain't tripping because your mug shot ain't up here in your ex-husband's house. Remember, the ex whose guts you can't stand? Why would you want your picture—"

"I know, Coco. It sounds silly, but—"

"But nothing. Forget him. You about to date a much classier man than Leonard. Shade Wilkins," Coco whispered in Alita's ear. "Shade. Shade," she kept repeating.

"Will you shut up, please?" Alita wanted to tune out her idiot sister. She longingly glanced at the photo of her son and his dad smiling into the camera as they stood outside a famous building: the Alamo. Alita remembered the time father and son went on the trip. She too was supposed to join them and go as a chaperone, but she had contracted the flu and couldn't join them.

"Why you all down in the mouth over some photos?"

"Because seeing that picture reminds me of something. When Leonard and I broke up, I begged him to let me have some of the baby pictures. He was like a maniac photographer back when we were married. He should have bought stock in Nikon. And yep, his camera took the photos, but I didn't see why he wouldn't be nice and just let me make some duplicates. But he refused. It was like he was trying to hurt me for filing for divorce. So that's why I'm a bit pissed right now."

"Oh, chile, you better get over that real quick. Leno has just turned sixteen. You may never see those photos ever again in your life; and don't worry about it, because the main thing is you have your son, you can remember when he was a baby, and that fool definitely can't stop you from having good memories."

Alita saw that Coco was trying to help, but she really wished her sister would be quiet. She started to regret that she had begged her to tag along. "Come with me," she said. Although it hurt her to see how well Leonard was living, they continued their tour. All the kitchen and laundry room appliances were top of the line. The family room had the biggest TV Alita had ever seen.

Something inside her whispered, *If you hadn't up and filed on this man, he'd still be your husband, and you would have this new house and everything that comes with it.*

Those thoughts made Alita feel even worse. She tried hard to block the nagging voices from invading her mind.

"Where is everybody?" Coco finally asked. "Where'd that maid go?"

"Let's go upstairs," Alita suggested. She walked to the rear of the house and began to climb the stairs until she reached the second floor. The first thing she saw was a game room decked out with TVs, laptops, and lounging furniture. There were hallways and a bunch of closed doors everywhere. Soon she heard noises. Joyous laughter. Happy voices. Alita followed the sounds. She stood outside one of the closed doors. She leaned and pressed her nose against the wood. She heard Leno talking. Alita knocked. The sounds inside the room were so loud it seemed no one could hear her. She turned the knob and allowed herself entrance.

Sitting comfortably on a king-size bed was Leno. He was shirtless and wearing a pair of gym shorts. He held a game controller; his other hand was clutched by the slender fingers of an unfamiliar female. From what Alita could tell, the girl's hair was dark brown mixed with blond highlights. She had sensuous lips, and she was wearing shorts.

A new thotsicle.

"Leno?" Alita said.

Her son looked up. He jumped out of bed. "Mama, we weren't doing anything, I swear to God. We were just playing the game."

"Baby, you don't have to explain. It's not like you were caught in the act."

Alita stared boldly at the young woman. The female had dark brown eyes, dimples in her round fleshy cheeks. She remained calm and smiled at Alita.

Alita noticed that the girls Leno came across were all kinds of beautiful. This one had long wavy hair that hung down her back; she had thick, pretty eyelashes, and, of course, the biggest boobs a horny man could ever want.

The sight of this girl with her son made Alita sick to her stomach.

"Um, what's going on, Leno? I called you like ten times, and you didn't pick up."

"Five times, Mama. Five times."

"Oh, so since you counting how many times I called, that means you ignored me on purpose. What if it would have been an emergency?"

"But I was all right, Mom. I was safe with my dad."

"I am not talking about you—" She wanted to add "dummy" but decided to hold her tongue for once. She could easily embarrass her child but no, not this time.

"I'm just saying something could have been going on at our house, Leno." She tried to calm down. "Anyway, I am here to pick you up. You do know that this is a school night, and you need to do that homework of yours that you haven't touched in days. You're lucky I let you go to the Texans game. Who won?"

"Our team won by ten points in OT," the young lady said with an excited smile. "It was so much fun."

"Um, who are you? My son is so rude; he should have been introduced you," Alita said, agitated.

Leno was quick to respond. "This is, uh, her name is Zaida. Like Za-ee-da."

"Does she have a last name?" Alita demanded.

"Rojo."

"What?" Alita scowled.

"It's R-O-J-O. The J is silent. So it sounds like Ro-ho."

"Hmm, I thought it would be something like that," Alita said.

"Mom!" Leno threw down his game controller and was keen enough to pick up on her veiled meaning. "Zaida is a nice girl. She moved here from Florida just last summer."

"Oh, so you've only known Rojo for a few months, and you think you know everything about her, son?"

Zaida's dark eyes looked puzzled. Then she said very sweetly, "We've gotten to know each other pretty well, ma'am. You have a smart, charming, and talented son. He's a true gentleman. I'm lucky to know him."

"You are lucky that you got to meet my son. But you aren't the only girl out here trying to know him," Alita said. She sized up Zaida. Besides a body and face to die for, this chick possessed a quiet confidence, almost smug, but it was cloaked in that sweetness that seemed to ooze from her pores.

"Leno, it's cool that you have a little friend, but please don't ignore my calls. I don't care if you spend the night with your dad, you will still show me respect, you hear me? Now come on, get your things so we can go."

"Yes ma'am. I'm sorry to worry you, Mama."

Alita's heart warmed. "It's okay, son, as long as you're all right. That's what matters."

Leno turned to the girl. "Our fun times with Daddy are done. Come on, Zaida."

Coco said, "It's good to see you, nephew. We'll leave you two alone so you can say goodbye." Coco grabbed her sister's arm and forced her to leave the room. She shut the door behind her. And they proceeded to wait outside the door. Everything grew eerily quiet. Alita shut her eyes tight and could only imagine what type of kissing was going on.

Alita said, "That chick looks like she's been getting dick since—"

"Since middle school just like me, right, Alita? Is that what you're trying to say?"

"This isn't about you. Your damage has already been done with your three point five kids. This is about my son and making sure he won't be a baby-making machine before he's ever had a chance to do something with his life. Coco, your kids are still young and innocent, but you best believe when they reach that age, you'll be pulling your Afro puffs and worrying just like me."

"Okay, Sis. You're right. If my kids end up doing everything I've done, my ass is in trouuuuble."

They waited a couple more minutes. Then Alita banged her fist on the door. This time a different door flew open. Leonard stuck his neck out.

"What are you doing in my house?" he asked as he started to approach her.

"Babe, I told you that you had company," said Desiree, who followed behind him. "But I definitely didn't let them in. Obviously, they're used to just breaking in—"

"Excuse me?" Alita said.

"I meant to say they must've invited themselves in, because I definitely didn't. And I have a problem with that. No, mm mmm. You can't just be going where you weren't invited," Desiree said. "That won't work at all."

"Leonard, who the hell is she?" Alita asked.

"I told you that I'm Desiree," the woman answered as she stepped in front of Leonard. "I'm the lady of this house."

"Oh, really?" Alita said, annoyed. It made her feel slightly better. Maybe Leonard had moved in with the woman because he was struggling financially.

"We live together," she continued. "So his house is also mine. And I don't want just anybody making themselves at home without being told that it's okay."

"Uh oh, I didn't,—" Alita clumsily stumbled over

her words. She felt so embarrassed. And angry. Why hadn't Leonard simply let her know his current situation? Then she figured it out. Because of the ways she'd acted in the past when she found out about his little girlfriends, that was probably why he neglected to inform her. He knew she had a temper like a teapot sitting on a fire ready to boil over.

"How long have you two been together? When did this happen?" Alita demanded.

"Look, baby moms—"

"The name is Alita *Washington*."

"Oh, yeah?" Coco interrupted in a loud voice. "But I thought you said you were getting your name changed back to Reeves. What happened with that?"

"Coco, please be quiet." By then Alita was exasperated. It shocked her to realize that feelings of envy had been exposed. The woman standing in front of her appeared sophisticated, obviously attractive, and although it was hard to admit, the lady might even be a nice person once you got to know her. And when Alita thought about how her ex had moved on, although it shouldn't have hurt, she still felt pain. She remembered how much in love he'd been with her in the beginning of their relationship.

Alita watched how Leonard protectively placed his arm around Desiree's waist, and she thought of Shade and wished she could see him or hear his voice.

Suddenly, Leno walked out of his bedroom with Zaida. They were holding hands, smiling, and seemed to be taking their sweet time.

"Oh, God," Alita said. "Let's get the hell out of here. We'll wait for him outside."

She raced down the stairs with Coco ambling behind her as she struggled to hold onto Chance.

Alita could hear Desiree's voice. "Look, next time she is going to have to respect our house and not walk all around like we're the damned Museum of Natural Science. My shit is insured, but so what? We don't know what she may have stolen."

"Wow," Coco said with a laugh as she followed behind. She waited until they both got back in Alita's car. "Lita, your drama with Leonard is making Calhoun Humphries look like Jesus Christ."

"Don't even try it. I wasn't given a heads-up about this situation, as usual with Leonard. He enjoys springing shit on you and sitting back to see the reaction on your face. He is the devil, I swear to God."

"To you all men are the devil."

"If I can help it, my son won't grow up being one. Did you see how Leno and Rojo was staring into each other's eyes, Coco? I know lust when I see it. You think they fucking?"

Coco covered up Chance's little ears. "If they are, there is nothing you can do about it, Sis. And that's the cold, hard truth."

"Like hell there isn't," Alita said. "I see the way he looks at her. It's different than when he was hanging around the thotsicles at his school. He was being friendly with them. But Leno's really feeling this chick."

"And if he is, and you try to break them up, he may run away from home . . . never come back . . . hate you for the rest of his life. Young love ain't no joke." Coco set aside her usually wisecracking attitude. Her sister was in pain but she needed to hear the truth.

"I know about young love. People fall in love and break up with someone new all the time."

"But if Leno loves *her*, Alita, don't mess it up.

Them Latina chicks don't play at all when it comes to love."

"If Leno's got to be out here living his life, why can't he at least find someone that looks like him? I'm not against interracial dating, but—"

"Oh, really?" Coco said in doubt.

"Leno can see who he wants, but it hurts like hell that my son brought a little Mexican to his dad's house. He's never brought no Mexican girls to our place."

Coco was stunned. "You sound like a straight-up racist, Lita."

"Don't label me. It's okay for me to wonder why my son can't find a pretty melanin girl? Why can't he fall in love with someone like me?" Alita knew that the high school Leno attended included Blacks, Asians, Hispanics, a tiny percentage of whites. But when her son chose a non-black girl for his love interest, it dragged a sharp dagger across her heart.

"He needs to stick to his own kind, pick someone that looks like or reminds him of his mama." Alita's words sounded hollow, for even she understood that most people couldn't help who they fell in love with.

Coco broke the silence. "With the way you act all the time, for all you know, you could be pushing your son away from black women. And if that's what's happening, it's your own damned fault."

"Coco, please—"

"No, no, Lita. You need to listen to me for one time in your life." She paused. "We are supposed to confront someone, right?"

"No!"

"Yes, we are. Sister Day says—"

"Fuck Sister Day," Alita said.

"What? Are you serious?"

Before she knew it, Alita's cheeks were hot and moist. She blinked rapidly; allowing the tears to splatter across her cheeks. Surprised, she wiped her face with the back of her hand. The thought that her own son could reject her by picking a woman totally opposite from her wasn't anything she expected. Didn't he know she would die for him?

"I'm not in no mood for no Sister lecture. Sister Assignment. Sister Nothing."

"You are a hypocrite," Coco said. "I knew you only liked this assignment shit if it benefits you. Only *you* can tell people off. Only *you* can keep it real with the sisters. But when we try to do the same thing you do—"

"I told you I don't wanna hear this," Alita said. "I don't care what you say. Some things are bigger than these silly ass assignments that Burgundy gives to us. Hell, I could come up with some juicier shit than her."

"Well, go on ahead then, since you think you can outdo B."

"I just might."

"Even if you do, it still won't change *you*, Alita. You are still bitter, hateful, moody, mean—and racist."

"All that? Really?"

"Yes, really."

"If you think that way about me, then you—" Alita swallowed her words. It felt like she wanted to release more tears, but once every few days was more than enough for her. She grew sober. "You know what? My bad . . . I should have followed my first mind. Handled this by myself as usual. You just don't understand, Coco."

"But that's the thing. I *do* understand. You're pissed off, Sis, and you got a right to be. You think that

Leonard has ruined your life. But why keep bringing up the past? How is it helping? Let the past go. That's what I do. I learned to just let the damned past go."

For once, and it was rare that it happened, Alita was in agreement with Coco. Holding onto the memories of what hurt you meant you'd stay hurt. And that's something she did not wish to do.

"You're right," Alita humbly admitted. She wanted to push Leonard Washington and every other dreadful memory far from her mind.

It took forever before Leno finally emerged from the house, and she was so ready to go.

"The past is the past," Alita admitted to Coco. "I'm all about my future—starting right now."

Exactly one week later, Shade and Burgundy were holed up inside the church bookstore. It was approximately two thousand square feet and as professional looking as any other brick-and-mortar store.

Burgundy stood by the cash register.

"Let's see," she said to a customer standing at the counter. "You want to purchase two children's Bibles, four pair of earrings, these T. D. Jakes books, this beautiful tote bag, a Travis Greene CD, *and* a Kirk Franklin CD?"

The female customer smiled and nodded as Burgundy calculated the order.

"Thank you for your business. And because you bought so many items today, we'll throw in a free Mary Mary CD."

The woman frowned. "Mmm. Actually I can't stand Mary Mary. You got Tasha Cobbs's latest one?"

Burgundy laughed. "I'm sure we do. Shade, can you go find the Tasha CD and then get some shopping bags for me? They're in the drawer. Thanks."

"My pleasure," he said. He located the CD that the customer requested. Then he had to squeeze past Burgundy in order to reach the drawer. They were in a very small space, and he nearly brushed against her behind. Shade placed his hand gently on her back so he would not bump into her.

Burgundy waited until he had gotten the shopping bags, then she proceeded to swipe the woman's credit card in the machine.

Once the lady signed the slip and left, Burgundy and Shade were alone.

She stared into space looking at nothing. Finally she sighed.

"Is there something on your mind?" Shade asked.

"Oh, no. I'm fine," she chirped.

"Burgundy, it's me you're talking to. You look like you want to talk about something."

She shrugged. "It's nothing serious. I guess I am so busy today I completely forgot to plan our dinner. And after church lets out I'll have to race to the grocery store and buy food that's quick and easy. Maybe cook a pot of chili, corn bread, and add something else that doesn't take a lot of time."

"You are quite a woman," Shade replied.

"Why you say that?"

" 'Cause you're always thinking about your man."

Burgundy wanted to laugh out loud. Shade knew her well, but obviously he did not know everything about her. She was the type of person who shared only what she wanted people to know.

"I do all right, I guess."

"I'm sure your husband feels lucky to have you and likes everything you bring to the table."

"Ha, sometimes I may not have time to bring something to the table. Sometimes," she emphasized.

"You're allowed that. I mean, nobody is perfect," Shade said.

"Not even you, huh?" She laughed and joined him at the table; she grabbed a sheet of labels and started applying them to a stack of books.

"How are you and my sister coming along?" she asked.

"Great. We actually had a chance to hook up twice this past week," he said. "She convinced me to do something I hadn't done in a minute."

"What?" Burgundy asked. "Have sex?" She laughed out loud even as she wondered what would make her even say that.

"Hey, how'd you guess?" Shade laughed.

Burgundy stopped what she was doing. "Shade Wilkins. I know that you aren't trying to get busy with my sister in the bedroom. That's not you at all."

Shade sighed heavily. "Pass me that book, will you?"

She picked up the paperback sitting next to her and checked out the title. *Sex in the Sanctuary* by Lutishia Lovely. "Who ordered this for the bookstore?"

"I don't know. Maybe the former manager? The one that was here long before we came on board."

"I was about to say," Burgundy replied, "I think this is a somewhat progressive church, but I don't think they're that progressive to be selling books like this."

"Why wouldn't they, though?" Shade said. "Christians have sex."

"Shade—"

"Now come on, Burgundy. Don't tell me that you're a prude. You can't be. You have two daughters."

Burgundy found herself blushing.

Shade had a pleasant smile on his face, but he wasn't above taking her to task. "Let's talk about sex."

"Shade?"

"Burgundy Taylor, do you really believe that the members that attend Solomon's Temple aren't bumping and grinding and getting their freak on in between a little Bible study?"

"Well—"

"Well, nothing. I know for a fact that some of these women around here will have the King James Bible on their night stand, right underneath an erotica book by Zane."

"You know about Zane?"

"From the look on your face, you know about her too." He couldn't help but laugh.

"Okay, fine," she said stubbornly. "But how do you know for a fact about what these women keep on their nightstand? Is your knowledge of them limited to their nightstand? Do you know what's in their drawers too?" She stuttered. "I meant, the furniture, not the—"

"I know what you meant, Burgundy." He gave her a teasing grin. "And to answer your question, I know all about where women store things in their bedroom, their bathroom, and every other room in their house."

Suddenly Burgundy grew very interested in what Shade had to say. "I thought you were a strict believer that goes by the rules."

"Huh? What you talking about, woman? I read the Bible, but I am a man too. I think I'm a decent man. I'm not out here tearing up the streets and breaking women's hearts left and right. And don't forget I told you about the woman that still goes to this church. She and I were in a long-term monogamous relationship."

"Meaning you had sex with her?"

"Every chance I could get."

"Oh. All right. Hmm." Burgundy's cheeks flushed apple red. She knew her older sister loved to have sex. Maybe not as much as Coco, but Alita definitely had her horny moments, of that she was sure.

"Well, what can I say?" she finally allowed.

"Don't judge me, Burgundy. We're friends. We'll always be great friends."

"Right, I know that. I, um, I was just wondering how you and Alita are doing. For real."

"We're hitting it off well. I'm enjoying myself. Did I tell you that we went bowling? She twisted my arm and made me take her to Dave and Buster's. I grumbled about it at first, but I ended up having a good time. She whipped my behind good." He laughed, and his eyes twinkled at the same time.

"I'm happy you two are hitting it off, glad you had a nice date." She paused. "You plan on seeing each other again?"

"I'm sure we will. And I must thank you for introducing me to Ms. Washington."

"You are very welcome," Burgundy said. "It's about time my sister started enjoying life again. In fact, I may call her up and get her take on things."

"Oh, you don't have to do that."

Burgundy froze. "What do you mean?"

"I feel like some stuff she may tell you, other stuff she may not."

"And how would you know that, Shade?" She was feeling a little territorial and was actually seething on the inside, but she did not want Shade to notice.

"I know it because she and I had a discussion."

"About?" she asked.

"She was telling me some stuff that she recently went through with Leonard and his new lady Desiree, and her son Leno and his new girlfriend Zaida. Alita was livid. I could tell. I let her vent. But afterwards I told her that now that we are getting closer, and I know how much she likes to vent, she may not want to blurt out every single detail about us to any and everybody."

"You said that to Alita? How'd she take it?"

"After she very nicely chewed off my butt, she said she understood. And that she agreed with me."

"I don't believe it."

"Believe it," Shade told her. He picked up the Lutishia Lovely book and went to stack it face out on the top of the fiction shelf.

CHAPTER 11

The Sex He Expects

After putting Natalia and Sid to bed, Burgundy stared at six-year-old Natalia's sleeping face one last time and quietly shut her door. She paid the same honor to Sid, tucking her in securely under the comforter then leaving her alone.

Burgundy hesitated, then ran down the front spiral staircase and went to her master suite.

Nate was sitting on one side of the king-size bed. He wore a big bath towel around his waist. He removed it and dried his legs. Then he asked, "You wanna wipe off my back?"

"Sure," she said in a chirpy voice. She took the towel in her hands and used it to absorb shower water from both his broad shoulders and his glistening neck. He smelled fresh and good and she quietly inhaled his scent, but concentrated on her task.

Nate suddenly reached behind him and pulled his wife toward him. He forced her mouth closer to him.

Made her kiss his neck. She complied with his request for a few seconds; her lips peppered him with light smooches. Then she rose up.

He sat and watched her. "You about to shower too, Burg?"

"Um, no," she answered. "I'd rather relax with a bubble bath."

"No, that'll take too long. In fact, you can skip that shower."

He walked over to Burgundy, staring at her with a dreamy look in his eyes.

"Nate, please," she said. "I smell funky. I need to clean myself."

"I'll clean you up," he offered. "Let me go get a face cloth and some soap."

"That's not enough. I don't want you down there—"

"I love your natural scent."

Nasty sex disgusted Burgundy. She preferred to be as fresh as possible.

"It'll be okay," he insisted. "I just want to eat you for a few minutes, all right?"

She grimaced, wanted to tell him, "You disgust me," but she wasn't in the mood to argue. She let him go wet a cloth with hot water and liquid soap. He returned to her then asked Burgundy to take off her clothes. She took her time removing her blouse, slacks, bra, and panties. Soon she was completely naked and shivering from a cold blast of air conditioning that suddenly filled the room.

Nate stood before his wife. He adored her body and had a good time observing her round tits, nipples, curvy hips, smooth thighs, athletic arms, and long legs. At thirty-two, she looked five years younger. She still made him yearn for her body. He knelt in front of Burgundy, placed his lips against her belly and kissed it.

"I love your stomach," he told her.

"Thanks."

He laughed, sounding almost giddy that he was able to be intimate with Burgundy. He then reached behind her and grabbed her ass with his strong hands. He caressed her butt cheeks, which were soft as a baby's bottom and had very little cellulite.

"Mmm," he moaned. "It's been so long. You know that, don't you."

She nodded. Boy, did she know.

As a woman, she learned a long time ago that females had something that heterosexual men wanted, and it wasn't peach cobbler. It was *coochie*. Men go crazy over it. They get demanding about it. Beg for it. Wear deodorant and shower and dress their best to try and get it. They'll lie to get it, cheat to get it, pay cash to get it, act nice to get it. They'll risk their health, their life, and maybe even their wife for it. They'll *wait* for it, and *wait* for it, talk about it, and get sentimental about it. Men can grow an erection just from dreaming about it. And if they feel that *your* coochie is *their* coochie, they might even kill another man for it.

With his eyes shut tight, Nate began to moan and purr. She knew exactly what that meant. His hands explored her like she was a rare treasure. Fingers rubbed her bottom over and over, caressing it; then his cold fingers were inserted between her butt cheeks. He wiggled his hand.

"How does that feel? That feel good?"

It felt awful, but she said nothing.

Nate could be freaky if she let him. He got settled

behind her, exploring every crevice. The tongue that was just on her lips was now in her behind. Licking, slurping, moaning and getting his kicks. She felt self-conscious but thought, *This is what he likes,* so she let him continue. He thoroughly enjoyed himself for a while as she let him poke around till he was satisfied. Then he got up and made her go lie on their bed. She climbed on the mattress and settled on her side so that her back was facing him. Burgundy's entire body stiffened the second he placed his hand on her hip. It was one thing for Nate to pat her ass, another thing for him to take things a few steps further. Her bones felt brittle as she held her breath and tensed up even more. But he never noticed her reaction. Completely lost in his erotic joy, Nate made a long trail of kisses: from her neck, to her nipples, to her kneecaps, to her ankles. She turned over on her back this time and let him do his thing.

Nate moved himself closer to her. He positioned his torso so that it was aligned near her mouth. His penis dangled in front of her. But then it was in Burgundy's face, close enough for her to smell it. Penis always smelled peculiar to Burgundy, like a rubbery scent, but she got used to it. He grabbed himself then rubbed the tip for a few seconds.

"Here," he offered. "Give me a hand job."

She wanted to argue, tell him no. But what good would it do.

Burgundy looped her fingers around his penis. Even though he had just rubbed himself, his male organ drooped and wilted, reminding her of a banana that was no longer ripe. And she hated it.

She withheld a sigh and dutifully began to stroke it with one hand. Up. Down. Up. Down.

Down. Down. Up. Up.

The task felt monotonous. Nate had about five inches, and he was pleased when it could expand to eight.

"Nate, babe," she gently said as she caressed him and he still didn't get hard. "You took your meds?"

She was referring to the tiny orange pill that his doctor prescribed, which was supposed to control high blood pressure.

"Mmm hmm," Nate answered as he moaned and shuddered.

She rolled her eyes. After five minutes of stroking him until her hands felt raw, his dick still felt squishy, like a banana gone bad that needed to be flung into a trash can.

Nate pushed his wife's head toward his banana; her mouth bumped against it. Its softness repelled her. She jerked back.

"Nate," she complained. "Sorry! But I-I've had a very long day. I'm so wiped out. I really don't want to—"

"There are a lot of things I don't want to do either, but I still do them." He reluctantly released his fingers from around her head. Nate went and reclined against several pillows that were stacked against the head-board. He stiffly folded his arms across his chest. He thought a few seconds. Then he picked up the remote and punched buttons that switched the channel to ESPN. He pumped up the volume and took an immediate interest in a sporting broadcast; he acted like his wife didn't just crawl next to him.

"Maybe tomorrow," Burgundy said lamely. She was close enough to him that their thighs touched.

Nate failed to answer. Usually he enjoyed placing an arm around her when she was in bed. They would snuggle together and he would hold her tight. But he did nothing.

It was like Burgundy was invisible. And right then she really didn't care.

How can I tell him that his penis doesn't do it for me anymore? I love everything else about our marriage, we get along great, we work well as far as our business ventures, but sex with him is like trying to make love to a two-year-old boy. I don't want a little boy.

Nate became consumed with the analysis of some recent NBA games. Feeling guilty, Burgundy got out of bed. She snuck away to take a quick shower. She cleaned herself well and pondered her dilemma.

It had been a long time for Nate, but it had been quite a while for her too.

As a woman she was no different than him. She also had needs. But what could Burgundy do if she wasn't being fulfilled? Masturbation was an option, but it didn't replace the feeling of a stiff, hot penis that fit snugly inside of her. She couldn't remember the last time she had enjoyed that type of sexual pleasure.

Burgundy quietly dried herself off with a towel, applied deodorant and lotion, and put several plastic rollers in her hair, then secured her curls with a silk bonnet. She flicked off the bathroom light and climbed back in bed beside her husband. She hesitated but then decided to cuddle up to him even though his eyes were still fixed on the television. She grabbed his hand and moved it toward her vagina. She was hairless down there, and she knew that he liked the feel of that. Hairless vaginas were his thing. He also loved her breasts. Everything about her seemed to turn him on, and she actually was glad about that.

Burgundy patted his hand.

"Go on," she whispered. "Finger me."

He turned around and looked at Burgundy like she had a lot of damn nerve.

"Oh, I can't get mine, but you still expect yours? You still want to come even though I didn't? Typical selfish woman."

"Nate, that's not fair." She snatched the remote from him and turned off the power, then tossed the controller away. It banged against the wall and rested on the hardwood floor.

"This is as much as your fault as it is mine," Burgundy continued in a controlled voice. "I told you to get some help. Just try the Viagra—"

"No!"

"Why not?"

"I don't need that. My dick gets hard . . . once you do what you're supposed to do."

"But, Nate . . . it takes so long for you to get aroused that my mouth gets tired. I've told you that a hundred times. I'm so exhausted from sucking you that I'm almost asleep by the time you're ready to penetrate me. And me being asleep while you're getting your kicks feels too much like rape."

"What?"

"All I'm trying to say is that . . . getting you ready just takes too long. And even then when the dick does get hard, it won't stay hard. Then we're forced to begin the cycle all over again."

"Don't you like pleasing me, Burg?"

Frustrated, she folded her arms across her chest. "I like a hard dick. A soft one doesn't do it for me. I-I can't pretend anymore."

He gasped, then glared at her.

Burgundy wondered if she'd been too blunt, if her honesty had severely wounded his pride. When she thought about their recent Sister Day assignment, it encouraged them to confront someone in a nice way. Well, she'd tried that method with Nate on several occasions. She had gone in easily by first making lighthearted jokes. And when he failed to laugh, she offered to help finance a pack of ten Sildenafil pills, which cost sixty-two bucks apiece. They'd have to fork over a total of six hundred twenty dollars just to get the dick to work.

He had complained for that amount of money he could buy an evening with ten whores.

She had laughed hysterically but wondered if he was serious. Was he *that* cheap, because they definitely had the money to buy those pills? Or did her husband have a different reason for not wanting to take medicine for erectile dysfunction?

It was true that when some men reached a certain age, they had trouble maintaining an erection, especially if they took medicine for hypertension. Supposedly there were plans for a generic medication for sildenafil citrate, one that would be decidedly less costly. Plus it treated high blood pressure. Double bonus. But who had time to wait on it to hit the market? Could her marriage afford to wait on a cheaper sex pill, or would something else have to happen first to get things going in their ice-cold bedroom? Burgundy hated knowing that Nate was impotent. She tried hard not to negatively judge him, but their issue was starting to take a toll on her, especially since she was hitting her sexual prime.

"Babe," she struggled to tell him, "I love you with everything I have—"

"I certainly wouldn't know it."

"Stop playing. You know I do."

"Then why won't you help me? I don't ask for much, do I?"

It was true. Nathaniel Taylor was like her Superman, one of the few men who were excellent at multitasking. He worked like crazy and was good at what he did in managing both the brunch restaurant and their barbershop. He also helped with the kids, took good care of their home, fixed many broken appliances, and he went to church semiregularly. He did more than the average guy out there. Burgundy knew she was fortunate, a woman who had a lot to be thankful for. Nevertheless, a hot dick was what she craved.

But she did have her marriage, and that's what she wanted more than anything, even if she did not have everything that she wanted.

"I think you should see a urologist," she suggested.

"I don't need to do that. I don't have time anyway."

"Nate, that's a lie. You're the master of your own schedule. Make time. Prioritize."

He quickly grew quiet on her. The silence felt painful. A closed mouth scared her, for she did not know what he was thinking. She couldn't begin to guess what her husband was feeling.

He finally replied. "Forget it. It's not that important."

"Really?"

"Yeah."

"Okay, now you're really lying."

"Are you accusing me of being a liar just because I said forget it? Burg, do you know what my schedule has been like lately?" he asked. "Even you are aware that ever since we have test marketed some new dishes, I've been very busy trying to keep all that under control. Trying to finalize those buttermilk wheat waffles and the fried chicken donuts. And the barbershop had an attempted break-in the other week—"

"It did?" she asked.

"Burgundy, I told you about that and how I had to replace a door. Weren't you listening?"

At that announcement, her face looked crestfallen. If it was true that his schedule was busy, then this was proof that his wife's was even more hectic because she could not recall the conversation about a break-in. Suddenly Burgundy's guilt multiplied. If he controlled his schedule, then she could control hers too.

"Babe, let's put this horrible incident behind us."

"It *was* horrible," he said, sounding like an inconsolable child.

"We can try again later this week, all right?" she asked in her sweetest voice.

But his dirty look shocked her.

"Nate, please don't be mad. It's not my fault, not yours, no one's."

"Didn't you just tell me I'm to blame, what, not even a few minutes ago?"

"No. Well, yes. It's your fault in that you refuse to buy those pills."

"They cost too damned much," he complained.

"Then it would be fair to say that your frugal ways are what's causing us to go through this sexual frustration."

"Burg, it's cheaper for you to suck my dick than it would be for me to take those damned pills. In my world that's not being cheap, it's called using common sense."

But Burgundy didn't want to suck dick. She never felt pleasure in giving him blowjobs. She considered the task exhausting. Besides, why should she have to work so hard to make his penis function anyway? A soft dick that had to get licked in order to grow as hard as a brick simply wasn't worth it to Burgundy.

But what could a woman do if she still enjoyed sex? She had gotten used to not doing it with Nate, and sometimes she convinced herself that she didn't miss it.

Other times, however, Burgundy found herself wishing that she could get away with stepping out on him. Nate was so trusting of her, he'd never even know. She sometimes wondered how it would be to enjoy one lovely evening in the sack with a man virile enough to keep her satisfied. She shut her eyes and imagined how wonderful it would be to have her fantasies come true.

Nate got up, retrieved the remote, turned on the TV, and resumed looking at ESPN. Burgundy gladly let him. She turned over in bed, pulled the covers over her head, and continued fantasizing. She knew the truth, but it would be a cold day in hell before she had the guts to admit her desires to her husband. And that's how it would have to be.

When a woman hasn't had any loving in months or years, sometimes she can go stark-raving mad.

Alita couldn't believe it. She was at Shade's house, lying right next to him, on top of his bed. Both of his lamps were on. The room was well lit.

Alita was fully dressed, but she still felt butt-ass naked. She was telling him, "Do I have a right to be in my feelings?"

"I'm not sure if you have a right, but you feel what you feel. You were married to the guy for what, over a decade?"

"Something like that."

"And how long did it take to fall out of love with him?" Shade sat perfectly still as he spoke with Alita.

He loved how the light shone brightly on her face, the way the ends of her hair were curled and touched the back of her neck.

"Oh, do you really wanna hear that story?" Before he could answer, she slid the sandals off her feet, kicked them off hard till they clunked on his ceramic floor. She took one look at Shade, then spread on out her stomach. Her dress pulled up a couple of inches exposing her legs, the backs of which had several dimples.

"I dunno, Shade. To be honest, I wasn't counting time. I was busy hurting."

He laughed and enjoyed the view from where he was sitting.

"Let me let you in on something. From what I've been told, if a couple has been together ten years and they eventually end the relationship, they've been breaking up for five years."

"Huh?"

He laughed again. He loved that way about her, an honest and unpretentious way that allowed her to not put on airs or to pretend she knew exactly what he was talking about all the time.

"Speak plain English," she said. "You know I only got to the twelfth grade."

"What I am asking you is if it took you years to get over Leonard? Are you over him? Do you have any love in your heart for him?"

"Ha! You don't even need to ask me that."

"Don't I?"

"What?"

"I've met a lot of women, all kinds of women, and one thing I've learned is that they may seem like they're all the same, but they're not. And, even if this one reminds me of that one," Shade explained, "I'm better off asking a woman very specific questions if I want to know the answers."

"That makes a lot of damn sense," Alita admitted. "And I feel like I can't stand the sight of my ex-husband a lot of times. The love I used to have for him died out probably two years after we broke up. I had to get my head straight, or at least try to, before I could even think about going out with a new guy. Not that they didn't constantly hit on my ass left and right."

"I don't blame them." He looked at her. "Hey, is it okay if I rub your feet? I've been told I have a great way of rubbing feet."

She smiled at him and shrugged. "Why the hell not? I could use a good rubdown."

At first she was going to simply lie there and let him lift up her feet. But she decided to be naughtily sexy. Alita unzipped the zipper and removed her jeans. She was now wearing just a size XL T-shirt. It made it look as if she was wearing shorty pajamas. She turned over on her stomach. That meant that Shade had an excellent view of the backs of her legs, which were gorgeous and alluring.

He wasted no time sliding one hand up and down her smooth leg. Her skin was soft like putty. His fingers sizzled against her skin. She tingled and felt goose bumps. Alita waited for Shade to lift her foot and rub lotion on it or whatever he liked to use.

But soon her feet felt wet. And then her toes were being hungrily pulled into his warm mouth. He sucked and nibbled. She fought to hold back a loud scream. Shade sucked her toes so well she didn't know what hit her. Him simultaneously sucking her toes and rubbing the back of her thighs felt like seduction overload.

Alita moaned over and over.

And when Shade asked her if it was okay if he removed her top, she nodded quickly.

"Do your thang, baby," she told him.

It had been so long. So very long since she'd better treated with such tenderness and care by a man. She was more than ready. She wanted to weep when she found herself completely naked in his bed. The breeze from the whirling ceiling fan made her feel chilly. But her loins began to pulsate with heat as she waited for Shade Wilkins to make love to her like she'd never been made love to before. He put his head between her legs. His long tongue found her clit. It was moist and ready for him. He licked and sucked on her slowly and gently. Over and over. She shuddered with each lick. Braced herself to feel what she hadn't felt in a long time.

"How's that?"

"Ohhhh," was the only response she could give to him. As he continued sucking on her, Alita got weaker and weaker. She gripped his head with both her hands, squeezing him so mightily she wondered if she hurt him. Alita's eyes rolled to the back of her head. When she came, she let go of his head and beat the mattress with both of her hands. Slapping it repeatedly, shaking, trembling, moaning, and wishing for that grand old feeling to last forever.

It took a few minutes of huffing and puffing for her to reluctantly admit that her orgasm had run its course. And after it was done, she gladly returned the favor. She took him in her mouth and gave him the best head he ever had. He smelled fresh and clean, and his penis was in good working order. Stiff and rigid, just the way Alita liked it. They fell into each other's arms pleasuring each other for the next hour. It felt so good not to

have to worry about exes and legal issues, family problems, and being broke.

After it was over, Alita couldn't believe what had
happened . . . that Cupid took his arrow and sneaked
upon her in the sneaky way that he did. And she knew
by the way she was blushing that she'd developed feelings for a man who seemed to care about her the way
that she cared about him.

"Thank you for that," she told him. "I needed that."

"We both did."

"Mmm, that's good to know," she told him, realizing it meant that his love was reserved for her and her
alone. And the fact that Shade was a generous lover
made Alita's heart feel emotions she had thought long
dead.

"Why did you do that to me? Huh? Can you tell me
why you did it, please, sir?"

"Do what?"

"That!" she said. "All that stuff that you did."

"What'd I do?"

"That toe-licking thing. Oh, my God."

He laughed.

"You made me feel happiness," Alita continued. "Made
me feel something besides disgust and anger and ugli-
ness. You even make me think different than I've thought.
So why did you do all that?"

She sounded so very serious that Shade was momentarily confused. Alita seemed almost bipolar with
how her feelings jumped from one end of the spectrum
to another.

"Look, I was just being myself, Alita. I-I'm sorry."

"Don't apologize. Are you crazy?"

"Me, crazy?" Shade laughed. "If I'm still with you,
after what you've shown me, then maybe I am."

Then he kissed Alita. She adored his kiss. It was sincere, meaningful, and it lingered. They continued exploring each other's mouths, and she let him suck her tongue for as long as he wanted. When she came up for air, she gasped then said, "I like that. Kiss me again." And he did, this time with even more fervency. She lay there wanting that very experience to repeat itself.

She sighed and held his hand.

"What you thinking about?" he asked.

"I hate when a man asks me what I'm thinking. Why you want to know? What can I tell you that I haven't already told your ass?"

He shrugged. "Yep, you're crazy."

"Shade, I have enjoyed myself so much, but you know how my mind gets to going here and there."

"So I've noticed."

"And like that singer Bobby Womack once said, 'Everybody wants love but everybody is afraid of love.'"

"Are you in love? Is that what you're saying but haven't yet told me, Alita?"

"I ain't saying shit."

"You know what? By the look on your face you really don't have to say anything." And he kissed her again.

Alita kept most of what she wanted to say on the inside. Good love felt good. And she liked the connection.

Unable to get her to open up any further, Shade excused himself to go use the restroom.

While she lay there and waited, one part of her wanted to get completely relaxed. But another tiny part of her wondered if she should search for her bra and panties and begin getting dressed. Go find her purse and car keys and be prepared to say goodbye so she wouldn't wear out her welcome. That's how this thing normally worked.

Before she knew it, Alita stood up; she was operating on female autopilot, trying to find her panties.

"Um, Alita?" Shade said after he returned from the bathroom.

Afraid, Alita was tempted to cover her ears in anticipation.

But Shade said nothing. He crawled into bed, then patted the empty side right next to him. She beamed again, then crawled into his arms and rested her head on his broad shoulder.

"Wow! Fucking church men!" she said with a loud laugh.

He cracked up too. Then he told her, "Ahh, don't even try it. Don't put labels on me. I'm a man."

"That you are."

"And you're a woman. A very desirable woman. Sexy. Interesting. Real. Hey, I couldn't help myself, Alita. And even if I wanted to help myself, it would have been hard."

"It was hard, baby, it was nice and hard. And you know how to work that thang too."

He laughed again. And Alita wanted to relax. Hearing his casualness made her want to let go of any anxiety. But when would an ax fall and chop off her head? Carve away the present happiness from inside her heart?

There were no guarantees about what would happen after a moment of pleasure, but Alita definitely wanted it again. She already believed that Shade Wilkins wanted the same.

CHAPTER 12

He Maketh Me to Lie Down

The Lord's Day started out looking the same way it always did. The sun shone as bright as ever with the promise of a glorious day.

Burgundy was in her gourmet kitchen stating directives to her daughters.

"Sid! Natalia! Put away your cereal dishes. Rinse them out good and make sure all of the Fruity Pebbles go down into the garbage disposal. Don't just leave any of 'em in the sink. And set the bowls in the dishwasher for now. Then go brush your teeth. And floss, rather you may try to floss, Nat. Count to sixty and then you're done."

"We already brushed, Mommy," Natalia complained.

"That was before breakfast. Brush them again. I don't want your breath to smell like sour milk. Do as I say then go wait for me in the corridor. We're running late and I hope there's no traffic on Forty-five."

"Yes, ma'am." Her daughters scurried off like obedient children. The kids bounded up the back staircase while Burgundy dashed off to her own bedroom.

As soon as she entered, she glanced at her bed. A large lump covered by a thick black-and-white comforter took over one side. Burgundy heard Nate snoring. She felt bad about needing to interrupt his sleep. But she put one knee on their bed and told him, "Nate, sweetie. I'm about to head out. I'm supposed to teach a class this morning, and I-I want my journal. I wrote notes in it. Have you seen it? The cloth journal?"

He moaned. She saw him shift underneath the cover. The clock was ticking.

"Wow, some people are so lucky," she said teasingly. "They get to sleep in on a Sunday."

"I'll see you at the usual time," he mumbled. "I don't know where your journal is."

"Shoot! All right." Burgundy opened a drawer and rummaged through a pile of wallets, Day Timers, stylus pens, and cell phone chargers. She found what she was looking for and grabbed it.

"Found it. Thank God. I'm going to have to really step on it. See you later? Maybe we'll meet up for brunch today? I'll text you."

Burgundy closed the door behind her and collected the rest of her things. Then she rounded up the girls; they were all loaded into the SUV and were soon headed for the eight o'clock service.

"Oh, shoot," she muttered to Natalia once she drove a mile away. "Mommy's getting old. I forgot to ask Elyse if she wanted to ride with us. I hope Nate remembers to bring her."

Burgundy kept driving. She forgot about how she had rejected Nate's sexual advances the night before. She concentrated on the biblical class she was about to teach. Topic? "Three Ways to Manage Stress."

Burgundy headed for the church and imagined herself teaching a room of one hundred people. She smiled to herself and promptly dismissed Elyse from her mind.

Unbeknownst to her, the youngest Reeves girl was tucked away in her bedroom, which was located down the hall from her nieces' room. It was the room closest to the back stairwell.

Elyse had suffered a difficult night, tossing and turning in bed, and she'd fallen asleep at two in the morning. Now, hours later, her brain still felt fuzzy, her body exhausted.

A large black Bible rested on top of her head. It was opened to the twenty-third psalm. Its soft onionskin pages touched her face . . . from the top of her forehead to the bottom of her chin. Her Bible was exactly where she'd carefully placed it the night before when she had said a prayer and then tried to go to sleep. The book was so big and heavy she could barely breathe underneath it.

Right then she took a deep breath, hoping to fall back asleep. But she heard a sharp knock on her door. She pulled the blanket over her head and waited.

Even though she'd locked the door, in seconds it was opened and then closed. Elyse clammed up. She took in tiny, sharp breaths. Her heart pounded so wildly she just knew he could hear her. She thought hard about what to do, how to escape.

The floor squeaked as light footsteps approached her bed. Then it grew eerily silent.

"She's gone," he whispered. "She's not here any-more." The fact that he whispered when he knew his wife wasn't in the house always made her tremble un-controllably.

"Get up."

Elyse dreaded the domineering sound of Nate's voice.

"Come on. I want to see you. Stop hiding from me."

He tried to sound welcoming, but Elyse crouched further in the bed. All she could hear was that creepy way he sounded whenever he talked to her. He stepped closer to the bed and shook her leg. She smelled the sweaty aroma of his body, felt his presence, and quiv-ered.

"Hurry up. I gotta get ready to go."

She knew he meant he had to go to church. She couldn't fathom how a man like Nate could attend church.

Nate reached out and felt underneath the cover till his hand touched the top of her head.

The Bible was pulled off her face; she heard it drop to the floor. He removed the blanket and looked at Elyse.

"What were you doing with that?" he asked.

Elyse wore an oversize baseball hat with her hair stuffed inside of it. Nate pulled the cap off and tossed it on the floor. "I hate when you wear that. Get up."

"Sick," she whispered.

"You're not sick." He continued to smile down at her with his painted-on grin.

He reached over and touched her hand. Nate's hand felt wet and slimy with moisture. He tugged at her tiny fingers and pulled on them until he got her to stand up. She whimpered as he led her from the bed to the large walk-in closet. Even though it was oversize, it still felt tiny. She hated feeling closed in like that.

He pointed to the carpeted floor.

"Lie down."

She shook her head.

"It won't take long," he told her. When she failed to respond, Nate grabbed Elyse by the shoulders and gently forced her to the floor.

He licked his lips and started removing his favorite flannel sleep pants. He wore no underwear. He reached in between the opening of his pajamas, gripped his penis and started stroking it.

Elyse started shaking and whimpering.

"Why you gotta act all scared?"

She knew he didn't expect her to answer. She sat cross-legged in the closet, trying to be as still as possible so Nate could remove all of her layered clothing. His entire presence blocked the door of the closet. He was tall and thick. She was petite and weighed less than 110 pounds. She knew there was no way she could get up and run past his body, run out of the bedroom, and escape down the stairs.

Elyse was wearing a long-sleeved flannel top that buttoned at the neck. Nate's hands were sweating as he unbuttoned it and removed her top. She wore another shirt, and he promptly took that one off too. He made her lie on her back so he could pull down her pants. Then he tugged at her cotton underwear.

"You could comb your hair sometimes and wear some makeup. What? You got something against looking pretty?"

Elyse didn't understand. Why would she want to look pretty for him? She didn't reply. She felt rigid and hideous under the glare of his glassy eyes.

The tips of her fingers felt like icicles; so did her feet.
She closed her eyes tight.
She recited scripture in her mind:

> *The Lord is my shepherd*
> *I shall not want*
> *He maketh me to lie down*
> *He maketh me to lie down*

Hot tears poured from her eyes. She waited.

Nate forced her to lie on her back. She froze up the second she felt his grubby hand advance up her thigh.

"Stop acting like a little girl. You're grown," he whispered. "Nice and grown."

She whimpered. He ignored her and moved his hand from her thigh to her inner thigh. From her inner thigh to her vagina.

His fingers felt cold as ice and hard as nails. He fumbled around, pinching her vagina lips together, then stuck his middle finger inside of her. She wished her legs were a large pair of scissors. She imagined herself closing her legs tighter together, slamming them shut and slicing off her brother-in-law's hands. In her head, she could hear Nate screaming from the pain. But the screaming noise frightened her. She eliminated her dark thoughts. She lay there allowing her mind to go blank.

"I got to have it," Nate told her. "Do you know how your sister treats me? Yeah, you know. You pretend like you don't know what's going on, like you can't see how she is sometimes. Stingy. And she calls me stingy. I give her everything. Everything a woman could want. What does she give me? She acts like she loves me, but sometimes I don't know."

Nate's hot breath brushed across Elyse's cheeks. He had wedged his penis in her by then, and his mouth was close to her ears, speaking to her as if she gave a damn about anything he had to say.

"She might hate me," he went on to say. "And I know she hates you. That's why if you tried and tell her any of your business, anything about what's happening in your life, she won't care. She got too much going on to care about anything except the stuff already on her plate. Our house could be engulfed in flames. She wouldn't notice."

Elyse's legs felt stiff as two poles. She grunted and bit the inside of her cheeks. Soon she tasted salt, the evidence that she bit herself way too hard this time.

She wanted to swallow but abhorred the taste of blood.

Nate pumped inside of Elyse's tiny, fragile, skinny, broken body.

How can he do this to me?

Why is he doing this?

She shifted when his body almost crushed her ribs. It was so hard to breathe. But maybe that was the point. Maybe he could smother her to death. She shut her eyes even tighter. Prepared herself to die.

But she didn't die. She just kept getting punished. The harder Nate thrust inside of her, punching against her sore vagina like he was outraged, the more she could see Burgundy's face.

What if sister catches us? Would he stop? Would she finally help? Would her closed eyes stay closed? Nate let out a loud moan that sounded like a scared animal.

Is he stupid? My sister might come back any minute. Is he crazy?

Nate yelled louder. The sounds he made caused her to start coughing uncontrollably. She could feel the tingly sensation of her legs falling asleep. She jerked around a bit, hoping he'd get the hint.

This hurts. Please stop. Leave me the hell alone.

Nate breathed in and out, like he was out of breath. His penis had been soft, then grew harder for a few minutes. Now it lay limp again. But Nate kept pumping into her, wasting his time and energy.

Elyse grinded her teeth together and tried not to feel anything.

"My, my, my," he said in a satisfied voice. "You feel so good, baby girl. I love this. I love this so much. I need this."

He looked at her face, saw her cheeks covered with tears.

"You must like this too, huh? I knew you'd like the way I make love to you. We need each other, baby girl. All we got is each other."

Elyse felt bile rise up in her throat. She wished she could let it out. Spit it out all over him. But she swallowed her hurt till it plunged back down her throat.

She waited and let Nate do what he did every Lord's Day. She thought about a Sister Day assignment. About telling the truth.

Sister needs to know truth. But she can't. She'd hate me. She'd blame me. I know she would. She'd make me leave. Then where would I go?

Truth hurt.

Truth ugly.

Truth caused pain.

Elyse wondered if she could do her Sister Day assignment for the first time ever and confront someone.

She wondered if doing so would change her life, or if this devastating secret would be hers until the day she died.

CHAPTER 13

Sudden Intervention

On that same Sunday, but late in the afternoon, Shade and Alita decided to meet up at Morning Glory. The restaurant served a jazz brunch every fourth Sunday. Shade picked up Alita from her apartment. She looked ravishing and felt relaxed. Her eyes sparkled with happiness. She seemed like a brand-new woman.

When they arrived, the first thing Alita did was look for Burgundy's car. She didn't see it.

Good, she thought, and they made their way inside. Shade and Alita found a nice booth and they sat next to each other on the same row. They stared at the menu and then at each other.

Their elbows touched. Alita sighed and said, "I don't know why the hell we looking at the menu. It's the same old stuff. You know what I like, Shade. Order for me."

"I'll do that, sweetie."

Alita spotted Burgundy first.

"Oh, hell, I knew it was a bad idea to come here," Alita said in a panic. "Why'd you want to come here?"

"I come here for the food, not for Burgundy."

"That's fine, but shit, my sister is the last person I want to see right now. And she's so busy sometimes she don't even make it in to this joint. Especially on a Sunday. But of course, today she's gotta be all up in the Morning Glory. I swear I do not have the luck of the damned Irish."

Shade chuckled as he watched her. "You're so cute when you're trying to be mad. Relax!"

"You relax."

"Oh, trust me. I am *very* relaxed."

"Oh, really? Wonder why?" Alita let off a big grin, and they both chuckled and touched hands briefly. Feeling his skin felt good to Alita. She wanted to hold onto him longer.

But she froze up again and let him go.

"She's so damned nosy," she ranted. "Just like a Reeves sister. Always gotta be up in somebody's business."

"You sound insane," Shade told her.

"She makes me act crazy."

Alita realized she was talking so loudly, Burgundy might recognize her voice. She tried to duck in her seat and shield her face behind the large menu. But soon Burgundy was standing by their booth.

"I don't believe this," she said with a shocked look on her face. "No wonder you had to leave the bookstore early today," she told Shade. "You had more important things to do," she said, then rolled her eyes at Alita.

"Hey, Sis," Alita finally said.

Burgundy stood there, noticing how her sister and

Shade were looking as cozy as an old married couple. Their elbows touched. Burgundy wanted to look under the table to see if their knees were touching too. She peered closely at Alita's hand. No engagement ring. Then she saw Shade grab Alita's right hand and hold it close inside of his big hand.

"Well, it seems like you two are truly hitting it off," she said in a chirpy voice.

"She's amazing," he said.

Alita wanted to chop him in the ribs but decided not to make a scene. "He's cool. He's my buddy."

Shade said, "I'm more than that, don't you think?"

"I don't know what to think," Burgundy murmured.

"I wasn't talking to you," he said to her. "I was talking to your sister. I said I think I'm much more than your buddy, Alita."

"Yeah, okay, all right. You're more than just my buddy. You've scored some major points lately. Damn. I can't believe this shit. Not again."

Burgundy got weak in the knees. She wanted to pass out. She knew the look of lovers when she saw it.

Those two have done the do. I know they have. I can't believe it. What a bunch of sluts!

Unable to think of anything more to say, she abruptly left them alone and returned to the business office.

Alita finally spoke. "She knows, Shade."

He shrugged. "She'd have found out eventually."

"I know, but still. I'm a hypocrite. I like to tell her stuff, but at the same time I don't want her to know everything. She'll try to run my life. Give me advice I didn't ask for." Alita laughed. "In some ways she is like me, but not in everything."

"Be you. Do you. I like you." He kissed the tip of

her nose. His words sounded so corny, but hearing them felt so good. Alita loved being with Shade, but it also scared her. When would the rug be pulled from underneath her? She wasn't ready to free-fall just yet.

"Anyway," she said, trying to act nonchalant, "you order for me. I'll be right back. I need to go check on Burgundy. She looked like she was about to have a damned heart attack. I swear that girl had 'hater' written all on her forehead."

He laughed. "See you in a bit."

Alita excused herself. She went through the double doors that led to the kitchen. That was where she bumped into Elyse. The girl looked as sick as a dog, like she was about to pass out any minute.

"You look like shit. What are you doing here? On a Sunday too? Where are Natalia and Sid?"

"Office."

"Oh, okay. How you doing, Elyse?"

Elyse's eyes flashed with anger. She sighed and shrugged. She was struggling to wash some dirty dishes. Beads of sweat scattered across her forehead.

"You don't look good at all. It's too damned hot in this kitchen. I'ma have to get on Nate about how hot he keeps it—" Before she could get the words out of her mouth, Elyse's mouth widened. She lurched forward. She tried to reach the sink, but she spewed a mouthful of vomit that spilled on the floor. She kept retching over and over again.

"This child is sick. Someone go find my sister."

After a while they were able to bring Elyse into the business office.

"What's wrong with Elyse?" Alita asked Burgundy. "I don't like her working here. This is not a good atmosphere for her. She probably is so stressed from

being around all these people that it makes her nervous. She needs to go see a doctor, because it looks
like she's losing weight, and she ain't that big in the
first damned place."

"I know. You're right. But I haven't had time to
take Elyse to the doctor."

"That's a damned shame," Alita said. "Hell, I have
a day off coming up this week. I will take her. Give me
the info. Doctor name, number, address. I'll make the
appointment."

"You're a lifesaver."

Alita unfolded her fist. "Give me some cash, though,
for the co-pay. Better add in some gas money while
you're at it. And toll road fees."

Burgundy sighed aloud but went into her purse and
fished out for Alita all the cash that she could find. "Let
me know what the doctor says."

"I will. You know I'll do that."

A couple of days later, Alita sat in the tiny examina-
tion room. Elyse was perched on the examining table.
The doctor stood before her.

"Hey there, Elyse."

Her thin shoulders jerked in shaky motion, trembling like she was cold.

Once the doctor finished up Elyse's exam, she left
the room for blood and urine tests. The doctor sat in his
chair. He typed in data in a tablet that he was holding
and quickly reviewed the young lady's medical records.

"Alita, I'm hoping you know the answer to this, and
it's fine if you don't. But . . . does Elyse grind her teeth
at night?" he asked.

"Huh? Hell if I know. Why do you ask?"

"I examined everything. I noticed that her top and bottom teeth are not aligned properly. I'm guessing she's been grinding her teeth. Have her gums been sore, or is there some other kind of pain that she's having in her mouth?"

"Sorry, doc. I dunno."

"It may be something she is subconsciously doing while she's asleep."

"Very possible. I can find out."

"Please do. She needs to go see a dentist right away. I know it may not sound very critical, but teeth grinding can lead to other serious problems, like muscular pain, headaches, cracked and broken teeth."

Alita gasped. "All that? Are you serious?"

Elyse returned to the room and sat on a chair next to Alita. After waiting a few seconds, she quietly got up and sat on Alita's lap. She buried her face against Alita's chest.

Momentarily stunned, Alita said to the doctor, "Um, I-I had no idea this was going on with Elyse's teeth. And it sounds real, real bad."

"I don't want to frighten you," the doctor said. "But please get some x-rays done and see what the dentist recommends."

Alita patted Elyse's back, whispering words of comfort. Elyse slumped on Alita's lap. She did not connect with the physician, and she never made any eye contact with him or any of the nursing staff from when the women first arrived at the medical office.

Alita's heart was moved by the young girl's need for comfort, but at the same time it embarrassed her how Elyse was so childlike. She wanted her to be normal, be grown, but she wasn't completely sure how to fix things.

Alita cleared her throat, which was clogged with pain. "Thanks for letting me know, doc. We'll make an appointment for her as soon as possible." Alita was ready to leave. She despised hearing bad news, especially when it involved young people. It made her feel powerless and defeated.

Alita snatched up her purse and made Elyse stand up. "Anything else?" Alita asked.

"As a matter of fact, there is." He paused. "I think that she has agoraphobia."

"Agora what? What is that?"

"Look at her," the doctor said quietly but respectfully. Alita stared at Elyse and tried to see what the man was talking about.

"I'm looking. That's how she always is. She's kind of odd. She talks like a kid and acts like one too."

Elyse shot Alita a hateful look that made her feel uneasy. Alita changed her description, saying, "Put it like this. I think my baby sister is a late bloomer. She's very shy. And she misses our mother." She explained that Elyse had fallen into a depression after their mother passed. Almost immediately they had noticed a major shift in Elyse's personality. Prior to that, the girl had been introverted, but it was never this extreme.

"I'm sorry to hear that. But agoraphobia is an anxiety disorder in which a person suffers from panic attacks, exhibits various fears. Fear of open spaces. I've noticed how she froze up whenever the door opened or closed. And I saw how you all did not take an elevator to reach this floor, not that that means anything, but now that I've observed Elyse, it all makes sense."

"Well, you nailed it doctor, because that's exactly how she be acting." Alita rolled her eyes. "She's too old for this. This girl will be twenty years old on her next birthday."

"Does she find it hard to tell you how she feels, what she's thinking?"

"Yes! All of that. I can barely get her to put three words in one sentence. She's a one-word person if I ever saw one. Drives me crazy."

"We'll let you know the lab results as soon as we have them."

"Thanks, doctor. I appreciate that."

Alita told him goodbye. She and Elyse exited the building and soon Alita was driving north on the I-45, back to the Woodlands.

When Elyse saw the direction that they were headed, she pointed frantically to her stomach.

"What Elyse? Hell, I'm not a mind reader, and I don't do sign language either."

"Hungry," Elyse said. "I want food."

"Okay, I could eat too," Alita said. "What you have a taste for? You want to go to Morning Glory?"

Elyse grabbed the door handle of Alita's car. The car was a late-model sedan and was falling apart. The seat cushions were ripped, the steering wheel needed to be replaced, and the muffler made loud noises.

Gripping the handle, Elyse rattled it and pushed her shoulder against the door.

"Girl, what you doing?"

Elyse unlatched her seat belt, then opened the passenger door. The door was heavy, and she struggled to keep it steady.

"Elyse, are you crazy? Shut the damned door."

Elyse cracked the door open a little wider. She twisted her petite body around to face it. She imagined herself jumping. Pictured herself falling out and land-ing on the road. And if she was lucky maybe a car would run over her since they were driving in the middle lane. Any car out there could do the job. It would be over real quick. And her nightmare would end.

Alita held the steering wheel with one hand. She leaned over and snatched Elyse's left arm. Elyse jerked back.

The sound of cars whizzing by filled Alita's ears. She glanced in the rearview mirror; an eighteen-wheeler zoomed behind them. Elyse saw the truck too. She opened her door wider.

"What the fuck you doing, little girl?" Alita was yelling by now. Her heart raced. Her mind felt confused. "All I wanted to do was take you to the doctor. I didn't sign up for all this extra drama. Why you trying to kill yourself?"

Alita wanted to slow down, but the cars behind her and on the side of them zoomed by at seventy miles per hour. Elyse rocked back and forth in her seat like she was bracing herself for the jump.

"Baby girl, please don't do this. *Please.* I love you, Elyse, can you get that through your thick head?"

Elyse shot a doubtful look at Alita. She turned toward her, but the door was still ajar.

"You love? Love me?" she asked.

"Yes, dummy. What do you think? Oh, my God. Why don't you know how much your family cares about you?"

If they love me, why they not save me? Why they can't see me, really see me? Why they not know everything not like it looks?

Elyse suddenly burst into tears. She covered her face with both of her hands, forgetting all about the swinging door.

"Girl, are you nuts? If you don't close that door I may push you out on the ground myself. Damn!"

Elyse ignored Alita. She wept and released all the pain and confusion and anger that had bubbled up inside of her for years. She wanted her mother. She wished she could find her father. She yearned for protection. She wanted an ending to every injustice she'd suffered.

Alita managed to pull over on the shoulder of the freeway. She got out of the car and ran to shut the door. Then she kicked it to make sure it remained closed.

She got back in the car and secured the locks. "Hell, if this is what I'll be going through, I need to get B to buy me a new car. If I'm the chauffeur *and* the fucking psychiatrist, I'm going to need way more than gas money and a free breakfast every now and then."

Elyse stopped crying and burst out laughing.

Alita was shocked. "You laughing?"

Elyse nodded. "You very funny. And crazy."

Alita started hooting and hollering. "Oh, my God. You have been paying attention, haven't you, Elyse."

Elyse nodded.

"Baby sis spoke two sentences in a row. It's a miracle. Somebody call TMZ. Somebody call *The Shade Room* please."

Elyse chuckled again until her laugh simmered down. Her stomach growled. And she felt light-headed. She angrily spoke. "Hungry, Lita. No breakfast. No Morning Glory."

"Okay, all right," Alita smiled. "We'll go wherever you want to go. Any place you want."

Elyse paused. "I want . . . go live with you. Can I?"

"What?"

Elyse nodded. "Please? I not trouble."

Alita wanted to laugh.

"Define trouble", she said.

"I not *trouble*, Lita."

"You're not trouble? Ha! I got a watch, I got a clock, but I don't have time for this shit."

"You love me?" Elyse asked.

"Of course I do, silly. More than you can ever imagine." Alita bit her bottom lip; her eyes filled with tears. "It's just that . . . I'm not in the position to handle all of this craziness. Trying to deal with Leno, and these recruiters that call me, and me having to work three jobs. I finally hooked up with a decent boyfriend, and I got bills." Just the thought of everything she was up against made Alita feel like she could barely breathe.

"You never see me," Elyse pleaded. "I be invisible. I be quiet. Please, Lita."

"Awww, sweetie. Let me think about it."

Elyse pouted. Her eyes clouded with fresh tears. She was sick of crying. What good did it do anyway?

Finding no answer, she quietly grabbed the door handle.

"Oh, hell no," Alita began to shout. "If you think you gonna try and manipulate me by threatening to kill yourself every time you don't get your way, then think again. Don't do this to me. I can't take it. I won't have it!"

Alita yelled so loud that Elyse snatched back her hand.

She cowered in her seat and made her body resemble a tiny ball. She leaned her head against the door and wished herself to sleep.

Wished herself back into the deep, black hole that was her life.

CHAPTER 14

Who Put You in Charge

The November Sister Day fell on the Saturday before Thanksgiving. When the ladies gathered at the nail salon for their fill-ins, no one complained about Coco being late. She was now twenty weeks pregnant. Coco waddled into the place, out of breath and fanning her face with an *Essence* magazine.

"Sorry, y'all," Coco said and made a whooshing noise when she collapsed on her seat.

Alita shrugged and shook her head as if she was used to Coco's pathetic ways.

Burgundy spoke up. "No apologies needed."

Alita didn't waste any time. "We still in the last Sister Day Assignment, right? Okay. I have been wondering about something . . . and I'll try to sound nice while saying it."

"What, Alita, what?" Coco said, assuming that she was the topic of Alita's complaint.

"It's not about you this time, Dark Skin, so chill." Alita looked annoyed. "My question is for Miss Queen B."

Burgundy turned and faced Alita. "Go ahead, Sis. What's on your mind?"

Ever since Alita had informed Burgundy about Elyse's medical analysis and the fact that she'd been diagnosed with agoraphobia and was suicidal, Alita's frustration had swelled. She felt that if Burgundy was too busy to notice that the girl was in deep trouble and needed immediate help, then she shouldn't be so insistent on being her caregiver.

"A lot of shit is on my mind," Alita replied. "But I don't want to overwhelm you since you're so busy and all. Let's start with this one: I want to know who the hell put you in charge of Sister Day. Last time I checked, I am the oldest—"

"Here we go," Coco groaned.

"Like I said, I've been in this world longer than you, Burgundy. Yet you the one who always barking orders, taking over everything, and acting all perfect like your shit don't stink."

"Alita," Burgundy said, ignoring her rant. "You gotta be joking. Stop playing."

"I ain't playing. This is a question that I want you to answer and not dodge."

"I won't be spoken to in a disrespectful manner."

"Fine. It didn't come out so nice and pretty. I'm sorry. But tell me this: Who put you in charge?"

"Wow, Alita," Dru interrupted. "I can't believe you'd go off on B like this just because she has a lot of initiative. Don't forget she hooked you up with Shade."

"Shade has nothing to do with this. This is all about Burgundy's annoying ass and how she acts so high and mighty coming up in here with her red-bottom shoes like she's going to a Broadway play or something. You don't have to show off your designer gear and thousand-dollar purses to us. Hell, since you got so much ched-dar, give me some of it. My rent is due, and the late fees are steadily piling up. What? Oh, okay, I thought so. You don't have money to truly help out your sisters, but you can fork over three hundred seventy-five dol-lars so we can get these mani-pedis every other month. I'd rather have the cash. My nails can stay jacked up for all I care."

"Alita," Dru said, exasperated. "Don't you have any shame? I don't understand you. Why can't you ever be grateful or happy about anything?"

"Because I can't. Not when it comes to certain things." She thought about how much Elyse had been suffering for God knows how long. And she recalled how the doctor had contacted Alita and recommended that Elyse begin seeing a psychotherapist; he told Alita that the girl should practice relaxation methods to help her with her anxiety. She might even have to start tak-ing medication, and Alita thought the girl was way too young to grow dependent on pills, even if they did straighten her out.

Alita stood up and grabbed her Walmart purse, whose threads had come loose and needed to be snipped off. The bottom stitching bore several obvious holes. Just one more thing that increased her anger and made her want to disappear.

She glanced around the salon, noting the fancy chairs, the glasses filled with complimentary wine, and the high, decorative ceilings. She felt like she was in Dubai.

"I hate all this fake-ass shit. What are we trying to

prove, huh? When mama was alive we didn't hang out like this. It feels so forced. It ain't from the heart. Burgundy got something up her sleeve, I can feel it."

"What?" Burgundy said incredulously.

"Yeah, I said it. You about as fake as these acrylic nails."

"Well, Alita. You can get solar if you want, I don't care."

"I know you don't care. As long as you showing us that you the house Negro and we the field slaves, that is all your bougie ass cares about." She wanted to tell everyone that their sister had almost killed herself, but instead she found herself spewing insults.

"I-I mean, hell, we never see our nieces looking dirty or with their shoes off. They're *kids,* for God's sake. Let 'em get dirty every once in a while, and stop treating them like they made of glass."

"Is that what you're upset about? The fact that my girls wear shoes when they're playing?"

"Yeah!"

"You sound like a fool, Alita." Burgundy's eyes flashed with anger. "Keep Natalia and Sid out of this. My kids are not your issue."

"I agree," Dru said. "Throwing the kids under the bus was a low blow. And it's obvious, Alita, that you're insecure and jealous of your own sister. You ought to be happy for her. She can't help it if she and Nate have successful businesses that the community supports. They work very hard at what they do, and because of that they can buy nice things for the kids. Be glad for them. What? You want them to be poor and struggling?"

"Tell her, Dru," Coco butted in, feeling satisfied that she wasn't in the hot seat. "Leave B alone. Everybody can't be as poor as you . . . and me." She cackled, then quieted down.

Alita's voice trembled. "I ain't say all that. I don't care what the woman has. My main question is why she thinks she has to run everything just because she has money. Money equals power, right? Money means status. Well, school me on how to get some of that. Maybe then I can have some fucking power."

Alita had said some of how she felt. But her real feelings were buried deep inside of her. For a rare moment, she lacked the courage to speak her mind when it came to how she truly felt about Burgundy. And if the sisters knew how negligent Burgundy acted toward Elyse, maybe they wouldn't be so quick to defend her.

"Alita." Burgundy sounded distressed and appeared embarrassed as the nail technicians kept rapidly talking in Vietnamese and eyeballing the sisters. "I don't feel like you should be attacking me, especially in this place of business."

"But see, have you forgotten you're the one that decided where we meet for Sister Day. You, Queen B, made up the rule that we must be honest. And if you don't want *us* to tell the truth, then stop pressuring us to tell it. Because, I swear to God, some of us couldn't take the real truth about what's really going on in this family."

"What she say? Oh, my God, this is so damn juicy all I need is some cheese popcorn and a Dr. Pepper," Coco hollered.

"Coco, this isn't funny; it's not entertaining," Burgundy said. "It's embarrassing."

"B, please. It's funny as hell and very entertaining." Coco was more cheerful than usual. "Y'all go on. Pretend like I'm not even here."

"This is unbelievable," Burgundy continued, looking sad and anguished. "Alita, sweetie. I'm not trying to be in charge. I just want to help keep us together as a family. If I hadn't stepped up and coordinated Sister Day, we might have gotten out of touch. And it would have been like pulling teeth to get us to come together. Then where would we be?"

"No one will ever know, because you didn't give any of us a chance to show what we could do," Alita argued. "For all you know I could have come up with Sister Day."

"But you didn't!"

"Say what? Why would you even go there?"

"What do you suggest then, Alita?" Burgundy spoke up. "You think you can do better? Do you want to be in charge?"

"Nope, not saying all that. What I'm asking is who the hell put *you* in charge."

"Mama," Burgundy whispered.

"Speak up, I can't hear you," Alita practically shouted.

"Our mama made me promise to keep us all together. She's the one that came up with this whole idea. And she asked me to run it."

"Whoa, uh oh, it's on now," Elyse said. It sounded so funny coming from Elyse that Coco laughed. Her sister reminded her of a three-year-old child who had just learned a new word.

"Whoa is right," Coco said. "When did all this happen, B?"

"A few weeks before she passed," Burgundy replied.

"How we know she ain't lying?" Alita said.

"Why would I lie about something like that?" Burgundy shot back. "I was never going to tell you all this. Or I would have waited years from now. But like it or not, it's the honest-to-God truth."

"I believe her," Dru spoke up. "Mama always said Burgundy was a planner and an organizer from the time she was little. Remember how she used to line up our shoes so that they were neatly set against the wall?"

"I don't remember that," Coco claimed with a frown.

"And she'd make us straighten up our closet and dresser drawers so that panties were in one drawer, socks in another." Dru looked at Burgundy in admiration. "While Alita would be knocked out asleep from staying up too late, Burgundy was the one who would wake us up in the morning so we'd eat breakfast and not be late for school. Mama probably thought B could start Sister Day and help us keep focused."

"Lord knows I couldn't have run it," Coco cackled. "And back before Mama passed, Ms. Thang here was fussing and fighting with Leonard Washington so much, Mama knew Lita wasn't ready to guide the rest of us."

"Shut up, Coco." Alita slumped, and she slid back in her seat, looking as if she couldn't leave the salon if she wanted to. All her energy shifted. She put her purse back down, then grew quiet and pensive.

When one of the salon artists walked over to Alita, she allowed the young woman to work on her feet and prepared the hot wax for the bucket. Alita's facial expression made it seem like her body was there but her mind was long gone.

"Some people can't handle the truth," Coco sang, pronouncing the words as if she were at church belting out a gospel song.

"Stop it. Be nice," Burgundy said. She cleared her throat. "If I have adequately answered Lita's question, I'd like to move on. We've lost a lot of time already, but it's cool. I was glad to finally get that off my chest. I didn't feel comfortable taking credit for Mama's idea. And she came up with the name Sister Day. So here we are. Let's give a round of applause to Mrs. Greta Reeves, may she rest in peace."

Even Alita shouted, "Clap clap, boom. Clap clap, boom."

"You're too much, Alita." Burgundy smiled. "Now, moving on. This month's assignment is: *Call, text, or email someone from your past to show it's not all about you.* That sounds kind of nostalgic, doesn't it, considering Thanksgiving is right around the corner?"

"I, for one, have nobody I want to get in touch with," Coco announced. "Let sleeping dogs lie and let 'em stay dead. I'm trying to keep my current situation straight, let alone trying to dip with somebody from my past."

"Coco, sweetie. I didn't say it had to be a man. It can be a woman, a relative, a former neighbor. It's just a suggestion."

"Oh, you saying that now, but if I don't try to do it, you'll have a fit. All I'm saying is I will have to think about this one, okay, Burgundy?"

"That's fine. Just give it some thought, all right, sweetie?"

"All right," Coco told her. "I will."

It didn't take long for Coco to figure out who she'd be calling from her past.

As a matter of fact, a few days before Thanksgiving, she had some free time on her hands. Her daughters Cadee and Chloe were hanging out at Burgundy's and having fun playing with their cousins. Coco was itching to get out of the big house. She buckled Chance in his car seat and gave him a loving kiss on his forehead.

"You rolling with Mommy today, little man." Coco felt nervous. She called Calhoun, even though she knew he was at work. When he answered his phone, she was surprised, but she quickly asked him which part of town he was working that day.

"I'm way out in Katy, almost near the Mills."

"I thought we might meet up for lunch, but I'm not going to be in that area."

"You too much, Ma."

Coco hurried and ended the call. She needed to be quick and careful.

She kept driving along, her mind deep in thought. Finally when she pulled her vehicle in front of Q's apartment, she felt as if the eyes of the world could see her. She had called his number from a pay phone a half hour ago. He was home alone.

It was like he was waiting on her, because Q opened his door before she could ring the bell.

Quantavius was tall and stocky like a running back. His arms were thick. They were easily the biggest arms Coco had seen in her life.

"What's good with it?" he greeted her. "I can't believe you brought your fine ass over here."

"Been a minute, huh?"

"More like a few years."

"Oh, please, it hasn't been that damn long. Anyway, I won't hold you. It already feels weird being here. But I thought you'd want to see him."

Coco nervously looked behind her before she stepped inside of Q's place. Before she could even speak another word, Q gave Coco a strong hug, then released her. She sat down to rest her weary feet.

Q examined Chance from head to toe. The last time he had seen Chance was four months ago; Coco convinced him to meet her out in public but way on the other side of town. Back then Q had sat the one-and-a-half-year-old on his lap, talked to him, played games with him, and enjoyed spending time with Chance.

And now, the more Q looked at the boy's handsome features, the more his chest began to swell. Chance had a similar bone structure, a pointy mouth, and pudgy hands. And his complexion was golden brown like Omari Hardwick's.

"What you thinking?" Coco asked when she saw him staring at Chance.

"I'm thinking it's a damn shame I can't claim him."

"Right, you can't. That ain't happening."

Q looked wistful. "Yeah, that wouldn't be cool. My boy and I are tight. We go way back. I ain't trying to fuck that up."

"Trust me, I ain't either."

"But at the same time, this my seed." His eyes misted, a rarity. He quickly recovered. "And that makes me not give a fuck about Calhoun."

"Oh, God, noooo, Q. Please don't say nothing. It would mean instant death for me, you, and definitely for the baby. Think about the baby."

Q relented, eager to stay clear-headed. "You right. I won't say a word for now. 'Cause this needs to stay on the low, low, low, low."

"You don't have to tell me twice." It felt agonizing

for Coco to harbor such a secret. Would Calhoun ever figure out what had happened? The fact that he suspected nothing so far made Coco feel somewhat relieved. Yet the very thought of Calhoun knowing the truth severely depressed her. She couldn't allow anything to come between her and the love she had for her man.

"But damn," Q said. "Why you gotta go get knocked up again? You fine as hell, but loading up all that damn weight make you big as a pig. You thicker than a Snicker."

"Q, don't talk to me like that. I don't wanna hear that."

"I'm just saying. You already a slice and a half. Now you eating for two. You gon' be big as a mafuck by the time this new one pops out."

"That ain't for you to worry about."

"Whatever."

"Well, I just wanted you to see little man. I didn't come over here for you to talk shit about my weight." Chance kept his arm tightly clutched around his mother's leg as she sat on Q's couch. He shyly stared at Q and refused to go to him when he gestured.

"Man," Q said in disbelief. "He have no idea that Calhoun ain't—"

"Right, and he never will. That's what you told me, anyway. I hope you can keep your promise."

"Can't be no other way."

"Good. It's settled." Feeling exhausted, Coco sighed. "I best be going. Calhoun knows my scent, and I don't want him to even think I've been within a mile of this spot."

"I heard that."

"And if he wanna come hang out over here after work, you need to make up a lie. Don't let him come over here for a couple of days."

"How am I gon' manage that?"

"I'm sure you'll think of something." She stuck out her hand. He opened his wallet and placed a few bills in her hand.

"Thanks," she said and stuffed the cash inside her bra. She leaned over and gave Q a kiss.

Surprised, he grabbed her around the butt and squeezed. She pushed him off of her.

"Don't get any ideas about that," she warned him. "You my boy, and I'm glad you staying loyal."

Coco rose to her feet and tried to suck in her stomach.

She strutted toward the door and turned around to gaze at Q. "By the way. Do Calhoun be having bitches up here when y'all hanging out?"

"What? Get the fuck out here, Coco. You ain't shit. I knew you were up to no good. You don't give a shit about me. All you care about is that bonehead."

"Is that a yes or a no?"

"Fuck off." He practically pushed Coco through the door.

"What a waste of time," she muttered and drove home feeling more frustrated than ever. "But at least I did my Sister Assignment like I promised Burgundy and got in touch with someone from my past. Yay for me!"

Coco could only deal with one issue at a time. And she promptly pushed the issue of Chance, Calhoun, and Q to the back of her head.

CHAPTER 15

Sometimes We Ate Bologna for Dinner

On Thanksgiving, a mild breeze combined with pleasant temperatures made the day perfect for family gatherings and socializing. The Reeves sisters were scheduled to assemble for an afternoon supper at Nate and Burgundy's.

Burgundy was in her first-level master bedroom suite perched in front of the vanity mirror. She opened her eyes real wide and stroked her long lashes with dark brown mascara.

"This is not cutting it," she said, finally giving up. "I need to break out my fake lashes today. I sure hope Alita doesn't notice."

She opened a drawer and searched for her cosmetic kit.

"Nate," she yelled from the cushioned chair. "Can you please go make sure Elyse and the girls are getting ready? My sisters will be here any minute. Except Coco," she said with a laugh.

Nathaniel popped his head inside the doorway. His long legs, thick thighs, and broad shoulders made him a towering presence. "Anything for you, my love."

Burgundy only wore a bra and a thong; she smelled like fresh bathwater and scented lotion.

"You're looking beautiful as always," he told her.

She playfully batted her eyelashes at him. Then she picked up a comb and started fussing with her hair. "Are you saying that because you think I'm gonna give you some, or do you really mean it?"

Burgundy still felt guilty; the majority of her energy was reserved for the girls, the businesses, and various civic duties. She knew her Viagra argument could only last so long. And this holiday week would feel like Christmas for her husband, because that's when she planned to offer him a pity fuck to tide him over.

"Look, woman," Nate replied. "I don't have to give you a fake compliment. You know you look sexy." And she did.

"Nate, you always know what to say."

"I'm not just saying it. I mean it."

"But why? Like, you don't seem terribly angry at me for holding out." She paused. "Does that mean you've found another lover?" She sat completely still, bracing herself for the confession she did not want to hear.

"No, babe. Ain't no other lover. I'm waiting on my one and only."

His words calmed and soothed her conscience. "Nate, I tell you, sweetie. I feel so lucky to have a husband like you. Any other man would have sought an affair. And if you did, it would be all my fault."

He just looked at her.

"And I-I really gotta do b-better," she stammered. "Do much better than I'm doing, because I would never want another woman to steal you away from me."

"Ha," he laughed in mockery. "No one is checking for an old man like me."

"Don't fool yourself, baby." She set down the comb and studied him. Her husband was a handsome, well-to-do guy. Any sane woman would be dying to be with Nate. "You still look amazing for your age. And trust me, I've noticed how those women at church are always up in your face, flirting, smiling, and acting like they want to ask you a question about scriptures and whatnot."

He couldn't help but laugh. "They're just being friendly. You have nothing to worry about, my love."

At his promises her heart wanted to melt. Other than his earnest yearnings for lovemaking, her spouse seemed too good to be true. Hardworking, attractive, church-going, and his pockets were padded, because if there was one thing Nate knew how to do, it was how to earn money. It made her feel good to be financially stable and to have the house and cars, wardrobe and jewelry.

"Nate, don't be naïve. I know women. I know hussies. I know home wreckers. And our church is filled with them. I got my eye on those women, because obviously you're too gullible to even know when someone wants you. Take Sister Glover, for example."

"That fat old thing. You know how I feel about obese women."

"Please. That fat old thing still has a big you-know-what, and she'd love to show it to you first chance she gets."

He grimaced. "Nah, Sister Glover is not my type."

"What did you say?" she asked with raised eyebrows.

Nate laughed again. "I said stop wasting time and get yourself ready for your family. Go on and get dressed before I do something to you that'll make you totally forget about turkey and dressing."

She smiled. "I'm so glad you have a sense of humor about all of this."

"I'll go check on the girls."

"Thanks, Nate."

She turned back to the mirror and made sure that every single hair was in place. Burgundy always felt excited when the sisters could hang out at her house. She had thought about wearing a fancy cocktail dress with her favorite red-bottom pumps, but mulled over what Alita had recently complained about her. She felt blessed to live a good life but genuinely didn't want anyone to feel uncomfortable. Burgundy put on a casual pair of white denim jeans, a simple blue-and-yellow printed V-neck blouse, and a warm pair of mink house slippers, then headed to the kitchen.

After Nate went to check on the girls, Burgundy asked him to go to the grocery store to pick up some last-minute items. She waved goodbye to him and rushed to look inside the oven at several pans of cornbread and desserts that she'd baked.

Five minutes later, when Burgundy opened the front door, she noticed how much Tyrique's eyes sparkled as he held Dru's hand tightly. She was even happy to see Alita; she had expected Shade to show up with her, but her sister told her she wasn't comfortable having him spend a major holiday with her dysfunctional family just yet.

Burgundy gave her the side-eye but greeted everyone else who came through the door. "Hi, my family. I'm so happy you all could make it. Where's Leno?" she asked.

"His dad has him," Alita answered. "First time in years he's been with him on this holiday. I decided not to fight it."

"Oh, I heard that. Thank God," Burgundy said as she invited everyone inside.

When Coco finally arrived, she waddled in huffing and puffing with all her babies in tow, plus Calhoun.

Everyone congregated in the gourmet kitchen.

"Hey, brother-in-law," Coco greeted Tyrique. She was grinning when she said it.

"Coco, you got jokes," Dru casually replied. She stood in the butler's pantry where the countertops were lined with bowls of every type of food imaginable: cornbread dressing, giblet gravy, black-eyed peas, collard greens, candied yams, potato salad, corn pudding, and other casseroles. She was tempted to grab a spoon and scoop up a bite of creamy mashed potatoes, but Tyrique jumped to her side.

"Let me help," he said.

"That's sweet of you, but I got this."

"Girl, you better let your future husband cater to you." Burgundy eagerly joined in on the lightweight teasing. She beamed at the crowd that had gathered in her kitchen. She winked at Tyrique. He blushed and helplessly shoved his hands inside his pockets. Tyrique wore his hair natural, and he was always seen in his black geek eyeglasses. Burgundy thought he was adorable.

"Hey, Ty," Burgundy said. "I haven't seen you in a

minute, and I'm always asking my sister about you. How is your animal lab job at the med center?"

"Busy. Crazy. But good," he responded.

"Umph," Coco sniffed. "You be around all them nasty research animals . . . I sure hope you wash your hands real good."

Tyrique laughed good-naturedly. "That is a no-brainer Ms. Coco." He reached inside his man purse and produced a miniature bottle of hand sanitizer.

"Dru?" he said. She obediently opened her palm. Tyrique squeezed a drop of liquid and watched Dru vigorously rub her hands while he did the same.

"Well, look a here," Alita said. "A true gentleman that won't even let his woman squeeze her own bottle. Bloop!"

"Hush, Alita," Dru told her. "Tyrique just notices a lot. He rarely misses a detail."

"That's the way a good man should be," Coco said, happy for her sister to have such a decent man.

"Queen B, does what's-his-face cater to you?" Alita asked point blank.

"Absolutely," Burgundy shot back.

"Where is he anyway?"

"Nate will be back soon. He went to the store to pick up some more drinks and bags of ice. He did it without my even asking him to," she said, telling a quick lie.

"She's going to always take up for her hubby," Dru stated matter-of-factly.

"Yes, I am. He's good to me so I'm good to him. That's the way it ought to be."

Alita bristled with envy. The house felt so ritzy that Alita was afraid to touch anything: Italian marble tiling in some rooms, plus lush carpet or Brazilian hardwood flooring in others. Decorative items hung from the ceilings or dotted the place, most of them made of crystal or glass. The spacious, well-furnished home reminded her of Leonard's, and the comparison made her feel depressed.

She thought about how she was struggling to maintain her overpriced two-bedroom apartment that was located on the third floor. Sure, she wasn't homeless, and she tried to keep the place clean and presentable, but she always felt self-conscious when recruiters came by to visit.

"Must be nice, B," Alita commented. "Looks like Kim, Kanye, North, and Saint live here."

"Might I remind you, Nate and I didn't steal this house," Burgundy said defensively. "We worked for it. We hustle hard. That's what we do."

"What you trying to say? That I don't bust my ass for my coins? I get three W-2's every February and let me tell you, I still don't own anything that comes close to this."

"Is that my fault?" Burgundy asked.

"Yes," Alita answered stubbornly.

"Sis, get real. It's not what you earn; it's what you do with what you earn."

"Are you serious, B? How can I do something with nothing?"

"Alita, please lower your voice."

"Why should I? Who we around besides family? Who you trying to impress this time?" Alita walked back and forth, using the thick heels of her boots to stomp on the Italian marble. "Word on the street is that you pay twenty-five grand a year in taxes for this house. Is that true? Y'all balling like that? Do you know what I could do with twenty-five G's? How many bills I could pay? The type of car I could have instead of that old piece of shit Chevy Impala that I drive every day?" She nearly wanted to burst into tears when she thought about the unfairness of it all.

Coco, Calhoun, Dru, Tyrique, Elyse, and the kids gawked at Alita.

"Alita, just stop it." Burgundy was fed up. "You're making a scene . . . again. That's what you do. For some reason, everything in the world is always about you. You are notorious for bringing up stuff that no one else is even thinking about, but I won't have you ruin the holiday. Not this year!" Burgundy took a deep breath. She didn't want Alita to hold that much power over her and waited until she calmed herself.

"Sweetie, look. I know you're struggling and trying your best. Everything isn't exactly the way you want them to be. But look on the bright side. You aren't homeless. You get paychecks every week."

"You call those pennies I make money? That ain't shit—"

"It's better than nothing," Burgundy told her. "Some people would be glad to get those checks."

"Oh, yeah? Want to trade places?"

Burgundy avoided the question. "Plus you get child support, Alita. Why do you keep going around with this 'woe is me, I'm poor, I'm so poor' sob story? What you doing with the money?"

Alita was shocked. "I-I'm stretching those dollars. I pay bills. I pay a car note."

"You're still paying a loan on a used car?"

"Blame the car dealer that gave me that ridiculous interest rate. It was a seventy-two-month note at eleven percent interest."

"Wow, why so high?"

"My credit score was six fifty," Alita flatly told her.

Burgundy moaned in horror. "You never should have agreed to such a thing. Learn to shop around. No one would have ever guessed your ex is a car salesman."

"Are we done with crucifying me yet? 'Cause I swear I'm just about ready to rise my ass from the dead."

"All I'm saying is that was then," Burgundy rushed to tell her. "But from now on, Alita, you need to make better financial decisions." She paused momentarily, wanting to lighten the tense atmosphere. "And if you keep guiding Leno in the right direction like I know that you will, you are well on your way to having good things, much more money, because we know Leno is going to be in the NBA one day. I'm sure his contract will be worth millions. Mmm hmmm. And he's going to buy you a nice house, girl. He'll move you out of Houston and into the suburbs. Wouldn't that be awesome? Plus, we all know you're working on having a decent relationship," Burgundy remarked. "So be patient, Lita. Stay positive. Keep your thoughts right. You have to see silver linings, not just the bad. And quit comparing yourself to other—"

"Ughhhh," Alita loudly groaned. "I can't take this sickening positive thinking you keep throwing at me. Y'all got anything strong to drink, B? My throat is parched."

"Parched?" Burgundy cackled. "What's with the big words? Knowing you, you've probably been sipping on gin and juice all morning."

"Hmm. I hella wish I *could* taste gin and juice."

Instantly, a female voice said, "Playing 'Gin and Juice' by Snoop Dogg from Prime Music." The bass line of the song began thumping. The Moog synthesizer riff wailed from the Amazon Echo device that was sitting in the corner of the kitchen countertop.

"What the hell?" Alita said, looking all around her.

"Oh," Burgundy said with a laugh. "That's Alexa. We bought that Echo not too long ago. And Alexa is nosy . . . dipping in our conversation. She probably thought I told her to play 'Gin and Juice.'"

Alita started rocking her head to the beat.

"You like that, huh?" Burgundy asked. "Nate *loves* Alexa. She's the only woman on earth that does exactly what he tells her. And she ought to, as much as we paid for her."

"See what I'm talking about? Y'all buy things you don't even need, like an Echo. What the hell is it anyway?"

"Voice control device. You ask it questions and it'll answer. News, weather, traffic. Obviously it plays music. And it even can open the garage door, turn on lights, turn on ceiling fans."

"So this device can do everything except fuck your husband, huh?"

"That's crude, Alita."

"It's the truth. You know we're all about telling the truth around here."

Burgundy wanted to laugh but knew it would come out sounding bitter. She gave Alita an odd look and stepped to the side to attend to her various baked pies.

Alita opened the refrigerator and found herself something to drink. She stood around, sipping on a glass of sparkling ginger punch, and tried to relax. "Hey, sisters, guess what? I was on Facebook this morning. Remember the Thompson family that lived across the street from us when we were growing up? I learned that they ended up moving to Jackson, Missis-sippi. But I still remember the oldest brother, Jay, and his baby sister, Charlotte."

"I remember," Burgundy said. "What about them?"

"Girl, I came across Jay's profile picture. He's fat."

"Who isn't?"

"And Charlotte? She's gay."

"Who isn't?" Burgundy shrugged. "People get fat and people get gay."

"And some are fat and gay," Alita remarked. "But I ain't one to judge."

Just then Nate stormed through the kitchen door that led from the garage. His arms were laden with twelve packs of soda, and his hands carried bags of ice.

Tyrique jumped to his feet, immediately grabbing a few cases. The others stood about in an open area; both the kitchen and cozy breakfast room faced the family room.

"You good?" Calhoun said, addressing Nate, then he went and got comfortable as he sat on the sofa in front of the TV; he wanted to watch the Cowboys play the Saints. Chloe, Cadee, and Chance followed after him.

When Alita stared a hole through Coco, then frowned in Calhoun's direction, at first Coco pretended she did not notice the way her man had up and left the kitchen. But Coco still had something to say.

"At least my man loves me enough to show his face with the family on a holiday. That's all that matters."

"Oh, don't give me that shit," Alita said. "He may as well have stayed home. His bum ass ain't lifting one finger to help nobody."

"Don't you see our kids on his lap? Watching the

kids is helping. Stop hating. Leave mines alone and try to hold onto yours . . . unless you already scared the poor man away."

"Huh? What you mean? Where you hear that?"

"OMG. She *did* scare Shade away. What you do this time?"

Alita gave Coco a frustrated look. She grabbed her drink and immediately fled the kitchen. Both Burgundy and Dru scurried after her. Alita went into a nearby powder room. She quickly locked the door and turned on the water faucet. She couldn't bear to look at herself in the mirror. If she did, the only thing she'd see were her reddened eyes. She always hated holidays. It was the time when she felt the most alone. Even though she was around a lot of people, it felt like she was on a deserted island.

Burgundy shouted from outside the bathroom door. "Please, Alita, unlock the door. I want to know what's going on."

"No. Leave me alone. I'll be all right. I'm just peeing."

"You are not!"

"Don't believe me? Listen to this!" Alita lifted her skirt, pulled down her cotton panties, and sat on the commode. She let out a blast of gas and made splashing sounds in the toilet.

"Ewwww!" she heard Burgundy say. "Please spray when you're done."

"Happy now?" Alita didn't care if Burgundy answered her or not. Her face was marked with anger.

I met a really nice guy. My son isn't locked up in jail. Why is it so hard for me to stay happy?

"Alita, it's Dru. Will you open the door for me? I have something I want to show you."

"Y 'all need to ease up and give me some privacy. I'll be out when I feel like it."

Alita flushed the commode, then washed her hands, and finally got the courage to examine her reflection in the mirror. She had inherited her daddy's big brown eyes and her mother's full lips and high cheekbones. Her complexion was considered redbone and her long hair was dyed reddish blond. Alita was a real beauty resembling an older Keyshia Cole. But for some reason her vision merely focused on the series of blemishes and dark spots on her cheeks, the ones that came from all the scratching she had done when she had chicken pox. She turned her head sideways and noticed a tiny black mole behind her left ear. She was the only sister with a mole. And her eyebrows were thin, not thick and beautiful like Dru's.

"What the fuck. It is what it is," she told herself. She found the air freshener, sprayed, then opened the door.

"Girl, don't you be scaring us like this." Dru pretended to choke Alita.

"I'm not a kid. I can potty by myself."

"We know this, Alita," Burgundy said. "It's not your *physical* condition that we're concerned about. What's going on? Are you still mad at me?"

"You really think you can get to me like that, B?"

"Okay, good. Glad to hear that. Then why'd you let Coco get under your skin when she asked you about Shade?"

"Did she touch a nerve?" Dru boldly asked.

"I don't wanna talk about it." Alita turned back around and went to lower the toilet seat cover so she could sit. Burgundy came into the bathroom. She stood next to Alita and lovingly stroked her hair. She talked in a soothing tone.

"I think I know what's wrong. This isn't about me, or Coco, or even Shade. We know you get this way every holiday. We remember how bad you felt soon after the divorce, when Leonard wouldn't want to spend time with Leno, and we know how angry you were. We understand, Sis. That happened so long ago. Yet you can't control anyone's actions."

"Just my own, huh?" she asked in a cryptic tone.

"Yep," Dru joined in. "You give that man way too much power. Y'all are through. He's moved on."

"Yeah, I heard he got married to that Desiree chick. He didn't have the balls to tell me."

"That was tacky of him," Burgundy replied.

"Even though me and him ain't cool like that anymore," Alita said wistfully, "I'd want him to be able to share that news directly with me . . . even if I had to pretend like I didn't care. But it hurt."

"Alita, your face looks busted. I hope that means you weren't thinking that you two would someday reconcile," Dru said.

"Nooo. It's not that. I just feel him getting married is another dagger in Leno's heart. I mean, his dad is trying to make things up to him now, but what if Leonard has kids with Desiree? How will my baby feel knowing his dad loves the news kids more than him? Leno is slaying when it comes to b-ball. What if he wants his dad to come see him at his games and he has to say no? Because now he has a new wife, new kids, other priorities? What if Leno gets discouraged and gives up because his own father doesn't have time to be in his life?"

"You're overthinking, Alita." Burgundy tried to

sound encouraging. "Sometimes we stress about the 'what ifs' when a lot of times they never happen."

Dru added her two cents. "In my opinion, the only thing you can do with an ex is forget him."

Alita spoke up. "You got that right."

"But also," Dru continued, "you have to learn any lessons that you were meant to learn from an ex and try to stay focused on any good things happening in your life. As far as I can see, Shade is nothing like Leonard. Why can't you see that? That every guy is different?"

"You really want to know why?" Alita nearly screamed. "Because the second I relax is the second these men pull a switcheroo." She took a gulp of her drink and set it back now. "Me and him are chilling big time. I'm enjoying myself with good old Shade. But sometimes I lay up at night staring at the ceiling. I want to pinch myself. Shade Wilkins ain't the first nice man I've met since my divorce. Remember Darwin?"

"Darwin was a slick little con artist with his Kevin Hart looking self," Burgundy admitted. "But you gotta go through the bad to recognize the good. Shade is the better man that I, I mean, that *you* found."

"Well, how do I truly know that underneath all that niceness that Shade isn't another con? I-I can't front, y'all. If he ain't the real deal, I won't be able to handle it." Alita's forehead was wrinkled with worry lines. "I-I like him. A lot. I wish he was here with me right now."

"It's going to be okay, Sis," Burgundy said. "I promise. If you take life one single day at a time and don't get overwhelmed with the details, it'll work out. Put your faith in God, not man. Man is going to let us down, because we're only human."

"B, you got the perfect husband out there," Alita

said. "How can you even relate to what I'm going through? You've never met anyone like Leonard Washington. Or Darwin, who cleaned out our joint bank account after I'd known him only five months."

"That was on you," Burgundy fired back. "I swear you are terrible with money. You should never get a joint bank account with a man that's not your husband."

"This was a second savings account that he convinced me to open with him. I feel like a fool for falling for that. But I was fresh off my divorce and—"

"Divorced two months. Divorced two years. Doesn't matter," Burgundy said. "You have to look out for yourself, sweetie. As women we have to do that. Or these men could completely take over."

"Oh, B, I'm sure you will never have that problem."

Burgundy sidestepped Alita's comment. "My point is you never should have fallen for Darwin's promises. You told me he only hung out at your house. That's a clear sign that he was married."

"Oh, okay! It's all my fault?" Alita was peeved. "When I did try and trust someone, I got the money snatched out of my savings. It was only three hundred dollars; that's beside the point. I never heard from Darwin again. *He's* the con artist, but because I got tricked, I'm the criminal?"

"You're no criminal, sweetie. But you never had to go in with him on a money deal. You could have said no. We all have the power to say no."

"But he—"

"It's not about him," Burgundy continued. "I love you, Sis, but you gotta stop playing the victim. See the role that you're playing in your failed relationships."

"Ouch. Shit. All right. I've been crucified, and I'm

officially rising from the dead." Alita dramatically spread out both her hands and tilted her head to one side.

"Stop playing, Alita. Didn't you just say you'd rather hear the truth, even if it hurts?"

Instead of answering, Alita swiftly brushed past her sisters and exited the bathroom. The sisters shrugged. "Moving right along," Burgundy said.

Alita, Burgundy, and Dru rejoined the rest of the guests, who by then had settled in their chairs at the dining room table, which was large enough to seat twenty. It was decorated with orange flameless candles and an orange tablecloth. The buffet was filled with meats, vegetables, side dishes, desserts, and mouthwatering breads. The room smelled like poultry, various seasonings, eggs, sugar, fruits, and flour, all wonderfully mixed together.

Once the women were seated, Nate said the grace and began to slice into a juicy Butterball turkey that Burgundy had spent hours roasting.

"Oh, wow, if only our sweet mother could see us." Burgundy beamed with pride.

"That's an odd thing to say," Alita remarked.

Coco started giggling. She nudged Calhoun. "Here we go. The shit is about to tear up the fan."

Burgundy's cheeks reddened. She was beginning to feel frustrated. It seemed no matter what she did, her older sister had to pour a load of crap on top of it.

"It's not odd, Alita. I'm just trying to say I miss Mama. I wish she were here. And she would be happy to know that all her daughters are together on the holidays. That's all I was saying."

"You sure about that?" Alita was bristling with anger. Why did it seem like Burgundy had everything? Smarts, money, influence, and one good husband that she was stuck with forever. And the whole thing made Alita want to be petty.

"I mean, do we really have to eat at your house every fucking Thanksgiving and Christmas?"

"Who cares where we eat as long as we eating?" Coco said. "That chick needs some dick. Fast. B, what's Shade's phone number?" Coco asked with a serious look on her face.

"She's already had some dick, from what I can tell," Burgundy said and cleared her throat.

"If you don't stop spreading my business, I swear to God."

"Uh oh. Lita got some?" Coco asked with a smile. "It must not have done the job, because she should be smiling and happy instead of frowning and cussing."

"I'm about to cuss your ass out if you don't stop with the bull," Alita snapped back. "My man does a great job at keeping me satisfied. But apparently yours don't, or else you wouldn't have had that in-between baby."

"Alita, are you serious?" Burgundy scolded. "Please knock it off."

"What? You're the one who started this by getting all up in my business," Alita claimed. "How would you like it if someone got all up in yours?"

"Mind your manners, Alita."

"I agree with B," Coco said. "We trying to eat and drink and be merry. But leave it up to Lita to fuck up the groove. Anyway, enough of her always trying to be the center of attention."

"Drink gas, bitch."

"Flavor Flav lookalike," Coco told her.

"Lick broken glass."

"Trailer park ho."

"Watch your back, you humpback crack ho."

While the others were laughing at Coco and Alita's outrageous display of behavior, Elyse found nothing funny.

"Stop hurt, stop hurt, stop hurt," Elyse said so loud that the sisters had no choice but to stop.

"Look, y'all, we're upsetting Elyse. She looks like she's been sick all day long anyway." Burgundy rose from her chair. "Elyse, you want to go lie down, sweetie? I can save your plate for you. Plus, she doesn't need to listen to all this crazy family talk anyway. Go on, Elyse, go get some rest."

"I will make sure she's okay," Nate said. "Come on upstairs."

Elyse gave a frightened look and gagged. Her mouth flew open and out flew the little bit of turkey, dressing, and potatoes she had hidden under her tongue. A greenish yellowish glob of gook sprayed from her mouth and dripped to the floor. Her throat contracted and she felt hot liquid rise from inside her belly. Soon Elyse's shirt was splattered. Her face reddened as she grabbed her head between her hands and trembled uncontrollably.

Nate clenched his hands into tight fists.

"Don't just stare at her like she's crazy. Help her," Coco screamed.

"That's just pathetic," Nate told Elyse. "We're talking about a thousand-dollar floor. You need to learn to control that!" He left the room.

Alita was ready to jump up and help, but Burgundy beat her to it. She darted to the kitchen and quickly ran warm water onto a fresh dishrag. She returned to Elyse and gently wiped her sister's mouth.

"Raise your arms; hurry," she ordered. She helped Elyse remove her top. "Natalia, be a big girl and get the vacuum out of the closet. You can help clean up the carpet." She scowled at first but then obeyed.

Alita covered her nose. "I've lost my appetite, I swear to God. Let's all just go chill in the family room. I can't stand that smell. It smells like collard greens mixed with donkey shit. Hell, I want to throw up too." Alita dramatically placed her hand over her mouth, then got up and raced from the table.

The rest of the gang reassembled in the spacious family room where they spread out on a sectional sofa. The football game was on, and smooth jazz was playing from the speakers.

Burgundy went to lower the volume of the music. "Sorry about what happened at the table," she said. "The main thing is that Elyse is okay now. We can continue to do our thing, y'all. Relax, have a good time. As a matter of fact, we will start a game of bones in a bit." Burgundy invited her guests to finish eating and told them don't worry about spilling food on the plush carpet.

"She's trying to lighten up and get the stick out her butt," Dru explained to Coco, whose eyes enlarged as she watched Burgundy try to act gracious and warm. "Relaxing is good for her. Everything doesn't have to be so perfect and serious all the time."

Just then the doorbell rang. Then there was a loud persistent knock.

Alita went to see who it was. Soon a middle-aged woman sashayed into the room.

"Hey, everybody," she said. "Long time no see."

When Nate saw her, his eyes grew wide.

She smiled and walked over to Nate and gave him a hug. "Hi, Baby Brother."

"Julianne," he said. He gave her a weak hug and stood back to observe her.

All big hair, oversize costume necklaces, and silver rings, Julianne sported her usual black high-low cocktail dress with a floral skirt. She also wore a delighted smile on her face and flashed her red-tipped fingernails.

"You surprised to see me, Baby Brother?"

"That's an understatement," he replied. "I thought you said you weren't going to be able to make it this year."

"I know. Plans changed. Now I'm here. Got any food left for a hungry woman?"

Nate forced himself to say, "Sure. I'll fix you a plate. Come with me. I got you."

Delighted, she put a little dance in her step and scurried behind him into the kitchen. He spun around and asked, "What do you think you're doing?"

"It's the holidays. I'm spending time with family."

"Yeah. Right."

"Baby Brother, we're all that's left. No more mama, no daddy, no grandparents. And definitely no more brother."

Nate flinched when she said "brother."

"It's just us two Taylors," Julianne told him.

Nate lowered his eyes at her, trying to see straight through her.

"Oh, Nate. I know that look," Julianne remarked. "It's like I could hear your thoughts. You wish there was just one Taylor left, don't you?"

"What? You sound crazy."

"But am I correct?"

He flatly ignored her question. "Julianne, you're welcome to visit, but you can't stay long. We all have other plans, and I'm sure you wouldn't be interested in them."

"Try me. What are they?"

"Family stuff."

Now she gaped at him like he was insane.

"Julianne, it's really nice to see you. Happy Thanks-giving, fam. And I'll be more than glad to fix you that plate to go."

"Hmm. That doesn't sound like a warm welcome, Nate. Not warm, not inviting. Just wow. Anyway, I've got nothing better to do, and since you and your *family* are still here, I don't see why I can't join you all for the holiday. I noticed all your sisters-in-law are here cele-brating with you." She frowned. "How'd you manage that?"

Speechless, Nate turned his back on her and ap-proached the counter that was covered with a large array of food.

"What do you want to eat?" he asked.

"Give me a little bit of everything," Julianne squealed and turned around in a triumphant circle. Nate rapidly spooned up a measly serving of a couple vegetables, a few meats, and cranberry sauce. He hastily arranged everything on a paper plate and made sure to grab a plastic fork while he was at it. He handed everything to her. "Hurry and eat before your food gets cold."

She shoved the cornbread dressing inside her mouth and nodded. "Mmm, it's good. I'm so glad I came over." She began to head for the family room.

Nate reached out and tugged on her arm.

"What are you doing?" his sister asked.

"Um, you can stay here in the kitchen and eat. They are watching TV and talking."

"Great." She shrugged. "Sounds like a plan." Ju-lianne abandoned him while she went to join the others.

There was an empty space beside Alita; she quickly patted the seat. "Come over here and sit on this couch. Tell us what's been up with you, Julianne."

"Nothing much. I'm renting a house in Angleton, which I guess that's why Nate rarely comes to see me. It's only seventy-five miles from here. But he acts like I stay out in Louisiana or something."

"Even if he did, that would be no excuse for you not to be around each other. You two should be closer," Burgundy said. "You're the last two siblings alive." Rueben, their eldest brother, tragically died at twenty-two.

"I know. Hey, I try to see him when I can," she replied. "But I practically have to invite myself over. Why is that?"

Alita spoke up. "Why you do your older sister like that, Nate? I thought you was better than that."

"She's welcome to stop by at any time," Nate said in a strained voice. "But she has to call first and let us know she's on the way."

"I'm family," Julianne counter-argued. "I don't have to call first."

"Yes, you do and yes, you will. It's rude if you don't check to even see if anyone is here. We are always in and out. Don't waste your time coming over if you can't call first."

"Hmm." Julianne crossed her legs at the ankles and started to say something. But then Alita made a comment. "You know he thinks this is the White House."

Coco joined in. "And security at that place is always on high alert." She laughed.

"You know you're wrong for that," Burgundy said in jest.

Appalled, Nate grabbed the remote. He pumped up

the volume until he drowned out the women's cackling voices. But they leaned closer toward each other and continued their conversation.

"My brother-in-law is cool, but sometimes he acts odd," Alita remarked.

"That sounds about right." Julianne nodded. "Fat Nat used to go off by himself a lot when he was like six, seven years old. He was a loner when he was younger." There was a sadness in her voice, a downward turn of her mouth.

"Did you say Fat Nat?" Burgundy asked.

"Yep," Julianne replied. "Fat Nat was his childhood nickname. He was a little overweight when he was in elementary and junior high, but obviously that's not true anymore."

"Well, now, he has it going on in Houston. Maybe my son can get some pointers from Nate."

"Hmm, I'll have to think about that one," Julianne exclaimed with a mystery laugh.

"Don't wait too long," Alita told her. "Leno will be graduating high school in a couple years and he needs a heads-up fast."

"Oh, right, you're the one with that athletic son. He's gonna be rich and famous one day." Julianne finished up eating and set her plate to the side.

"I think Leno is already famous . . . for wanting to do the wrong thing," Alita said. "But we're still working on the rich part. In fact, what can we do to keep these little skeezers off of him? I'll bet Nate has all kinds of women lurking around the barbershop trying to find a baller. Or trying to get in good with the owner of the business."

Coco cut in. "I've been to Baller Cutz plenty of

times. And it ain't nobody in there but some crusty old men. Middle-aged guys trying to stay relevant."

"What you doing hanging out at the barbershop, Ma?" Calhoun asked Coco.

"What? I-I have business to take care of sometimes." She exchanged uneasy glances with Burgundy.

"Business like what?"

Burgundy explained. "Coco helps me out from time to time with certain tasks. I've given her the key to our PO box and a couple days a week she has agreed to go pick up our mail. Or she comes by to get two thousand flyers and brochures that need to be sent out via bulk mail. So she helps with that too, organizing them by zip code and putting the rubber bands around them. It gives my sister something to do while she's sitting around waiting on you," she said with a friendly wink.

"Oh, yeah? I didn't know that," Calhoun said.

"Just because you're her man," Alita said, "it don't mean you're supposed to know her every move. Coco, don't tell that boy—"

"Boy?" Calhoun said.

"Excuse me. I meant to say never let a man know every single thing about you. You hear me, Coco? I already know Dru don't roll like that."

"I'm just saying," Calhoun explained. "She usually be running her mouth when I get home letting me know everything that happened that day. I didn't know she be out there at the barbershop and the post office like *that*."

"Man, you act like she's going to check in at the crack house," Alita said sounding annoyed. "There're a lot of things men won't know."

"That's true, Alita," Julianne cut in. "And not just

men. Most people see what they want to see. Because
you may be impressed with this lovely house that Nate
Taylor bought for his wife, his family. You see expensive cars outside, a swimming pool in the backyard,
this pricy furniture and top-of-the-line electronics, and
all that damned food in the kitchen. Enough food to
feed an entire army, plus the homeless population."

Burgundy beamed at Julianne. "We enjoy the fruits
of our labor," she said. "I can't deny that."

"Because truth be told," Julianne continued, "when
we were growing up, we didn't eat steak and lobster
every day."

Burgundy leaned in, her ears itching. Nate saw all
the women staring at Julianne's mouth. He picked up
the remote and powered off the TV.

Julianne was saying, "Sometimes we ate bologna
for dinner."

"What?" Coco said. "We've had bologna sandwiches for dinner too. Maybe there's hope for me and
all my children."

Everyone laughed.

"I'm just saying," Julianne said. "At one point in
our life, money was tight. I could look clear through to
the back of the refrigerator. Or we would eat beans
from a can with weenies. No bread. Sometimes dinner
would be cereal with water. On a good night we'd have
grilled cheese sandwiches with a glass of Kool Aid. No
dessert. Kool Aid *was* our dessert, right, Nate?"

"Wow," Dru said. "Sometimes in my work, I come
across children with malnutrition. So bony and sickly
that it feels odd when they try to give me a hug. And I
never would have guessed that Nate went through that
as a kid. You just never know about people sometimes."

"Ha," Julianne said, "I could tell you some stories. Nobody knows people like family."

All at once, Coco, Alita, and Burgundy tried to chime in. Their voices fell on top of each other.

They were noisy and boisterous. The women agitated Nate. He stepped into the center of their gathering and blew a whistle till the voices died down.

"Hey, I have a little something I want to share with everyone," he said.

"What it is?" Burgundy asked.

"Actually, it's a brief video. Um, I loaded it in the DVD player, and if you don't mind, I want you all to look at it."

He started the disc, and soon the big screen displayed a video recording featuring all of the Morning Glory and Baller Cutz employees. The Morning Glory crew wore their grey uniform polos and pants. The Baller Cutz crew wore their black and red aprons. Men and women. Young and old. They all were smiling and waving. There was a big "Thank You, Nate Taylor" banner suspended from a ceiling. It looked like they had all gathered at a clubhouse.

One by one, several employees looked directly into the camera and spoke.

"I want to thank Mr. Taylor for that huge unexpected Christmas bonus," said one man who looked to be in his late forties. "Now I can buy my four kids some toys and get an entire turkey and all the side dishes. And I can pay my outstanding car note."

"Wow, Nate, that's pretty nice of you," Alita said. "Where's my bonus?" She stuck out her hand.

Several employees expressed their gratitude about having such a generous and thoughtful boss. He'd announced to them that they would each receive two-thousand-dollar checks, and they weren't shy about blabbing the amount he'd presented to them. In the history of both businesses, this type of windfall courtesy of its owner had never happened.

Burgundy exchanged an uneasy glance with Nate. "Aren't you full of surprises?"

He himself hates when the unexpected happens, but I'm glad for the staff. But then again that money is supplemental wages and it's taxable income for those clueless employees. Nate must be up to something.

She focused in on the recording and wondered who had filmed it.

"Mr. Nate is the best," declared one female, a waitress and single mom.

"Hmm, that's debatable," Alita said. She peered at the video. "I don't see Elyse thanking you. Did you give her any extra money? She needs it. Bad."

At hearing her name, Elyse froze up. Everyone turned around and smiled at her.

"Hell, she's an employee too," Alita continued. "She busts suds, sweating like a criminal in that hot-ass kitchen. Nate, you gon' have to do her right and give her two G's just like you did everybody else." Nate turned off the video and refused to face Alita, who by now had gotten off of the couch and was trying to force eye contact.

"Why am I talking to your back, Nate? Be a man. Look at me."

But he gave his attention to the disc player, fiddling with the knobs and tuning her out.

"That's a shame," Alita complained. "I just hope you do the right thing and give my sister the money within the next few weeks."

He finally turned around. "What would Elyse do with that kind of money?"

"Plenty. Like move in with me and help me pay rent. And that's all I'm going to say about that."

"The hell she is," he snapped back. "Ain't no way."

"And why not? Who died and put you in charge of my family?"

"Your mother."

Everyone gasped. Although Nate laughed and said he was joking, Alita wanted to punch him. But Burgundy came and stood protectively next to her husband.

"Everyone calm down, please," she said. "You have to excuse Nate. He doesn't like surprises at all. And this is our first time hearing about you wanting Elyse to live with you. It sounds strange. I thought you were busy raising Leno and hanging out with your new lover."

"And what's that got to do with the price of tea in China?"

"Never mind. We can talk about this later." Burgundy's voice trembled. So did her hands.

She never liked being embarrassed in front of a lot of people, and God knows she would not allow it to happen on her own turf.

"Let's go back to having a good time. Nate, turn off the video, and thanks for sharing that rare surprise with us. Ty, can you please find some music to play on the stereo? Wait. Never mind. I got this. Alexa," she said in a loud voice, "play Bobby Brown from the eighties."

Alexa said, "Shuffling songs by Bobby Brown."

Soon they heard the thumping bassline of "Don't Be Cruel."

Alita asked, "Don't be cruel? You trying to be funny?"

"I was five when this song came out. Mama would play that album all day every Saturday. Remember?" Burgundy snapped her fingers and rocked her head back and forth.

In short time, everyone forgot about money and Elyse, food, and arguments. Coco grabbed Calhoun, bounced around with her pregnant self, and belted out the lyrics. "Don't be cruel. 'Cause I would never be that cruel to *you*."

Even Dru and Ty started dancing. The rumbling of the music could be felt underneath their feet, the throbbing bass line pulsated through the wooden floor. The room sounded like melodies from a rhythmic tribe. Burgundy couldn't take it anymore. The music got to her so much that she felt she had to keep moving, dancing, and freeing herself from all the stress. She sang and twisted. Whooped and dipped. Burgundy grabbed Alita and hit her hip with her own, forcing her to do the bump.

Coco joyfully sang the lyrics and was happy to let her hair loose.

Alita immediately joined in. Yelling, twisting her ass, and moving her arms around. "Eighties music was the good shit. Sing that song, Bobby! With your crazy old ass."

Everyone sung the chorus, smiling and bonding.

Julianne tried to get Nate to dance; he flatly turned her down and bolted from the room.

The kids ran around screaming and yelling, collapsing to the floor and laughing hysterically.

Two hours later, it was difficult for Burgundy's guests to leave the holiday gathering. By then she was sweaty and exhausted, but peaceful and giddy. She held a drink in one hand, sipped on it, and tried to keep from falling over and bumping into walls.

"Y'all go ahead and make a plate. Make two or three. There's plenty. Me and Nate can't eat all this food." She burped and giggled.

"That's a damn shame. Spending that money and wasting it like you the federal government." That was Alita.

"Hush, Alita. I-I-I enjoyed you. All of you. Y'all come back now, you hear?" Burgundy said with a big smile as she saw everyone out the door. She waved goodbye and leaned her woozy head against the door and sighed in relief.

"Free at last, free at last, thank God almighty we's free at last."

CHAPTER 16

Cupid Strikes Again

In early December, Shade met Alita at her son's high school to watch him play on the varsity squad. They were three weeks into the season. The game was about to begin.

The cheerleaders wore their red-and-white uniforms, and the crowd made whistling sounds and yelled the moment the players entered the gymnasium.

Shade was seated next to Alita three rows up on the metal seats. The room was packed with students, staff, parents, and siblings. Alita felt excited with nervousness.

Leno's varsity squad was up; so far they had a perfect record, 13–0.

"There he goes." She beamed as Leno was introduced in the starting lineup.

"He takes after you," Shade told her. "Nice looking young fellow."

"Oh, hush."

"I mean it."

"I know you do." Shade quietly grabbed her hand. His fingers felt warm and strong. She couldn't stand fingers that felt cold, rusty, and dry.

Once tip-off occurred, Alita kept her eyes at the action on the gym floor. Shade mostly stared at Alita.

"Can I get you anything? You straight?" He doted on her throughout the first ten minutes.

Alita told him, "Nah, I'm not thirsty right now. I'm good." Shade rose up and left anyway. A few minutes later when he returned, she didn't argue when he handed her a cold bottled water.

"Here, drink this."

"Why? I told you I'm not thirsty."

"Yeah, but you've been screaming so much that you sound hoarse."

"That's because those refs are full of shit. I like things to be right. And I get pissed when they're not."

"I can see that."

He twisted off the cap for her, and she took a long swallow. She said thanks and shivered. Shade immediately removed his jacket and placed it over Alita's shoulders. She stared at him suspiciously.

He laughed, "It's freezing in this place. Here it is December and they acting like it's July. I noticed that you were trembling like you were cold."

She laughed and blushed again, feeling embarrassed for judging his kindness. Alita arranged the jacket so that it fully covered her shoulders. She inhaled. The jacket smelled like expensive cologne. It smelled just like him.

"What am I doing with a man like you?" she asked.

"What do you mean?"

"You seem decent. You not broke. You don't live

with your mama or your grandmama. You're educated, cultured."

"And?"

"Why would you want to kick it with me at a damned high school basketball game? You should be at a Rockets game checking out James Harden, or somewhere in New York watching the Knicks and sitting next to Spike Lee or something."

"Are you serious? C'mon, Alita. What's wrong with me being here with *you,* young lady?"

"That's the point. I'm not young. I-I—"

"Are you a centenarian?"

"A what?"

He laughed. "I meant to ask if you're a hundred years old."

"Hell, no."

"Then your young self needs to stop stressing, start relaxing, and simply enjoy the moment, with me. Do it! Because now you're starting to piss me off."

She gave in and laughed. "Hey now, Shade! I like that."

"I'm serious. Let's enjoy the moment. Just do it. Together."

As simple as his words sounded, they seemed as sweet as a slice of fresh watermelon. She nodded and told him all right. She was angry, so angry at herself for not being able to see the bigger picture, to realize that life was meant to be enjoyed with whomever you were blessed to have in your life.

Feeling sheepish, Alita grabbed his hand again and intertwined her fingers in his. He smiled at her, then winked. She wanted to explode with happiness.

"There you go again," Alita told him as she leaned against Shade and enjoyed the strength and the warmth of his masculinity. "You do all the right things, every little thing that make me feel so good."

"And it seems you want to destroy it all?"

"No, Shade, never that. I-I want every good thing that you give me. And that's what I'm scared of. Me admitting that this is what I want. The decent guy. A stable life. My son to do well—Woo, watch it now." She took her eyes of Shade and monitored Leno, who had just hit the floor in a hard fall.

"Get up, baby." She quickly rose to her feet. She bit her nails and mumbled a brief prayer. She only calmed down when Leno's teammates pulled him back up to his feet. She felt relieved when she saw her son walking around without assistance.

Alita sat down and groaned. "See, Shade, that's what I'm talking about. This game makes me crazy. I have to be here at every time he plays. I lose money when I come here because I turn down work, but you know what? I am having a good-ass time. And I wouldn't have it any other way."

Shade nodded. "Was that so hard to say? Feel? Think?"

"No, it wasn't."

"Now I want to ask you a question," he said. "How would you like for us to spend Christmas together? That's only in a few weeks. I don't know if you've made other plans."

"No, we usually hang out with the sisters. So, yes." Her heart pounded. She would have to introduce him to her sisters. Was she ready? Were they a couple?

"Yes, what?" he asked.

"I wanna see you around the holidays. May as well. But now I need to ask you something too, Shade."

"Ask away."

"What are we?" she said.

"What are we? You tell me."

Right then a timer went off indicating the end of the first half. Leno's team was trailing by four points. Alita stood up and said, "Can we go outside to the food truck? I'm hungry for some tacos, and I need to use the ladies room. Come on."

Shade followed right behind Alita as she walked down a few metal steps. Once she reached the floor of the gym, he grabbed her by the hand and led her to the main hallway. They broke away from each other outside the restrooms so she could go into a stall and relieve herself.

Once they reconnected again by the water cooler, Alita saw Shade talking to a female. Immediately, she wanted to react with rage. But Alita forced herself to remain calm, then she marched right up to them.

Alita heard the woman saying, "I just moved to this district. My daughter goes here. She's a freshman and a cheerleader."

"Oh, all right," Shade said. He turned around and noticed Alita standing idly by.

"Alita, meet Monica, one of my former co-workers. We used to be in the same department at Shell. Till she got laid off a few years ago." Monica smiled and extended her hand.

"And Monica," Shade said. "This here is my lady. You may call her Lita."

"Okay, I can call her Lita. And what do you call her, Shade?"

"You'd have to be there."

"Uh, that's enough." Monica frowned and smiled at the same time. "That's too much information."

"Don't ask and I won't tell," he said, laughing.

"Your man is so crazy, Lita. Good to meet you. He always had people in our department laughing. They would always frown or either crack up because his jokes were so corny and straitlaced."

"That's my man all right," Alita said.

Monica spoke to them a couple of more minutes, then said goodbye.

Once they were alone, Alita spoke up. "I really respect what you did, Shade."

"Do you?"

She leaned over and kissed him. Openly, unapologetically.

"Now you believe me?" she asked.

"Hell, yeah," Shade told her.

They rushed outside to a food truck, and he bought them some tacos and drinks. They made their way back to the stands.

"Cupid," Alita said aloud. "He struck again."

Shade beamed at her.

"Don't get me wrong. I like this, being here with you, feeling connected like this. It's been a minute." Alita wanted to cry tears of joy. To have such a decent man claim her felt like a dream. Shade seemed incapable of harming her, but it was still too early to know.

"When my mother was alive," Alita told him, "she and my dad had a pretty decent marriage. I mean, Daddy was always around. He never slept one night away from the house unless he had to take a road trip to visit our relatives in Mississippi."

"That's where you're from?" Shade asked.

"My father's side is from Jackson. I went there a long time ago when I was a kid. Hell, I barely remember anything about it. But I do remember every time we crossed that Horace Wilkinson bridge that goes over that big old river. There'd be all these cars, and trucks, and the traffic would slow down. And we'd be stuck on the bridge. And I was scared to death being stuck over all that water, but I tried to act brave."

"Your daddy could see right through it, huh?"

For a minute Alita could not reply. The thoughts of her childhood brought warm memories, but deep in her psyche, she knew that everything wasn't as rosy as she recalled.

"My daddy was my protector," she finally answered. "He always calmed me down, saying, 'We gon' be all right, Lita. You can close your eyes but you don't have to, 'cause we gon' be all right.'"

Alita smiled at the memories of the first man who had ever made her feel safe. "But anyway, all throughout my life Daddy was around a lot, being the only man in the family with all us women." She laughed. "He stuck around even throughout Mama's sickness. But I could tell that seeing her body break down like that hurt him. Seeing him watching her health fail made me run to him and tell him that things were okay. But they weren't." Alita's voice grew distant and hard. She knew all too much about how good things turned into bad. How good things appeared like they'd be good forever, but overnight they could change . . . and destroy an entire family.

"My daddy might've acted strong, but I can tell when a man is trying to show everyone that he wants to be there for his family, but deep inside he wants to escape. He wants out."

"And?"

"And so he did," she said with a pained laugh. "Once everything was over, Mama passed, and that body was finally in the ground, Daddy . . . what can I say? I think he mourned, briefly, then he was on to something else."

"Something or someone?"

"He remarried. Fast. Just like my ex—"

"Does it bother you that your ex-husband remarried?" Alita had shared that info with Shade just as soon as she heard how Leonard and Desiree up and went to the courthouse one day. She called Shade, venting and stressing, then she abruptly shut off the conversation once she no longer wanted to talk about it anymore.

"Hell, yeah," she finally said. "It bothered me."

"At least you're honest."

"I'm honest, but not in the way you think. My concern is always for our son."

Shade watched Leno score another two points. When he tossed the ball, it would seamlessly glide through the air, fall into the basket, like it was destined to do what it did.

"Your son seems fine, Alita. And you probably stress more than you need to."

"Is that a criticism? Because if I did not come to all these games . . . if I didn't care who Leno dates, who he hangs out with, then what kind of mama would I be?"

"Be concerned about him, Alita," Shade told her. "But don't kill yourself worrying about every detail. You couldn't fix his dad. You won't be able to fix his son."

To Alita that sounded awful.

"Meaning what?" she asked.

"Many things are not in our control."

"Hmm. That's what I was scared you were going to say." All at once it seemed as if the pleasing feelings of sheer joy that Alita had enjoyed with Shade were instantly deflated. Her emotions were so up and down that she knew she needed to learn how to manage them so she could stop tottering over from every negative thing she heard or experienced.

"I don't want to get religious on you," Shade continued.

"I must be psychic, because I knew this would happen one day," she exclaimed. "Go on."

"Somewhere in the Old Testament, there's a scripture that talks about how we make plans, but God's way prevails."

Alita looked like she didn't know what the heck he was talking about.

"What God wants is what will happen," he explained. "We don't really run a thing. Our job is to trust him no matter what happens."

"But . . . I don't like how that sounds."

"It's called reality, sweetheart. Are we only to be thankful and praise him when things go our way, but hate him when they don't?"

She could not reply.

"If God wants to stop anything bad from happening," Shade explained, "then he can do that, but what if he doesn't? And it's also true about good things. Nothing can stop them either. But we still want to trust even when things don't go our way."

Alita yearned to believe Shade, draw strength from his words, but to her it felt like closing her eyes and allowing someone else to lead her. And putting her life in another person's hands was something she'd been afraid to do.

Alita gave her attention back to the game. Leno charged his way down the court and caught the ball when it was passed to him. He slammed the ball in the basket and pumped his fist when the crowd yelled his name.

"You think my son got a chance to go pro?" Alita asked as she watched Leno earn eight more points.

"I can tell he has talent," Shade told her. "But it's going to take so many things to get him in the professional leagues. Just keep working with him. Surround him with the best coaches, decent mentors. He has as good a chance as any other young hopeful out here."

"Thank you." This time she meant it.

"But, sweetie," he said in a measured tone, "also know that only one in five million will make it in the NBA. And just like you're preparing him to play for the pros, you gotta also make sure he's prepared with his Plan B."

"You mean prepare him for a 'what if' because Leno might not make it? Is that what you're saying?"

"Alita," he said. "Don't get angry."

"I'm not angry—"

"Hear me out. Be quick to listen, babe, slow to speak."

She calmed down, nodded. "Okay. What were you about to tell me?"

"You're being a good mom if you tell your son the realities of the world, and I think you try to do that. And if you really want to keep it real, make sure Leno understands that studying is important, education is number one, and make him gain those transferable skills he needs to secure a good job. Because even those that go pro only play in the league for twenty years, tops. They must have a Plan B and stay prepared for the unexpected."

"I hear you," Alita responded. "Dream big, but not too big, because something can come and take your dreams away . . . see, that's exactly why I act like I do. The stuff you love, the thing you thought was yours, gets snatched away."

"Oh, it's all right to have dreams, to want big things."

She nodded. "It's hard to dream sometimes, you know what I mean?" she boldly told him. "Some people just luckier than others. You're a decent man, and you have a good relationship with God. I can tell he has your back. Well, me and Jesus don't roll that way. Maybe he's paying me back for all my sins. And I have more than you can count."

"Don't say that. He's for you, not against you. If you're all right with me, then you're all right with him too."

"Oh, so you God's chief of staff?" She was partially joking but kept her annoyance hidden. Although he encouraged Alita to be herself, she wasn't a hundred percent sure she could do that. If he really knew her for all her faults, would he still encourage her?

"I can't speak for God," Shade replied. "No one can. Not even the preacher man. But hey, if we feel led to say something, we give it a shot. That's fair, right?"

"I guess. I can't imagine God wanting to say anything to me. So if I gotta hear it through y'all, then I guess that's just how it's gon' be. *Going* to be."

He laughed. "Stop. It's okay. Relax. You are beautiful and acceptable the way you are."

He grew bolder and reached over to caress a mole on her neck.

"Hey!" Alita protested.

"Every inch of you is beautiful. Own it."

During the rest of the game, she pulled out a mirror, glanced at her reflection, and tried hard to see all the beautiful things that Shade saw in her.

CHAPTER 17

Tribal Matters

A couple of weeks later, Alita was at work. Ten minutes remained in her lunch break. She was about to call her brother-in-law and check on the bonus check for Elyse.

Before she could dial Nate's number, her phone began to buzz. Caller ID informed her it was Leonard.

"Hello," she said, sounding cautious.

"Oh, I am surprised you picked up."

"I'm surprised you're calling me, ex-husband. Aren't you supposed to be on your honeymoon?"

He laughed. "I just wanted to check on you. See how you doing." He paused. "Where are you?"

"Why?"

He quieted down as if he was listening for sounds that would give him a clue.

"Alita, I don't want anything much."

"We already know that—"

"But I did want to tell you that Leno has reached out

to me about taking him to Villanova. He wants to visit their campus."

"He does? Leno never told me that."

"He might have forgotten. So is that okay with you? What's your schedule like this week? We can coordinate so it won't impact you. In fact, Leno told me that on Tuesdays you work at that catalog customer service job." He paused. "Is that where you are right now?"

"Leonard, what do you really want? Get to the point."

"I want to go ahead and buy airplane tickets . . . for me, Leno, and my new wife, of course. We'd leave for Pennsylvania in a couple of days. It would just be for Thursday through Sunday."

"What? That means Leno would miss two days of school. It's getting close to the end of this term. He needs to stay focused on his classes."

"I know, but he really wants to go. And I want to enjoy the experience of taking him. It would be cool if my son could attend college, since you didn't go."

"Excuse me. You don't have a degree either."

"I know, and that's why I really want to help Leno explore a college campus since . . . you know, you would die first before you let him become a car salesman like his daddy."

Based on his comment, Alita knew that her son had told his dad the things she said about him behind his back. That pissed her off. But at the same time, his taking Leno on the trip could be a good thing. Yet, she felt left out. It seemed just like the time father and son visited the Alamo together.

"Um, Leonard. I don't know about this. I don't appreciate how you springing this on me at the last second. I'll have to think about it."

In reality, Leonard already knew that there was

nothing for her to think about. He'd been testing Alita since he first called, just to see how she'd respond.

"Too late for that, Alita. To be honest, the tickets have already been bought. They're nonrefundable. And Leno is going as far as I'm concerned. So be a good mother and help our son pack his suitcase. I'm picking him up tomorrow night around seven."

Leonard never even gave her a chance to argue.

He said, "Bye," then hung up.

"Fucking bastard," she said at the dead connection. "It was a set up all along. He made a fool out of me."

Alita's hand trembled uncontrollably. She didn't want to return to her job feeling and looking emotionally unstable. But she went back to her workstation and put on her headphones.

As soon as she sat down, the telephones started ringing.

She answered, giving her usual spiel, and tried to listen as a customer told Alita she wanted to place an order for some clothes and shoes.

"What is your name and phone number? Do you already have an account?"

She rolled her eyes as she verified the customer's identity.

"Okay, what you wanna order? You know the catalog number?" Alita knew that she wasn't going by the script. But right then she didn't feel like doing the right thing.

"What you say? You don't know the item number and you want me to look up every item for you?"

She mouthed "Fuck" and tried to make her voice sound happy and helpful.

"I will be so delighted to help you with your order today. Now you say you need some drawers? What kind, ma'am? What size? How many? What color? What fabric?"

Alita forced herself to act like she cared about all the clothes the old lady said she wanted to buy to impress her new twenty-year-old boyfriend.

"Yes, his name is Fred. And he is hot. I think this is the one."

"You's just a big ole fool, lady. That young man ain't thinking 'bout you. You wasting your money trying to impress him 'cause he probably lying up with some other bitch right now."

"Excuse me?" the caller said. "Were you talking to me?"

Before Alita could respond, a stranger walked up to her holding an envelope. He waved it at her and tried to get her attention.

"Um, may I place you on hold?" Alita didn't wait till the woman said okay. She cursed herself. She had hoped that her customer couldn't hear her when she was commenting about the lady's personal life, and Alita had already been written up once before for her unprofessional conduct.

Alita glanced up at the man who stared at her with no expression. How did he get in their secured area? Alita noticed one of her coworkers scurrying away from the room. Maybe she had let him in.

"Um, you're not supposed to be in here, sir. How may I help you?"

"Are you Alita Reeves Washington?"

"Who's asking?"

"I'm just wondering, because that's what your badge indicates right there. It says you're her, ma'am."

"Then why you asking, if you already know I'm Alita?"

"Fine, Alita. Nice to meet you. This special package is for you. Please sign."

Alita paused but signed his manifest. Once he left her cubicle, she shrugged, tossed the envelope on her desk, and tried to regain her composure. She resumed the conversation with her customer, completed the order, and disconnected the call. She stared at the envelope and hoped another call would come in. But since it didn't, she reluctantly opened the brown envelope and reviewed its contents.

After reading a couple of paragraphs, Alita powered off her computer, located her boss, and told him that she had a chronic headache and needed to go right away. Alita couldn't afford to leave work a few hours early. It meant she wouldn't receive a full day's pay. But she couldn't stay.

Burgundy didn't think anything unusual when Alita showed up unannounced at her door midafternoon. Burgundy typically left Morning Glory around two o'clock each weekday and came straight home unless she had errands to run or civic meetings to attend.

"Hey, Sis," she greeted Alita who, after ringing the bell, slumped in Burgundy's doorway with her eyebrows furrowed.

"Hey."

"Come on in, Lita. What's popping?"

"Are you busy tonight? Is Nate gonna be here?"

They retreated to the kitchen, where Alita made herself at home by perching on one of the breakfast bar stools.

"Nate and I were going to go to midweek service."

"He can go, but you can't. I need you." Alita explained that she had got off work early and would camp out at her house until that evening.

"Okay, Sis. What's going on?"

"Sister Day needs to be Sister Night. Tonight. I want all of us to meet. I can't wait till next month . . . I can't."

"Girl, you are scaring me."

"Can we make it happen?"

A few hours later all the sisters had gathered in Burgundy's family room. She completely understood the curious stares they gave her when she passed around a big bowl of chips and dip. She set up a table filled with sodas, water, iced tea, and freshly squeezed lemonade.

"I know this isn't the normal eats," Burgundy explained, but . . ."

"B, why you drag me out here tonight?" Coco said. "A new *Empire* episode is coming on."

"Tape it," Alita snapped.

"I am, smartass, but I still wanted to watch it live—"

"*I* called this sister meeting, not Burgundy. I really wanted to see y'all and talk to you and be around people that . . ."

"That love your dumb ass?"

"Gee, yeah, thanks, Dark Girl." Alita removed a letter from the brown envelope she'd placed on the coffee table. "Some jerk got me to sign for this today. I'm so mad I could scream."

Dru snatched the letter and began to read.

"Wow, this is messed up," Dru remarked. "Basically, it is stating that Leonard Washington is seeking full custody of his son. And he wants to hold a hearing and allow a judge to decide if he can have Leno. He claims Alita kept him from his child's life, that she has verbally and physically abused Leno, and that she has prevented Leonard from exercising his parental rights throughout his formative years. Well, we all know that's a lie from the pit of hell."

"I could have predicted this one," Coco responded. "My nephew balling so good; why wouldn't his father want to jump on that?"

"Tell you what. Let's talk about the November Sister Assignment," Burgundy suggested. "Not that it is the end-all or be-all, but it helps us all be of one accord and have the same mind if we take this seriously." She withdrew the document she had created that listed all the year's assignments in advance.

Burgundy laughed, then started reading. "Remember it says, 'Call, text, or email someone from the past to show it's not all about you.' Has everyone done that? Dru?"

She nodded. "Yeah. I tried to look up my high school sweetheart."

Coco said, "Ooh. You must be checking for Jerrod Dawson. I remember him. You two used to get on my damned nerves, y'all hung around each other so much. Remember that, B and Lita?"

They both nodded.

Coco laughed. "Umph, well, look at you with your sneaky self. Does Ty know what you did? And were you able to find your ex, Dru Boo?"

"Not yet."

"Not yet, as in Ty doesn't know what you doing behind his back."

"Knock it off, Coco. I'm just trying to complete the November assignment like everyone else. I'm not keeping anything from anybody," she calmly replied.

Coco smirked. "Yeah, right. Anyway, how long does Dru have to get herself into some trouble by looking up her ex?"

Burgundy rescued Dru, whose eyes began to flash with anger. "Coco, sweetie. We're not doing this assignment so we can get into trouble. We might want to look them up so we can forgive someone, or we might need closure from somebody. That's all. If we're good to someone from our past, we can prove that we are the bigger person."

Alita, who'd been quiet all this time, was about to open her mouth.

"Don't even try it, Lita," Coco warned her. "Enough with the fat jokes. I'm only this big because I'm carrying a baby."

"You can believe that lie if you want to," Alita said with a hearty laugh. Then she sobered up. "There is nobody from my past that I'm trying to get in touch with."

"Maybe the person from your past that you need to get real with is Leonard," Burgundy said.

"Are you telling me that I need to forgive him for filing on me?"

"I'm just saying there's probably a good way to work this assignment into what you're going through right now."

"What?" Alita said, feeling like she was about to explode. "Meaning?"

"Meaning no matter how hard it is and how much you don't want to do it," Burgundy replied, "you're going to have to find it within yourself to make this thing with Leonard not just be about your feelings."

Alita snatched the strap of her denim handbag and arranged it across her body. She stood and fled the family room.

"Alita," Coco called after her. "Bring you bony ass back here. You called this meeting, and you damn sure not leaving after five minutes."

"Sister sad," Elyse said softly.

"Yes, Elyse," Burgundy said. "We're 'sister' sad, but for Alita's sake we gotta be strong. We're Reeveses. We know how to go through hard times, no matter how hard things get."

Alita sprinted back into the family room. She leaped toward Burgundy and shoved her chest until the woman fell backward with her legs awkwardly sprawled on the sofa. Alita practically lay on top of her, her face close to Burgundy's face, as she stared at her sister's mouth.

"Dang, what you do that for? Get off me." Burgundy wiggled her tiny body underneath Alita, but the older sister solidly pinned her to the sofa.

"I'm sick of you talking all this crap when you ain't the one that has to go through it. You always give silly-ass advice that sounds good to you, but it means nothing to me. Until you walk a day in my shoes, don't open your mouth any more about my life. And unless you really ready to help me, really help a sister out, shut your damned mouth, because until you exit your ivory castle with the Italian floors and step inside my, or Elyse's or even Coco's shoes for a day, you know nothing about real life."

Breathing so hard that it sounded like she was having an asthma attack, Alita gave herself a couple more minutes to control her temper, then she angrily lifted herself off Burgundy.

The second oldest Reeves sister had never been in a fistfight a day in her life. It just wasn't who Burgundy believed herself to be. She had always been dignified. Self-controlled. A lot like her daddy. But not one hundred percent like him. This is why, after she composed herself but then thought about her sister's vicious verbal attack, something uncontrollable rose up in Burgundy.

She got in Alita's face. "You think you're the only one that knows trouble, Lita. Huh?"

Alita withheld her anger and said nothing.

"Just because I don't wallow around in sorrow and because I don't call all my sisters up every single time I feel depressed, or miserable, or frustrated," Burgundy continued, "it doesn't mean that I don't have real issues, real problems. Because I do." She ran over to her purse, opened it up, and pulled out a dildo. It was big, hot pink, very wide, and made of latex. It could also light up when she squeezed it.

"Does a truly satisfied woman have sex with sex toys?" she asked.

"Some do," Coco said. "They get it in any way they can. Literally."

"I'm being serious," Burgundy told her.

"You're being ridiculous," Alita cut in. "Just because you're kinkier than I thought and you enjoy getting off on one of those things . . . seriously, B? That's all you dealing with? That ain't shit. Why'd you get one anyway? Nate's dick not working like it used to?"

"No." For once Burgundy decided not to put on airs. "Not anymore. Not how I want it to."

"But why is that thing in your purse? Oh, never mind," Alita said.

"Oh, Burgundy." That was Dru. Coming from Burgundy, that topic seemed so taboo that Dru barely knew what else to say. But right then she realized that all the sisters had their own issues.

Coco only allowed a sad shake of her head.

And Elyse gave a tiny, feeble grunt that everyone ignored.

"Okay. Big deal," Alita finally said after thinking about the situation. "So you get your rocks off on your plastic boyfriend, your chick stick, your weapon of ass destruction, as some like to call it. It ain't the end of the world. I'd still trade places with you, my sister, in a minute. Would you trade places with me?"

When Burgundy failed to reply, Alita knew she had the answer to her question.

"But check this out, y'all. This is why I called this emergency meeting," Alita continued. "Not only did Leonard spring this legal shit on me, but I also got fired from my customer service job."

"Oh, Sis," Dru murmured. "I'm so sorry. But what did you do to get fired?"

"Yes, anyway," Alita said in a loud voice. "On top of that, Leonard didn't ask me, he *told* me he's flying Leno out of state to go to Pennsylvania on Thursday. To go on a college campus tour and see if he likes it enough to pay their athletic director any serious attention. Villanova been reaching out. And so Leonard *told* me that I need to have Leno ready on Wednesday night so he can spend the night with his dad. There is no co-parenting here. Just him giving orders. Him living life exactly the way he wants, and I'm just supposed to say okay and obey him." Alita quickly brought them up to speed on every unfavorable thing that Leonard Washington was doing. Last-minute things. Things that made Alita's head spin. Things that made her want to kill somebody.

While it was true that some couples who broke up had amicable dealings with each other, it wasn't always the case for others. Alita was *the* poster child for the unusual cases.

"So, Lita, what you gonna do?" Coco asked in a serious tone. "You gon' let Leno go on the trip?"

"Hell, no. When it comes to Leonard, I'm afraid to

let my baby out of my sight." She gasped for breath as if the thought of anything happening to Leno was unthinkable. "Him hanging out with his dad in Houston is one thing, going out of state is another. And this is where you come in. I need a favor. Can one of the sisters let Leno stay at your place on Wednesday and Thursday? Maybe Coco can pick him up from school on Wednesday and he can go spend the night with one of you. Leonard is not taking him to Pennsylvania. And I refuse to give him what he wants when he's hardly ever given me what I want."

"But legally, can you do that, Alita?" Dru wanted to know.

"Do I look like I care about it being legal? Hell, is it legal for Leonard to try and take my only child away from me . . . after all this time?"

"He's just being greedy. He wanna hurt you, Sis," Coco said. "That's how men get when they feeling themselves. He's got that really nice house, a pretty new wife, some new pep in his step."

"She ain't that pretty." Alita refused to give in to the positive statements Coco was saying.

"You right, Lita," Coco continued. "Desiree isn't pretty. That woman is gorgeous. She looks like a damned celebrity and acts like one too. She's the upgrade."

"If you know what's good for you, you'd stop talking right now, Dark Skin. And forget about Leno coming to stay with you. Dru, I hate to ask you this, but can you please watch him for me? You and Ty have no drama in your house. I trust you to do the job."

Dru squirmed in her seat. "I dunno, Lita. I can't help you."

"C'mon, Dru Boo. We family. We supposed to be

there, be supportive. Even you said that at one of our Sister Day meetings."

Everyone glanced at Dru as she easily responded. "I remember what I said, Lita, but Ty and I are actually having problems."

"Bullshit," Alita said.

"I know it sounds shady. But it's the truth. I swear on a stack of Bibles."

"I don't believe it," Alita said. "You're just being your usual self-centered self. You don't care about me and what I go through. You just like B, with that 'my life is perfect, don't get me involved with your drama' type of attitude. Damn."

With her options seeming to run out, Alita looked like she had no idea how to handle her problem. There was no way she'd let Leno and Leonard and his new wife get on that plane and travel more than 1,400 miles to enjoy a pleasant weekend in the northeast. But if no one was willing to help her out, what else could she do but let him go? A painful lump formed in her throat.

"Is this how family do? Turn their backs on you when you going through a little something?"

"That's the thing," Dru said. "You are always going through something, Alita. And yes, we are family, we love you, but you can wear out your welcome when we constantly are expected to cheer you up, bail you out, magically fix up every wrong thing that's happening in your life. A life that you chose. Why we have to rescue you when you make these poor choices?"

"Are you serious, Dru? Because I don't remember you having that attitude when Coco is going through it." Alita asked.

"Alita, you're the oldest, and you ought to know better by now."

Alita came this close to pouncing on Dru, just taking off her shoe and hitting her, pulling her hair, and shaking her one good time. But Burgundy picked up on Alita's violent intention and quickly came and sat beside Alita. She held her hand, talked soothingly.

"Don't worry, Sis. Leno can come over here. I will pick him up. He can hang out with us until further notice. But I do have a concern," Burgundy said. "If Leonard gets wind of us hiding his child, we don't want it to turn into a custody battle. I haven't seen him in a while, but he could easily look up on the internet, see where we live, and start all kinds of trouble even in this gated community. We have to fully think of the implications of this and come up with a concrete game plan. This is serious business, Lita. We want to help, we will help, all of us, in one way or another, but let's put our heads together."

The sisters all gathered around Alita, forming a protective circle. They came up with every single question they could think of, plotting, scheming, and trying to act like a true family tribe, laying aside their own personal agendas and thinking more about the one in need. Burgundy reminded them that they were Reeveses. "This is what Mama would want us to do. She's smiling down from heaven and is happy that we're figuring out how to help each other."

By the time they were done talking, Alita was all smiles, reenergized and filled with confidence instead of moping around with anger and dread.

That Tuesday evening, Alita stole Leno's cell phone. She knew his password, and she quickly looked up Zaida's phone number. Then she fished around till she found another number. She promptly placed a couple more calls. She knew that Leno was in his bedroom, hopefully studying. Alita sat on the couch and waited.

Ten minutes later, the doorbell rang.

Alita opened the door and greeted Tiffanie, one of Leno's high school classmates that had a deep crush on him. The girl was wearing a T-shirt bearing the school colors, along with a cute pair of shorts. She carried a backpack decorated with all kinds of key chains, lapel pins, colorful buttons, and tiny bottles of hand sanitizer.

"Hi there," Alita said. "Don't you look cute? Glad you could make it. How'd you get here?"

"My mom drove me." Tiffanie hesitated. Alita peeped over her head and looked outside. "Oh, your mother waiting on you so she can give you a ride home? Don't even worry about it. I'll drive you home later. I have a feeling you might be here a while."

"That'll work. Thank you, Mrs. Washington."

Alita laughed and invited the girl farther inside the apartment. She offered her a drink and asked her to be seated. This was the second time Tiffanie had been over to their place. A few weeks ago she had finagled her way over to Leno's apartment after school one day when Zaida was sick and had missed classes. Tiffanie noticed how much Leno had been coughing and sniffling while he was in school; she offered to go home with him and fix up a homemade remedy that would get rid of a nasty cold. He said okay. That's when Tiffanie had first met Alita, a woman who seemed to be excited to see her with her son.

Right then as she sat on his couch again, Tiffanie felt really good that Leno's mom had taken to her so fast.

She and Alita chatted for a couple more minutes. Then Alita excused herself. Minutes later the doorbell rang.

Tiffanie sat and waited. The bell rung again. She heard a light knock. But neither Leno nor his mother came out. Tiffanie got up and went to open the door. The second that she saw Zaida Rojo, she felt a sudden burst of energy. Tossing back her hair, she said, "Hi. May I help you?"

Zaida appeared stunned. She didn't know what to say at first. Then she coughed and cleared her throat.

"What are you doing here, Tiffanie?"

"I was invited. By his mom."

Zaida looked crushed. "That's impossible. His mom knows that I'm Leno's girlfriend."

"Obviously she doesn't, because the woman called me on my phone and asked me to come over." Tiffanie's eyes darkened.

"You have no business being over here, even if she did ask you to come. You know he's my man."

"Zaida, girl, shut the fuck up. He's not glued to you. He can hang out with whoever he wants. Especially if his mom doesn't mind."

Zaida tried to enter the apartment. But Tiffanie slammed the door shut before the girl could get in. Zaida dialed Leno's number. He answered.

"Hey, what's up?" he said.

"I'm at your spot. At the apartment. Standing outside your front door that got slammed in my face. Leno, what the fuck is Tiffanie doing over at your place?"

"What? She's here? I didn't even know."

"Don't lie, Leno. Y-you've never lied to me, right?"

"You know better than that, Zaida."

"Where are you, babe?" she asked. Zaida thought about how she did not trust Tiffanie and how the girl could just be toying with her for the hell of it.

"Are you even at home, Leno?"

"Yeah," he said. "I'm here chilling with my mom. I was in my room. Mom came in. She said I had company. But I thought it was Phil."

"Leno, your company is not Phil. Hurry and open the door. Tiffanie won't let me in. What the fuck's wrong with her?"

"Uh, all right. Be there in a sec."

By the time Leno reached the front door, his mother had already let Zaida inside. Then Alita joyfully gazed at both young ladies.

Zaida started in immediately. "Leno, you busted. I can't believe this, Papi. Why are you doing me like this? We're in a relationship."

"People break up all the time," Tiffanie chimed in. "And you two aren't married. He can be friends with and date anybody he wants. Me and him are chilling."

"Stop lying, Tiffanie," Zaida insisted.

At that point, Tiffanie unzipped her fancy backpack and pulled out an article of clothing. She unfolded Leno's letterman jacket, gave it a good sniff, and said to Zaida, "If we weren't cool, why did your man let me hold this for over a month?"

"Leno?" Zaida said. "How'd she get your jacket? Don't lie to me."

Before he could respond, the doorbell rang again. Alita answered. It was Shamicka Beach, another high school classmate, looking tall, regal, and stunning.

Zaida took one look at Shamicka and bolted out the doorway, rushing to the sidewalk and heading as far away as she could get.

Leno started to run after her, but Alita stopped him. "No, no, no, son. Never want anyone that doesn't want you. She's mad now, but give her time. Let her have some space. I promise you, she'll get over it."

Alita closed the door and feigned innocence; it was an attitude that infuriated Leno, but he knew better than to cause a scene.

"I thought you all would want to study together," his mother explained to him and the remaining girls. "I know the semester is almost over, and you have tests coming up. So I set up this study date."

"That's true, Mrs. Washington, and I'm glad you thought of this," Shamicka said. She came and sat down at the couch and was about to pull out her textbook.

"Oh, no, sweetie, I've set up everything so you can study at our dining room table. Go right ahead. Make yourselves at home."

The following day, Leno was so miserable and angry at Alita, all he could do was try and talk to Zaida, but she blocked his calls. Every time he attempted to approach her at school she told him he needed to get his priorities straight, then she avoided him.

Later that evening, when it came close to the time that he was to be picked up, Leno ignored his dad's texts.

Burgundy was visiting them at the time. She sat back and watched as Alita peppered her son with questions. "So you sure you don't want to go on the college tour, son?"

"No!"

"I thought you were looking forward to spending time with your dad." She paused. "And come to think about it, Leonard has never taken you on a trip any-where since the day you left fifth grade. I wonder why all of a sudden he wants to get involved with these college campus trips. Have you ever wondered about that, Leno?"

Leno let out a curse word. He left, and they could hear his door slam when he went into his bedroom. Later on Leno finally answered his phone and let his father know he wasn't in the mood to go out of town. When his father told him off, Leno promptly hung up on him. He did not hesitate to take up Burgundy's offer when she suggested that he needed to get away from everything, and he could come stay with her for the weekend.

Leonard Washington was furious that he had wasted money on the nonrefundable airplane tickets and called Alita to complain about it, but Alita did not care one bit.

Later that night Alita got on the phone and thanked Burgundy for taking in Leno.

"How's he doing, B?"

"He hasn't eaten a thing."

"Oh, give him another hour. He'll tear through your refrigerator real good."

Burgundy laughed. "It's fine. I feel bad for him, though. He looks depressed, Lita."

Tiny needles pricked at Alita's conscience, but she ignored them. She was the parent. He was the minor, and in this world, the parents held all the power.

"I hate to hear that he feels sad about that stupid girl. But he don't need her. And he can't be letting his dad take him somewhere far from me and put a lot of crazy shit in his head. I did what I had to do as a mother to protect him and to send a strong message to Leonard. He can't screw me in the ass and expect me to like it. He can't rape me and expect me to not retaliate."

"You are being overly dramatic, Alita."

"How about this? How would you act if someone tried to take away Nat and Sid? You'd act like a crazy person and would do anything to protect them just like I did."

Burgundy did not argue.

After a few days of nonstop threats, Alita met up with Leonard in person and finally managed to calm him down. He agreed to rethink his custody lawsuit.

"Don't do this, Leonard, please. Not now. Enjoy your wife. I've always let you get Leno whenever you've wanted to. As long as you keep him here in Houston. Let's stick to that plan, please; for his sake and yours, don't do this full custody thing."

Leonard stared at his ex-wife and suddenly had a change of heart. He promised he'd back off, and Alita felt like one good deed deserved another.

"Thank you, Leonard." She choked back tears. "I hate legal shit."

"I know you do."

"And somehow, I will pay you back the money you lost on buying Leno's ticket."

"Don't worry."

"How much was it?" she asked.

"Four hundred."

"Oh, shit."

"Don't worry about it."

"Okay, then. If you say so," she told him. "Thank you. Thank God."

They sadly stared at each other, shook hands, and called a truce.

CHAPTER 18

I Made a Mistake

Coco was home with her kids. She was in the living room trying to place decorations all over her Christmas tree, a surprise gift that Calhoun brought home the night before. She recalled how last night she had given her man a suspicious look when he dragged the live tree through the front door. It smelled like pine cones and left a trail of debris across the hardwood floor.

"Hello to you too, beautiful," Calhoun said, ignoring her stare. He stopped to give her a kiss on her cheek, then set up the tree in the corner of the room next to the fireplace. He told her to find something pretty to put on it.

"You dumbass. We've never had a tree before," she hollered at him. "I don't have any ornaments lying around. I have nothing."

"Then our good smelling tree will be looking crazy."

"Why don't you go get the rest of the stuff and not be so half-assed?" she said, challenging him.

Her directness brought on an entirely new argument. They spent the next hour fighting, until Calhoun begged Coco to shut up and come give him some loving. She complained but obliged. Even though she was twenty-four weeks pregnant, and didn't really want to have sex because she felt self-conscious about her size, she did it anyway. Anytime he asked. Every time he asked.

And now, she felt happier because Calhoun brought home several bags of ornaments. He even brought lawn decorations, an inflatable Santa Claus and reindeer that lit up. It was beginning to really feel like Christmas.

Coco was impressed with the pine cones, red-and-gold decorations, and the strands of red, white, and purple lights.

"Glad you like everything," Calhoun said. "Make everything pretty for us and make this place feel like a home."

"I thought we already had a home."

"We do, but we can make it even better. I know what you going through. I know I can do better."

"Thank you for saying that."

"I ain't blind. Not a total asshole."

"Thanks for saying that too."

He laughed and pressed his thick, wet lips against her neck and made a trail of kisses.

"Ma, you know I gotta work today, but I trust you to do a good job." He swatted her on the butt. "I'll be back later to see what you working with." He winked and left.

Coco ran to the window and watched as Calhoun drove off. She yelled for Cadee to bring her a footstool.

Coco concentrated on placing ornaments on the lower part of the tree. She felt guilty when she saw little Cadee was all out of breath as she tried to drag the footstool across the floor.

"Stop making all that noise. And be careful. We can't be scratching up the hardwood. What if I want to sell this place one day?"

Cadee started crying and stopped dragging the stool.

"Bring it here. Oh, never mind. Damn. I'm too pregnant to be standing on this stool anyway. If I didn't know any better I'd think my man was trying to kill me."

Coco knew that Calhoun would be at work for several hours. She used her cell phone to call Q, feeling deliciously naughty about what she was getting ready to do.

"What you doing?" she asked Q, trying to sound nice but overly sexy.

"I'm out and about. Getting some gas. 'Bout to go get something to eat. Why? You miss me?"

"Shut up, fool. Stop playing."

"I ain't playing. You know what I told you."

Coco couldn't believe Q was counting the days till she wasn't pregnant anymore.

"Yeah, I remember, but I wish I could forget. Anyway, drop everything you doing. I need help with my Christmas tree."

"What kind of help?"

"I was hoping you could help me put some decorations on the top. I can't reach it."

"Where your man at?"

"Your best friend is at work just like you know he is. Don't even front."

Coco's palms began to feel moist. She never liked to talk to Q on the phone for longer than a minute or two. She never wanted Calhoun to check her phone records and know she was holding long conversations with his boy.

"So what you gonna do?" she asked him. "Can you come?"

"Oh, baby, you know you can make me come anytime, anywhere."

Coco's face flushed. She hung up on him and wished she had never called. She didn't know why she even bothered with him. Their one sexual encounter rated a seven out of ten, nothing to jump up and down about. But Q's swagger made her curious and gullible enough to play with the fire he presented to her each time he came around.

Ten minutes later Q showed up. She made Chloe and Cadee go to their room and watch their little brother.

She came back to the living room and barked orders.

"Hurry up," Coco said. "I don't have all day."

"That's not my problem, though."

'In a way it is," she retorted. "Because when you come over here, you on a time schedule, so make it quick."

Q placed all kinds of ornaments on the tree as Coco handed them to him as he stood on the ladder. Every time she raised her hand toward him, her chest rose up. And when her chest rose up, so did his eyes. He stared at her breasts, her luscious lips, and that huge behind. He nodded with approval and licked his lips.

The room smelled like pine cones and peppermint sticks, cinnamon and bayberry candles. The few lights that Coco wrapped around the tree were now twinkling off and on.

"This shit is popping," he said, impressed with how things were coming along. "I'm feeling kinda sick, though . . . helping you out like this."

"Why? Are you saying it should be your tree?"

"Not just that. It's Christmas," Q explained. "That boy is my seed. You should be my woman."

"Boy, you must be out your mind."

"Boy?"

Chance waddled into the living room happily talking to himself. He smelled like apple juice and cheese. A speechless Q quietly observed Chance. He was well dressed in his red "Let It Snow" pajamas. And the boy had the fattest cheeks Q had ever seen.

Q suddenly stretched out his arms gesturing at the boy. Feeling happy and excited, Chance galloped toward Q.

"No, no, uh uh. That ain't happening. You gon' have to leave." Coco ran and scooped up their son. "I think he's getting too attached to you."

"That boy ain't dumb. He knows—"

"He's only two. His brain ain't developed. He knows nothing."

"But I do."

Q was one of those types who barely showed emotion. He always acted as if nothing bothered him. But by the pained look on his face Coco could clearly see that was a lie.

"Look, I'm sorry, Q." She stopped handing him ornaments. "I think this is enough. You did good."

"We only half done."

"We'll have to call it a day. I can do the rest myself."

"Stop lying."

"Or I can get Chloe to stand on the ladder for me."

"Coco, motherhood is a waste on you. You still ain't shit."

Coco gasped. "What you say? How dare you call me out with your irrelevant ass." Coco knew she demanded the impossible: for Q to be a loyal keeper of her sordid secrets. She expected him to play along with a game that no longer felt like fun. It felt torturous and deceitful.

"Look, Q. I'm sorry. I'm pregnant, I'm stressed. My blood pressure has been high. I'm sorry."

Q told her, "Okay. It's cool." He sighed and said, "I guess I'm done with the tree. But before I go, I have something for little man."

"Something like what?"

He hesitated, then reached in his jacket pocket. He pulled out a Chevy racing car with spinning wheels, headlights, the hood that could open, doors that opened and closed. It even had louvers, and the entire thing was painted blue and white, Chance's favorite colors.

"What are you doing, Q?"

"It's Christmas."

"But this wasn't the agreement, and you know it."

"I still got rights." His voice sounded threatening. And hearing him sound so adamant made her heart race.

Chance's eyes lit up. "Give me," he said.

"Dammit, Q."

"I bought this toy a couple weeks ago. It's a good time to give it to him."

"Lord Jesus, please don't do this. I made a mistake. A huge mistake." Her voice trembled. "Q, I'm sorry, but you gon' have to go. Now!"

Chance screamed at the top of his lungs. Coco heard a door fly open. Chloe and Cadee peeped out of their room, took a look at Q, and their eyes widened.

"Get your nosy asses back in that bedroom before I beat the black off you."

The girls screeched and slammed the door shut. That made Chance cry even louder.

"How can you talk to kids like that? You fool, don't you ever talk to them kids like you crazy."

"You can't tell me how to raise these damn kids," Coco argued. "Now get the fuck out."

"I can tell you what to do with mines."

"No, you cannot."

"Oh, this is some bullshit." Q's voice croaked. He kicked the wall as he walked past. His shoe left a black mark the size of a quarter.

"And you got the nerve to call me crazy?" Coco felt dizzy with anger and nearly fell over from stress. "Q, man, why you do that? Really? See, that's what I'm talking about. I'm in no condition to deal with all this stress you putting on me."

"I'm putting on you? You expect me to pretend like—"

"This is not going to work, and you know it's not. Stop tripping. You yourself said we gotta keep it on the low. So play your role."

Q getting to see the boy felt like a mistake, but not on his part. It felt as if his feelings did not matter. And he wondered why couldn't a father openly acknowledge his kid?

With the toy still clutched in his hand, Q glanced at his son.

Chance raised his own hand, his hopeful eyes bright

and clear and completely glued on the blue-and-white car.

"Give me," Chance demanded again.

"No, baby boy," Coco quickly told him in a much nicer voice. Then to Q she said, "Please leave."

When Chance began to cry again, nearly snorting from anger, Q gave Coco a hateful look. And when Chance dropped to the floor and kicked his little legs in the air, Q had had enough. He opened and slammed the door so violently that the walls shook. Paint chips fell from the ceiling. Coco heard Q's car start and its tires screeched as he backed out of the driveway and sped off.

"I hate I ever messed around with that fool."

Coco took time to calm down Chance. He was screaming and yelling like he'd been bitten. She went to the refrigerator and filled his sippy cup with some apple juice and diluted it with a little bit of water. She said sweet words to him, and sang to him and forced him to take a nap. Then she hurriedly swept the floor and mopped and carefully got rid of the paint debris.

She wound a long string of garland around the tree and nearly broke her neck trying to set a wire angel on top. She had the girls climb up a tall ladder and put the rest of the ornaments on the tree.

Coco stood back and admired her handiwork, feeling happy and proud that the decorating had turned out nicely; she loved how the lights seemed to magically illuminate the entire room. And she couldn't wait until Calhoun got home so she could see the look on his face.

Coco talked to her girlfriends on the phone to pass the time. A couple hours went by. She hadn't heard from Calhoun since he left, and her mind raced.

She picked up her cell, thought about calling, but changed her mind.

She played games with the kids until another several hours had passed. By then it was bath and bed time. She gave the girls a bath together and washed up Chance real good. She was so drowsy that her eyes opened and closed every time she yawned. After the kids climbed into bed, she looked out the window at the driveway, but Calhoun's parking spot was empty. She thought about going out and searching for her man, but her car was low on gas.

"Fuck it." She dialed Calhoun's cell. It went straight into voice mail.

She punched in Q's number and hung up before it could ring even once.

Coco lowered herself to the floor. She scooted back until she sat against the living room wall. She stared blankly at the pretty blinking lights, listening to classic carols and singing softly until exhaustion forced her to fall asleep.

By the time Christmas Eve arrived, love, peace, joy, and harmony seemed to raise people's spirits. Even though she still hadn't found another job, Alita wasn't worried or angry.

In fact, she spent that afternoon baking a few dozen peanut butter cookies, a chocolate cake, and two apple pies. She carefully packaged the baked goods, set them in the trunk of her car, and drove off. She arrived unannounced at Burgundy's door around five-thirty that evening. Darkness had just settled, and the evening air was marked by a crisp, wintery chill.

Alita pulled on her long-sleeved jacket and was glad when Nate answered the door.

"You remind me of Julianne," he told her in a not-so-nice manner. "You just show up at my house whenever you ready."

"Yeah, um, thanks for letting me in through the gate. I wanted to drop by here tonight and give you all these desserts. I thought I'd get to spend the holiday with you all tomorrow, but I won't. I'm supposed to hang out with my boo thang and Leno. But you can eat the dessert and think of me."

"How nice," Nate dryly told her. "Can't wait."

Before Alita could give him a piece of her mind, Natalia and Sidnee entered the hallway. They both squealed in delight when they started sniffing and noted the sweet aroma of fresh apples, peanuts, and chocolate icing.

"How's my two little nieces?" Alita asked and gave them each a hug.

"We're good," Natalia said. "My daddy is so nice. He gave me a Christmas present just now, even though it's not Christmas yet."

"Oh, don't you mean Santa Claus gave you the gift, Natalia?"

"No, Auntie. My daddy is my Santa Claus." She went and held his hand as he patted the top of her head.

Alita felt like she was about to get even more annoyed.

"How nice. Anyway, is she here?" Alita sweetly asked her brother-in-law.

"She who?"

"Who else? Burgundy!"

"Don't sound so impatient, Alita. Remember, two of your sisters stay here."

"Right! My bad."

"It's cool. The wife is doing some last-minute shopping. I will put your desserts in the kitchen and let her know you stopped by." Nat tried to grab the food, but Alita shook her head.

"That's okay. I can wait here till she gets back. I need to tell her something."

Nate gave her an odd stare. "Sorry, but that won't be necessary. If you need to tell Burg something, just pick up the phone and give her a call. She's at the mall. I think Target closes at eleven, so you might be waiting awhile."

"Nate, are you trying to get rid of me?"

"No, no. I just don't want you wasting your time hanging around when Burgundy won't be back for hours. I know you have better things to do on Christmas Eve."

"Yep, like visiting Baby Sis. I'll go up to her room for a minute."

Nate looked as if he wanted to say more, but he changed his mind.

Alita ran up the front staircase. She walked over to Elyse's bedroom door and twisted the knob.

"Damn, why she lock the door?" Alita reached inside her purse and took out her pocket knife.

She unsecured the lock, then entered the room.

"Baby Sis?"

Elyse's yellow-and-white-striped comforter remained unruffled, pillows intact.

By sheer instinct, Alita ambled toward the closet and swung open the door. Elyse was on the floor, sprawled sideways. A wool blanket covered her from the waist down.

Thinking her sister was asleep, Alita got on her

knees and gently shook her until she stirred. The closet smelled like sweat and ammonia.

Alita violently shook the girl again. Elyse sat up with a start and quickly pulled the blanket up to her chin.

"Sorry if I scared you, Sis. You all right? Why you in here?"

Elyse smiled awkwardly. Her eyes reminded Alita of Chance after he'd been crying.

"Baby girl, why you in here all by yourself?"

Elyse smiled even wider and nervously played with a black hat that she was wearing. She didn't say a word.

"Elyse, we need to talk. Last time we had a real good conversation, and I loved how you opened up to me, but now you acting scared again." She paused and closely examined Elyse and everything around her. "You haven't done anything to hurt yourself, have you?"

Elyse's eyes widened. She shook her head no. Her eyes swept past Alita. Nate was standing in the doorway, quietly staring down at her. He reminded her of a judge sitting on his bench, and she felt like the criminal waiting to be sentenced.

Alita scrambled to her feet. "Nate, do you know why she's in this closet?"

"I have no idea. Maybe she's playing a game with her nieces. Hide and go seek, maybe?"

"My sister is not the type to play these kind of games. I think I may need to take her back to the doctor."

"Did you say the doctor? What are you talking about?" Nate asked. His tone was sharp.

"Um, nothing," Alita said. "Never mind. Family business."

He glared at her for so long that Alita finally said, "Okay, I think I'd better go now. Um, you sure you okay, Elyse? You want to come spend the night with me?"

She stared down at her lap, then grabbed her pillow. "I all right. Just sleepy."

"Then go get in the bed like a normal person."

"I had accident. In da bed."

"Then go take a shower. Damn!"

Disgusted, Alita decided to leave. She wanted to make Elyse go home with her, but she decided to hold her tongue and avoid any arguments. She left the house and walked outside and stood under the thick, slow-moving clouds. She placed a call to Burgundy, but the woman didn't answer. Alita made a mental note to call her sister back in twenty minutes. She got in the car and headed toward home.

Meanwhile, Burgundy had been catching last-minute sales for hours. Her final stop was at Target, where she scooped up adorable winter wear for Coco's kids. She found a couple of small appliances for her kitchen and grabbed a few holiday bedspreads and pillows that caught her eye.

Even though it was getting late, and she really needed to use the restroom, there was one more item on her list. Burgundy was dying to surprise the girls and buy them something really special. It was called a Disney Princess Carriage Ride-On, a battery-operated pink carriage that could fit two people. It went backward and forward, and it cost four hundred dollars. Earlier that week, after Natalia sweet-talked him, at the last minute Nate had secretly had a conversation with his wife, and he agreed the girls could have one.

So Burgundy was in Target, on a shopping list mission. But this store was out of them; after doing a search and placing a few calls, Burgundy gleefully discovered that a Walmart located fifteen miles away still had a few left.

"Please hold one for me. My daughters will die if they wake up and this carriage ride-on is under the Christmas tree."

"Yes, ma'am. I'll hold it for you."

Burgundy hurriedly drove to the Walmart Supercenter and rushed inside.

The pickup department was located in the back of the gigantic store. A lot of shoppers were milling about. As Burgundy walked to the rear of the store, she sneezed very hard and felt a trickle of urine wet her underwear.

"Damn it," she said to herself as she raced down the aisle. "I can use the bathroom first, then pick up the toy."

When Burgundy went into the women's restroom, the room seemed quiet. She noticed there were four stalls on the right-hand side. She began to walk toward them. But as she approached the first stall, she noticed that the door was closed. A handwritten "Out of order" sign was taped against it.

"Dammit," she said.

As she kept walking she noticed that all the doors had the same sign taped on them. When she reached the last stall there was no sign on it. The door was slightly ajar. Feeling relieved, Burgundy tucked her fingers on her slacks and was about to pull them down.

She pushed open the door and gasped.

A heavyset woman was already seated on the toilet.

Her underwear and pants were resting around her ankles.

"Oops. I'm so sorry," Burgundy said as she began to back away. But then she got pushed back into the stall by someone behind her. The person shoved her so hard that soon her lips touched the shirt of the woman sitting on the toilet. She was so close she could smell the chick's perfume.

She grunted and wanted to tell the lady sorry again.

But before she could do it, Burgundy felt something hard being shoved against her back.

"Hand over your purse, lady. If you don't do it, you're dead." A female voice behind her made her knees weaken. She locked eyes with the woman on the toilet, letting her know that she needed help. But the lady just gave her an amused smile and held out her hand.

Burgundy realized that a scarf was being tied around her head, and she could no longer see anybody. She heard the women laughing and digging around in her purse. The woman rose up and she aggressively pushed Burgundy until she bumped her head against the stall door. Then she collapsed to the cold, hard, smudgy floor.

By the time it was all over, and Burgundy was sure that she was alone, she got up and yanked off the scarf and grabbed her purse. It felt much lighter than usual. Burgundy cupped her mouth with her hands, left the bathroom, and practically ran out of the store.

By then she knew she'd totally wet her pants. She felt dirty and naked, disrespected and violated. She kept looking behind her hoping that no one was following her.

Burgundy managed to get inside her SUV and quickly

locked the door. She turned on the ignition, pressed her foot on the gas, and backed out of the parking space.

As soon as she was a mile away from the store, she burst out crying. She searched around in her purse. Her cell phone and wallet were missing.

"I can't even call the police," she said. Her mind raced as she tried to think of what to do next. She ended up driving to a gas station a couple of miles away. The store clerk let her use the phone to report the robbery.

"Thank you, sir. Now I need to call my husband. My driver's license was stolen, all my credit cards, my cash."

"I'm sorry to hear that, ma'am. Go ahead, take your time."

Her underwear was drenched in urine, and she could smell herself. For the first time, she realized that even a woman like her could hit rock bottom.

Burgundy let out a moan and dialed Nate's phone number. It rang and rang. She hung up and called their landline. When no one picked up, she slammed down the phone.

"Where is everybody?"

The clerk watched Burgundy, her face puffy by now due to the tears she openly let fall from her eyes.

"No one is ever there when you need them," she said aloud. "You give and give and give. You try to be supportive to the people that you love, but they don't even care when you go through things." She laughed and shrugged, by then not caring that she was talking to herself. "Maybe this is what I deserve for acting like I have it all together, that I'm on top of the world, like they need me more than I need them." She let out another frustrated groan.

Burgundy decided to go home to the Woodlands.

Even though she was upset, she drove the speed limit, not wanting to draw attention to herself. And when she stepped foot inside the door of her house, it was eerily quiet.

"Nate?" she called. "Elyse?"

Alita had left already. It was Christmas Eve and pretty much the worst night of Burgundy's life. She went into their bedroom. And there her husband was, knocked out on his back, mouth open, his face buried in the pillow, and she could hear him snoring.

Burgundy thought for a second, then went over to Nate and violently shook him until he sat up. He blinked and scowled when he saw her glaring at him. Her eyes were void of light; they were dark, sad, and hollow.

"Why didn't you answer the phone when I called you? I tried to get you like ten times, Nate. I called your cell, the house. Why didn't you pick up? Were you even here?"

"Where else would I be?" he answered and scrambled to his feet. But the big man immediately fell back down on the bed. He was drowsy like he'd been aroused from the deepest kind of sleep.

"I was knocked out cold," he commented. "I-I didn't hear the phone." He closed his eyes for a long moment. "Did you finish getting that Disney thing for the girls?"

"No!" she snapped at him. "I couldn't."

"What do you mean you couldn't? They ran out of them or something?"

"I did not buy the fucking toy because two low-down women robbed me at gunpoint. When I went to the restroom, they forced me to hand over my wallet and cell phone. I hate Walmart. It's so ghetto, and I won't ever go there again." She broke down for a minute. "Here I am once again. Trying to do good for others, make someone else happy . . . but where are the people that want to make me happy. I am so tired, Nate. Tired of you, tired of my sisters, tired of everything. I give and give. But people take and take."

"Burg?" he said, now more alert. "Are you blaming me for what happened to you?"

"You weren't there for me, Nate."

"Burg, come on. I'm sorry about what happened."

"You sure don't act like it. You act like it means nothing to you. You don't seem upset at all."

Now Nate was really listening, as well as thinking. He thought about what he'd been doing while his wife was getting a gun pointed into her backside. What if the situation had grown worse and her assailants had shot her and left Burgundy for dead? Nate blinked a few times, wondering how it would have been if the worst has happened to his wife: his wife getting gunned down while he was getting Elyse to service him for the second time that night. The first time was right before that stupid-ass Alita decided to pop over. And after he got her to leave, Nate went to Elyse for a second helping. Man, it felt so good. Releasing the stress, getting rid of his sexual frustration. And now this? All of this was Burgundy's own fault.

He came back to the present and saw his wife's lips moving, her hands frantically waving as she went on and on about how she was the real victim of the family.

"My sisters, they have nothing to lose. But me?" She barked out a long list of what she brought to her family, to the community. Nate quietly and skillfully tuned her out. He nodded but pondered evil thoughts. He wondered what gunshots would sound like if the robbers had pulled the trigger. Would it take four bullets to bring her down? Or would two have done the job? What would life be like if Burgundy wasn't around any-more? Who would be her replacement? Could a wife as giving as Burgundy Reeves even be replaced?

The instant Nate realized where his mind had gone, he mentally apologized to her. This was his wife, for God's sake. When he imagined his better half no longer being around, he felt stiff and cold inside.

Nate allowed himself to become more present in the moment; soon he heard the sound of his wife's voice again.

"Nate, it was so scary. I never ever thought any-thing like that could happen to me. Women victimizing women. Of course, both of them had to be black. Why'd they have to be black?"

"Would you have felt better if they'd been white?"

"Fuck you, Nate."

He walked over to Burgundy, hugged her tightly, then calmly told her that they'd need to make some calls.

"I'll tell them to cancel all those credit cards. And we'll go and apply for a replacement driver's license as soon as we can. And we'll buy you a new smart phone, and a smart watch too."

She said nothing. Nate finally told her he was glad she got home safe.

"I'm glad about it too," Burgundy answered. "But I still didn't get the girls their toy. I wished I could have gotten that for them, Nate."

Instead of answering, he crawled into bed, turned his back, and stared into space.

CHAPTER 19

Pow! Pow!

Christmas came and went. The mood at the Taylor house was somber. Burgundy soaked in the tub most of the day and read her Bible.

Alita and Shade hung out together and tried to cheer up Leno, who was still depressed about Zaida.

But on the day after Christmas, when Alita got in touch with Burgundy to ask how her holiday had gone, her sister informed her about the robbery.

"I'm sorry you went through that, B. Anything I can do to help?"

"Yeah, I need to take care of this little bit of business concerning my medical ID cards, gas cards, checkbook, and other shit that got stolen, but why don't you drive over to my house and check on Elyse. Nate's gone to work already. Maybe you can talk to Elyse and spend some time with her. I'll be back at Morning Glory later on. You can bring Baby Sis to the restaurant for me." She paused. "I'll give you the gas money when you get here."

"No problem. I'll be happy to help out," Alita told her. "I'm on my way."

Her drive to the Woodlands took an hour. Elyse let her inside. Alita went and sat on the family room sofa. The TV was on, and Elyse was still sitting around in her pajamas.

"How was your Christmas, Elyse?"

She shrugged. "I dunno."

"Did you get anything special that you wanted?"

"What I want . . . it can't be put under a tree."

"Oh, okay," Alita said, feeling happy that the girl was talking.

"And what type of present you want Santa to bring you?" Feeling silly and elated that she was there spending time with the girl, she said, "You want a new baby doll, Elyse? Do you still play with dolls?"

"I'm not child. I grown."

"Oh, really?" Alita told her. "You hardly ever act like it."

"You don't know how I act. How I be. You not with me all da time."

This was the most revealing thing Elyse had ever said to Alita.

"You're right." Alita sat down next to her. Even though they were blood-related, a family member could be mysterious. Yet the love was still there.

Alita reached over and kissed the girl's forehead. She grabbed her hand and squeezed it.

"What happens when I'm not with you? Tell me."

Elyse cast her eyes downward. "I a woman."

"You're a what?"

"I do it. I do what women do. With a—"

"You mean, you mean that you have sex, Elyse? With a man or with a woman?"

Elyse tried to relax as she noticed Alita's sudden interest in what she had to say. She fiddled with her fingers and examined them. Her nails were looking terrible. Elyse thought that maybe it was time for her to take care of herself, make herself look pretty, because going out of her way to make herself look ugly wasn't working.

"I have sex with man. Only a man."

Alita felt lightheaded. She stared at the girl. "With a man or a boy? Tell me, baby."

"A boy," she quietly told her, stuffing bravery back into her heart. She knew the truth would cause a family war. She had to keep this a secret for as long as possible.

"Oh, yeah? What boy? I've never seen you with a boy since you were in ninth grade."

"He at Morning Glory."

"Elyse, what? You been fucking with one of the customers that come in there?"

"No."

"Oh, shit. Then you been getting it on with your co-worker?"

"Yeah."

"But," Alita said as she began to think, "I don't know if there's a lot of young boys there. You're the youngest employee at Morning Glory. Who is it, Elyse? Tell me his name."

She violently shook her head. Her body began to tremble. She swallowed deeply. She had met a boy there. His name? Gamba, a Zimbabwe name that meant "warrior." For the past several weeks, Gamba had been eating lunch at Morning Glory every day. He'd talk to her whenever Nate wasn't around. He told her about life, the ways of the world, and how she needed to take control, and she listened. Gamba became Elyse's only friend, her one true ally. And she didn't want any of her family to know that he existed.

"Elyse," Alita asked in a frustrated tone. "Why you shut down again? It's like you hiding shit from me. Don't hide in there," she said, staring into the girl's eyes, looking for any sign of life.

"Is his name Darius, Elyse? Tell me."

"No. You crazy. You hurt people."

"That's what I'm supposed to do. If someone hurts my family, I'm supposed to hurt him."

Hurt *him*. Isn't that what Elyse wanted? She thought about Nate and his disgusting ways. But she also considered Burgundy, who seemed to worship the ground he walked on.

No, she could not destroy her sister's happiness. But Alita wouldn't let up unless Elyse told her *something*.

"Yes, his name is Darius." The lies spilled from her mouth. "He touch me, kiss me, put his thing in me."

"Where, though? Where does this happen?"

"Morning Glory. That's where it happened."

"That's sick. While customers are out there eating breakfast, he's in the back having sex with my—that old man is about to regret ever putting his hands on you."

Alita made Elyse go to her bedroom. She found some non–work clothes for her to wear. She combed Elyse's hair, and they got in the car and left.

Alita arrived at the restaurant, and the first people they ran into were Nate and Burgundy.

When Elyse saw the two of them, she went back and got into the car.

"Oh, okay," Alita told her. "Wait for me here in the car. I won't be but a minute."

Alita marched right up to Burgundy. "We've got a problem. And I need you to get rid of your employee right now." She looked at Nate in disgust. "Do you do background checks on your employees before you let 'em work in this joint?"

"Of course we do. Why do you ask?"

She pulled Burgundy by the arm. "I told you I wanted to whip that cheating man's ass from day one."

"Who, Lita?"

"Darius. The cheater. The flirt. The married employee whose been seeing our sister on the side."

"No way."

Burgundy had already figured that Alita was referring to Elyse. She was the only sister Alita got very emotional about. Burgundy asked Alita to take a seat and then allowed her to spill information that she wasn't ready to hear.

"It's been going on in front of our faces. I guess since I refused to give him any, he went and got him the next best thing. A younger Reeves woman."

"Darius and Elyse? Alita, I'm sorry, but I just can't believe this."

"That's because you're naïve. You want to think the best about everybody, even when the dirty truth is staring you in the face." Alita threw up her hands. "I knew this Sister Day shit is a joke. We don't even take it serious. I am telling you the truth, Burgundy, and what do I get? Doubt. From my own sister. What you want me to do? Make up a lie to make you feel better about reality?"

Pow! Burgundy felt like she just took a bullet. The shrapnel was still stuck in her heart, her gut, the very place where she felt every emotion. And this type of attack, a criticism of something their mother created, felt wrong.

"Why bring Sister Day into it?" Burgundy asked.

"Because the person running Sister Day is nothing but a fake."

Burgundy jumped up in Alita's face. A finger waved in front of Alita's eyes, which were burning with fire.

"Just because I don't do things the way you think they should be done doesn't make me fake. I-I do the best that I can. I work hard. Wait a minute. Why am I explaining myself to you?"

"Oh, yeah, right. Because you the *important* Reeves. You and Dru. The rest of us ain't shit."

"Don't even try it, Lita. You are the main criticizer of Coco. And I don't know why you're taking a sudden interest in Elyse."

"Somebody has to. I can't depend on anyone else in this family to step up, including you."

Pow! Pow!

Burgundy emitted a tiny scream and abruptly sat in a chair. She hid her face in both her hands. Trembling. Moaning with frustration. Her mind felt cluttered, disorganized. This wasn't typical of the woman who always seemed to keep things together. But lately . . . lately the pressures of life were eating at the seams of Burgundy's heart. She took several moments to just air out all negative, hateful, vengeful thoughts that she'd had about Alita.

Then she decided to get back to the main topic.

"First of all, Lita, let's say that Darius is a cheater

who has fallen into an affair with Elyse. Even if it were true . . . Elyse is a grown-up."

"A grown-up? Are you insane? She's childlike. She needs help. Plus that girl don't care nothing about that man. Have you ever seen them hanging out around this restaurant?"

"No, that's why it's hard to believe this story."

"Well, you ain't here all the time, and things can happen when you gone, or even right under your own nose."

Burgundy vehemently shook her head, then stopped.

"Stop being in denial, B" Alita continued. "I'm sure your little Darius is hounding our sister for sex. His wife ain't giving it up, and that makes him go stick his dick in another woman's wag. I can't stand guys like that."

"Do you know all of this for a fact, Lita? It sounds like you're making up anything just to find someone to blame. And that rumor is something I can't afford to rely on. We're talking about a very good employee here; we've never had a single moment of trouble out of him."

"So you're taking his side over mine?"

"I don't even know his side," Burgundy told her.

"Why don't you call him then? Ask him to come back to work. See what he does the second he looks in my face."

"Oh, no, you won't be anywhere nearby when I confront Darius." Burgundy stared at the ground, wishing desperately that she knew how to handle this situation. It could get ugly, and God knows she did not need any type of trouble surrounding her businesses.

"I need to discuss this with Nate," Burgundy continued. "And then we'll figure out a plan of action. But thanks for telling me." She started to walk in the direction of the business office.

"Hey, Sis. Are you crazy or just stupid?" Alita asked.

"What are you talking about?"

"Why haven't you even gone to the car to see how your sister is doing?"

"I-I don't—"

"That's it. She's moving in with me. I don't care what you or your husband says. I have a lot on my plate, but this will just have to be added to it. For you to be so smart, so together, you really are as much of a fuck-up as I am."

And Alita turned around, got in the car, and sped off without a second thought.

The next evening Alita was ready to execute her plan. The last time she had spoken to Burgundy she'd told her that she should use her common sense, admit that she was being stubborn, and she needed to allow Elyse to live with Alita. Burgundy told her no and calmly hung up on her.

But now Alita had a plan that she prayed would go well.

It was a Thursday. Alita drove over to Morning Glory. She hoped that Elyse would be there, for she knew that on Thursdays Burgundy did other things while Nate worked late; and usually was the one to drive Elyse home after the last worker left for the day, usually around five-thirty.

When she looked around the parking lot, Alita did not see any of the cars that Burgundy liked to drive. Good.

She picked up the phone and called Dru.

"Dru Boo, what you doing?" she asked.

"Studying and eating."

"Okay, do me a favor."

"Why are you the sister that always needs a favor?"

"Because I am; are you going to help me or not?"

Dru's lack of response irked Alita even more. "Are we even related?" she asked. "Why are you taking so long to agree to help your sister?"

"Because I can," Dru answered.

"Funny. Anyway, this one is easy. I need you to make a phone call." Alita went on to explain that she simply wanted her to call Burgundy and engage her in a conversation. Keep her occupied. Ask her the regular questions that she'd ask that required long-winded answers, specific inquiries like the upcoming holiday and all her plans.

"And when I call you back, that's when you know it's okay to end the call."

"What are you up to, Alita?"

"I'll tell you about it later. Now promise me you'll make the phone call. Count to two hundred, then dial her."

"What if she doesn't answer? You know how busy Burgundy can be, and she'll let a call go into voice mail in a minute."

"Keep trying till you get her," Alita said. "Now, I'm about to hang up. Start counting. Bye."

Alita then made her way inside Morning Glory. She walked past Darius, who nodded his head slightly at her.

She decided to stop and chat for five seconds. But she didn't have a lot of time.

"Hi, there. Have you seen my baby sister?"

"Yeah, but not lately."

"Okay, I'll check in the kitchen."

"I don't think she's there," Darius said, but Alita kept going and ignored him.

When she saw that Darius was telling the truth, she went to the business office. The door was shut, which wasn't unusual since the noise of the restaurant tended to be so loud that Burgundy preferred to keep it closed.

Alita turned the knob, but the door was locked.

"Hmmm," she said. She walked back to Darius. "Is my brother-in-law here?"

"Why do you want to know?"

"Please don't act this way, Darius. We have a family emergency." Darius looked like he could not care any less. He proceeded to drop some waffle batter on the waffle maker and completely shut out Alita's pleas to help her.

She picked up her cell phone and dialed Nate. But the call went straight into voice mail.

"Dammit. Where is she?"

She tried to call Elyse, but she had never known the girl to answer a cell phone. She had no idea why she even had one, because she definitely didn't use it for talking.

Frustrated, Alita went out to her car not knowing what to do and needing a quiet place in which to think. She saw Elyse sitting in the backseat with her eyes closed. Stunned, she asked Elyse how she was doing. When the girl spoke not a word, Alita dialed Shade. "Babe, I know you think I'm crazy, but I-I think some foul shit is going on with my baby sister, Elyse." She sniffled, hating that she was forced to share family drama with the man who she wanted to love her.

"But it's going to be all right. I just wanted to hear a friendly voice."

"Sweetie," he said. "Where are you? You need me to come to your place?"

"No, I'm at Morning Glory."

Before she could say anything further, Shade told her, "On the way."

By the time he arrived, Alita had a clearer head. She briefly told Shade what was going on. Together they walked over to Darius, and she politely asked him if he had a moment.

He stopped what he was doing, and he followed the two of them outside.

"Darius, I know you and I didn't start out on good terms and I'm sorry 'bout that. I really am. But something serious is going on with my . . . Elyse told me that . . . Do you ever . . . um, have you ever . . ."

"What are you talking about, lady?" Darius said.

"Have y'all been fucking?"

He frowned and turned right around to go back inside the restaurant.

"Darius, please just let me know did you have sex with . . . with my sister?"

He stopped walking. Turned around. "That's it. I've had it. Forget this shit."

He walked back inside. He went to the business office and told Nate that he was quitting.

"What?" Nate said. "Why?"

"I can't deal with this shit, man. Your family is crazy. That sister-in-law you got. She needs to be locked up."

"Don't let that woman keep you from working here, Darius. You're my best employee."

"As long as she keeps coming in here harassing me and accusing me of—"

"Of what?"

"She thinks that I have had sex with Elyse. That girl is young enough to be my child. And for the record, I haven't touched her. And if she says I have, then she's crazy like her sister. I'm done, man. I'm out. Mail me my last check."

And just like that, Darius was gone.

CHAPTER 20

The Treason, the Reason, and the Season

"Elyse, what the fuck is wrong with you, girl?" Alita said in a high-pitched tone. "Don't you know that if we had gone to the police and filed charges against that man and they found out you lied, then your black ass would have went to jail?" Alita was livid. "And guess what? I would not have bailed you out either. If you went to jail for filing a false police report, you would have gotten just what you deserved. You would have ruined a man's life. For nothing. Stop playing these silly-ass games and grow the fuck up."

The two sisters were in Alita's car. Elyse sat in the back. She was trembling so much, she looked seriously ill. But Alita did not care. Not this time. Caring too much got her into too much trouble. And she was getting weary of dealing with family drama.

"I sorry I lie."

"Why did you lie?" Alita tried to be patient. "Sweetie, have you or have you not been having sex?"

"I-I made it up."

"What? Are you serious?"

She hunched her bony shoulders.

"Elyse, do you understand what you did? Number one, you made a big fool out of me because I trusted you. And number two, I don't think I can ever show my face at Morning Glory again."

"Good!"

"Oh, Lord, did she really say 'good'?" Alita had to laugh. "And see, not too long ago you swore to me you wouldn't be any trouble. I see you lied about that too."

"I sorry. I wrong. I-I—"

"Look, Elyse. Forget it. I'm not going to stay mad at you. But I'll be honest. It will be hard for me, or any of the family, to trust you after this. Do you understand what I'm saying?"

Elyse nodded and felt horrible for making a bad situation worse. Something had to give. She was screwing up big time and could not afford to alienate the only family ally that she had.

"I promise to do better. I learned my lesson."

"Wow, you spoke two whole sentences, and you sounded halfway intelligent for a change." Alita could not help herself. She climbed in the backseat and told Elyse, "Come here."

"Okay, Lita."

The two women hugged each other tight. When it was over, Alita sighed. "It's been a horrible holiday so far. It has to get better. I'm worn out, Sis. Thank God we have a few more days to the New Year, and Dru's birthday is in a few days. That should bring a little bit more cheer our way."

"Yeah."

"'Tis the season to be jolly? Yeah, right. I sure hope this New Year hurries up and gets here," Alita said. "'Cause I cannot wait to say goodbye to this last one."

"Me too, Lita. Me too."

They laughed again and sighed and quieted themselves, hoping to get some rest and peace of mind before the night closed out.

A few days later, Alita cornered Burgundy after they'd gone out to eat.

"B, we need to talk. I want to know a good time for me to pick up Elyse. She's going to live with me. I can do a lot to help her out. Because, as I see it, me losing that job was a blessing in disguise. It gives me time to focus on her, focus more on Leno. It's a win-win situation."

Burgundy shook her head. "It doesn't work that way, Alita."

"What you mean?"

"I mean that you can't make that decision for her. You said it yourself that the girl is emotionally disturbed. She'll need to see a few therapists."

"I know that. I'd be happy to take her."

"But would you be happy enough to pay for her medical bills?"

The color drained from Alita's face. "Oh, so we're doing things like that now? You assume I am flat broke and can't afford to take the girl to the doctor?"

"It's not an assumption, Alita. You're just not the

most suitable person to take care of Elyse's very critical care. Nate and I will handle things."

Alita was stunned and angry. "Other than a fat bank account, what's so great about you two?"

"I'm not about to have this conversation. Anyway, we're about to go to the house."

"Okay, fine. But when you take Elyse to see a psychiatrist, make sure and go to see one for yourself."

Alita couldn't sleep at all that night. And the next day she drove over to Burgundy's. She saw her sister's car, but Nate's vehicle wasn't there.

She went to the front door. Burgundy let her in and they walked straight to the home office. She closed the door and folded her arms over chest as she glared at Burgundy.

"Why are you looking at me like that, Alita?"

"We are not done with our conversation. I could kick myself for not being brave enough to tell you the things that are really on my mind . . . but you need to listen to me and listen good. We're sisters, and I love you, but you're married to a perverted man."

"Alita, I don't want to hear it."

"I figured it out. He is the one that's been messing around with Elyse."

"What? Are you serious?"

"Yes, you know it's the truth. That's why you carry around a dildo in your purse, B. Instead of you having sex with each other, you do it with your plastic dick, and he does it with Elyse."

Burgundy gritted her teeth and abruptly raised her hand, but Alita blocked her.

"Don't hit me, B. Just think about it. Think about every time you've wondered about your own husband.

When he said things that don't add up. Anytime you had a weird feeling in your gut. I know, B. I've been there. When my ex was lying and cheating and acting strange, the signs were all in my face. Your signs are there too, so please open up your eyes and admit what's going on, okay?"

Alita said her piece and started to walk away from her sister, but Burgundy called for her to stop.

"If you don't acknowledge it," Burgundy said in a tiny voice, "you don't have to face it."

"Accept that your man is having sex with another woman. Your flesh and blood."

"When you think positive, negative stuff cannot hurt you."

"Oh, B, seriously? What fool told you that, and why would you believe it?"

"You are telling me things that you want me to believe, right? Well, I feel like I don't have to believe everything I hear."

"Okay, B. Fine. But what about the things that you see? Can you believe it if you see it?"

"What are you getting at?" Burgundy said.

"If I tell you what *I* saw, would you believe it?"

Burgundy's entire face seemed to scream no. It was true that her sister talked a lot, but much of what she said hardly ever made sense to Burgundy. She knew full well how dramatic Alita could be. She felt that the woman did many things for attention. And maybe this was one of those times. Alita's theory about Darius had been way off. In fact it was laughable. It had caused a man to quit his own job. And it proved that Elyse was a pathological liar. So there was a good chance the little girl was also lying about Nate.

"I doubt you saw anything—" Burgundy replied.

"Listen to me for a moment, B. Please."

"What, Lita?"

"I know you're not going to like what you hear, but this is what I saw." Alita knew this would be the hardest thing she'd ever have to say to Burgundy. Much harder than the brutal judgments she'd given her about being an uncaring snob who was stuck on herself.

"B, I did something I should not have done and yes, I came over to the house without calling first."

"Alita."

"And I followed another car inside the security gate. I did. I drove around the neighborhood half scared to death trying to talk myself into doing this confrontation thing. I wanted to find Elyse and whip her little behind for embarrassing the hell out of me. But, B, I was lucky in that I drove in the driveway. And I did not go to the front door like I normally do. I walked around, and I came to the gate that goes to the backyard. And it was unlocked."

"Alita, please."

"The gate was unlocked, B, and I opened it and came into the backyard. And it was so quiet, so very quiet that it was like nobody was left on earth. I didn't even hear or see any birds or anything."

"This is getting ridiculous, Lita."

"No listen up. I walked around the back of the house, and you know y'all like white folks and you like to keep the window blinds open all the time and so I easily could look inside of your house. I saw inside of the castle. I saw the king and queen's bedroom window. And B, I saw the two of them, in your bedroom."

"I don't want to hear it—"

Alita kept talking, telling her eyewitness account of what she had seen that day. As Burgundy listened, it seems her ears grew bigger and bigger. And the more she listened in horror and hated what she heard, it seemed like her ears began to shrink.

"I saw through that window. And Nate was wearing just his plaid sleeping pants. He wore no shirt . . . just the pants."

"So what? I've seen him plenty of times walking around the house in just the pajama bottoms."

"But Elyse was wearing the matching top. And it was unbuttoned. And—"

Burgundy covered her ears.

Alita snatched her sister's hands from her ears and shook her shoulders. "Listen to me, B, or at least explain to me, what was the girl doing wearing his pajamas? Doesn't that seem strange to you?"

Burgundy gave Alita a cold, stony look. "If you told that to a court of law, they'd laugh at you and toss out the case."

"Oh, Burgundy," Alita said in a pleading tone. "Don't do this. Don't reject truth. Truth is what we're about, right? Am I right? Or are we supposed to play along with this fucking family fantasy that you've come up with, but you don't even believe it yourself? What? Why waste the sisters' time? You really think this what Mama would have wanted?"

"Leave Mama out of it."

"No, let's bring Mama into it. Because our precious mother isn't as angelic as we've painted her to be." Alita burst into tears. Her mother wasn't perfect by far, but she still missed the woman's voice, her smell, her touch. Alita cried for a while until she got rid of her anger and hurt and sorrow.

"So anyway," she said as she wiped her nose, "do you really believe that our mama would want us to be like this, B? Lying to each other? Because ain't it true that our own mother was the type to lie to herself?" Alita began to sob. "Mama was a pretender too. I guess you grew up to be just like her."

Now Alita was laughing. And going from weeping to laughing within minutes made it feel like she was losing her mind.

"Sister Day is like a big cover-up."

"Alita—"

"No, be honest. I don't know who we trying to prove something to and why we gotta act like we're Reeveses, as if that means anything."

"Right now what you're saying isn't making any sense, Alita. And I believe you are sincere. You think you saw something, but I'm telling you it was nothing. Don't go looking for trouble either, because if you do, you'll always find it, even though you haven't proved a thing."

"Okay, fine. I give up. Keep living in your fantasy world, Burgundy. But I won't let Elyse continue to stay here with you two. Is that understood?"

"I will have to discuss it with Nate—"

"Burgundy."

"We're married, and we have to be in agreement. My husband is my covering. If I go against his wishes, then bad things will really happen in our marriage."

"What? Who told you that?"

"My church."

"Oh, hell, no. Keep those people out your business."

"Alita, don't be upset. I told you let me discuss this with Nate. And I'll let you know."

"You know what, you are so smart, yet you're stupid as hell. It's okay, B. You not the first woman to get played by her man. In this present world, just about every woman has an ex-husband, you hear me? We survive the bullshit and go on to find a much better man than the lying-ass, cheating, fucked-up, delusional, wife-beating, whoremonger, jailbird, bitch-ass punks that treat you like shit and act like he's the victim. These men out here suing women for child support, trying to get that spousal support, having side babies while they married, and acting so shocked when she gets fed up and ready to leave his ass. So if your man is doing any of this shit, B, it's time to make a decision. Fuck what he wants. You either leave his ass or you stay and keep dealing with it."

"Hillary stuck by Bill."

"She's stupid," Alita yelled.

"And Camille Cosby stuck by Bill."

"Two stupid-ass wives. Wait, hold up. That lets us know we need to stay the fuck away from men named Bill."

Burgundy cracked a tiny smile.

"I hear what you're saying, Alita, but God hates divorces."

"He hates child molesters too."

"Please don't call him that."

"Oh, all right. I get it. You a stand-by-your-man-no-matter-what type of woman. Like that lady that stuck by her husband who molested all those boys in the locker room. You disgust me."

In all her life Burgundy had never been judged so harshly. The glare of the spotlight shining upon her insecurities and weaknesses was almost more than she could bear.

And Alita knew she had touched a sore spot. She knew that this entire scenario was something that Burgundy never would have expected. "He believes in

God, he's a good man, Alita. This has to be some sort of mistake."

Alita's eyes burned with anger.

"For once in my life, it feels good to know I'm not the only foolish woman out here."

"What do you mean?"

"Get out! Leave him."

"We have kids. They worship him."

"So what? They can still know their father, but I don't even know that I'd want them to know that sleaze-bag."

"Lita, you assuming stuff. Assuming is the lowest form of intelligence. We can't make critical life decisions based on assumptions and circumstantial evidence."

"You're a fool. But if it's fine for you to be a fool, you gon' pay a big price for staying with that man. 'Cause if you staying, then you paying."

"Alita, how many times I have to tell you that I have no proof? Why should I take anybody else's word over my husband's? Even my sister's. My emotionally unstable sister." She paused. Nate wasn't perfect, but she refused to believe he was the devil either. And in spite of their few differences, she knew she still loved him. That was all that mattered. That's all she could let matter.

"That's my husband. Something that you could not hold onto yourself."

Before Alita realized it, her arm flew out like a baseball bat. She slugged Burgundy across the cheek.

Burgundy's eyes enlarged. She rubbed her cheek, which was made hotter when she placed her hand on it.

"Don't make me go there, Lita," she finally said. "You don't want to see me go there." Burgundy blinked her eyes several times and prayed no tears would fall. She had to be strong, resilient. She had to keep it together no matter what.

She walked out before Alita could answer. She went to her bedroom and locked the door. The room was dark. She heard loud snoring. She turned on the lamp and stood there looking at her husband. A mixture of love and hate filled her entire heart. Burgundy reached down and smacked him on top of his head. Nate woke up startled. She hit him again. And again.

"Burgundy, what's wrong with you? What you hit me for?"

She cried and kept striking him, not very hard, but enough to let her husband feel her pain. Truth felt painful. Truth was ugly. Truth caused people to face things they did not want to face . . . like horrible, unimaginable secrets that could destroy families.

And while Burgundy was letting out her frustrations on Nate, Alita was upstairs, getting Elyse to grab a couple of things. She took her by the hand, and they sneaked down the back staircase. They quietly closed the door behind them and got in Alita's car. Instead of starting the ignition, she put it in neutral and had Elyse sit in the driver's seat. She pushed the car down the driveway and a few houses down. Then she hopped in the passenger seat and encouraged Elyse to start the car.

They drove off in the darkness of the night. Alita was ready to face whatever consequences would come her way. For her, Sister Day had just got real.

Stay tuned for what happens next
In the tension-filled sequel
A SISTER'S SURVIVAL
Available now wherever books are sold

And keep an eye out for
A SISTER'S POWER
Coming Soon
Cydney Rax
And
Dafina Books

Connect with Us

Visit us online at
KensingtonBooks.com
to read more from your favorite authors, see books
by series, view reading group guides, and more.

 Join us on social media

for sneak peeks, chances to win books and prize packs,
and to share your thoughts with other readers.

**facebook.com/kensingtonpublishing
twitter.com/kensingtonbooks**

Tell us what you think!

To share your thoughts, submit a review,
or sign up for our eNewsletters, please visit:
KensingtonBooks.com/TellUs.